# CARPE DIEM, ILLINOIS

## ILLINOIS

### A LEO TOWNSEND NOVEL

**KRISTIN A. OAKLEY**

**LITTLE CREEK PRESS®**

A DIVISION OF KRISTIN MITCHELL DESIGN, LLC

Mineral Point, Wisconsin USA

Author's Note: *Carpe Diem, Illinois* is a work of fiction.
All characters and events are products of my imagination.

*To Caitlin and Jessica,*
*my toughest critics and strongest supporters:*
*you are masters at seizing life.*
*Love you.*

# 1

At the corner of Tiger Whip Road and Highway 20, Patrick Holden slumped over the handle bars of his idling Harley. The motorcycle's black leather seat and saddle bags were creased with age, the twenty-year-old fenders dusty but barely scarred. Patrick hadn't aged as well as his bike. Years of fighting school administrators, education tsars, and a weird mix of politicians had creased more than his outward appearance; it had creased his soul.

The motorcycle's headlight illuminated the decaying façade of an abandoned shed. Swirling farm dust mixed with dry hay made Patrick cough, leaving a gritty taste in his mouth. He ran his gloved fingers over the neat stitches holding the cycle's seat together and regretted the late night meeting.

He had been persuasive, articulate, and even-tempered but the meeting had been a disaster. Illinois State Senator Christopher Shaw, in all his patronizing benevolence, had refused to see the obvious dangers of his legislation. Instead, threatened by reason, the senator stormed out of his office. When the door slammed, Patrick realized he was no longer sitting. His skinny, six-foot frame leaned over the senator's wooden desk, his hands splayed on the maple, leaving damp prints.

What had he done? Perhaps his father was right. Perhaps he had gone about this the wrong way, screwed things up, and jeopardized the future of Carpe Diem.

The idling purr of the motorcycle's engine soothed some of Patrick's despair until a semi trailer roared past. He shielded his eyes from a tornado of dirt and gravel and watched the truck cut a path of light on the dark highway.

Cutting a path through the darkness, what an idea. Turning the motorcycle back onto the two-lane highway, he fish-tailed, then accelerated to eighty miles an hour.

Alexandra Shaw steered her silver BMW down Highway 20 toward home. She had spent an inspiring day in Chicago at a novel writing workshop, followed by dinner with other passionate writers. She had been told several times that her story would make an excellent book. Thrilled, she hummed along to the sultry voice of Norah Jones on the radio. She couldn't remember ever being this happy.

She slowed through a small Midwestern town, passing three churches and a corresponding number of neighborhood taverns, then sped by endless farmland crawling with late night tractors lighting up rows of dried corn stalks. At a sharp bend in the highway, she spotted the sign, "Carpe Diem, 5 miles." That sign always intrigued her. Now she took it as a good omen and even considered stopping for a cup of coffee until she heard the muffled *Won't you take me to Funkytown?* ringtone of her cell phone. It was probably Natalia, eager to hear about her workshop.

Alexandra grabbed her purse from the passenger seat and felt inside but couldn't locate the phone. Her eyes on the road, she dumped the bag's contents. She riffled through gold pens, a mini notepad and her leather wallet. *Won't you take me to Funkytown?* She had it. She looked at her right hand. A packet of tissues.

She snatched another glance at the road. *Won't you take me to Funkytown?* A single light came over the nearest hill. A car with a busted headlight? A motorcycle? Yes, now where was the damned phone? She reached between the leather seats. Nothing. She felt on the floor and found a hardened French fry. The phone stopped asking her to take it to *Funkytown*. Why hadn't she listened to her husband and gotten the car's Bluetooth option?

The BMW's interior brightened. Alexandra jerked her head up. The motorcycle was driving in her lane. Straight at her. She punched the horn but the motorcycle didn't swerve. She yanked the steering wheel to the right, her foot smashing the brake pedal, the car's tires screaming. It wasn't enough. The motorcycle slammed into her.

The wrenching scream of tortured metal filled her ears. She buried her head in her arms. Shattered glass spit at her, pinpricking her bare hands. She tasted blood. The steering wheel's air bag crushed her against the driver's seat. The driver's door smashed inward, the side air bag deploying too late.

The car began to roll. Compressed, gasping for breath, strapped into the tumbling car, Alexandra flipped over and over as if on a crazed amusement park ride. *My book will never be published. Natalia, I'm sorry.* Right before passing out, she saw something bounce off the air bag—the delinquent cell phone.

# 2

Leo Townsend rubbed the scar on his bristled jaw and wondered what the hell he was going to say. If he played it cool and answered the questions directly, maybe, just maybe, the prosecutor wouldn't ask for his source.

He shirked off his leather bomber jacket and rolled up the sleeves of his white button-down shirt. What he wanted, what he *needed*, was to redeem himself. The last couple of months he'd been lazy, careless, and way too drunk.

If he uncovered an injustice and wrote a great exclusive, the story of the century, then maybe all of his personal and professional transgressions would be forgotten. Otherwise, his life would be meaningless backwash in the bottom of yet another empty beer bottle.

He reached for his tie but decided against loosening it even though the knot at his throat felt like a noose. A loose tie would be taking the casual look too far. He took a deep breath and willed his shaky hand to push open the heavy wooden courtroom door. He managed to move his feet forward, step inside. The sight of the crowd stopped him. The closing door bumped his back, pushing him further into the federal grand jury room.

Leo scanned the chamber. To his right, twenty or so jurors sat in three tiered rows. Murmuring to each other, they hadn't noticed his entrance. Directly in front of him was a large conference table. At the far end, a court reporter sat adjusting the tape in her machine. Another woman stood shuffling papers behind a small podium in the middle of the table. She wore a charcoal grey suit and a scowl a pit bull would envy. She had to be the Assistant United States Attorney. The federal prosecutor.

Leo noted the lack of a witness stand, a jury box, a bailiff, and even a judge. This didn't surprise him. He had never been before a grand jury but his editor had told him what to expect. The prosecutor would run the proceedings while trying to prove she had enough evidence to indict former gubernatorial candidate Carl Smithson on corruption charges. The jury would decide if she succeeded. Leo hoped she could succeed without having to know the name of his source.

That source had led him to information exposing Smithson's illegal activities. Skimming millions of dollars from teachers' unions was frowned upon, even in Illinois. Leo's resulting *Chicago Examiner* story almost won him a Pulitzer, but cost Smithson the governor's race. With a grand jury indictment and potential subsequent trial and conviction, Smithson could lose his freedom as well. The stakes were high. The prosecutor would demand the name of Leo's source, but he couldn't, he wouldn't, give that name. Keeping quiet was his only chance to save his job and any remaining dignity. But keeping quiet might land him in jail.

Leo ran a damp, shaking hand through his wavy brown hair. If he could take charge of the situation, he'd feel better. He shuffled forward, cleared his throat. The room quieted. The jurors stared. He wondered if they noticed his fingers quivering. Attempting to appear calm and in control, he tilted his head toward the jury and slowly smiled. Some people nodded, some smiled back. A few jurors actually sighed, and not all of them were women.

"Well, Mr. Townsend," the prosecutor barked. "You've found the grand jury room." Her words quelled whispers from the crowd.

He tried to speak, but the sound caught in his throat. He coughed then tried again. "I'm sorry I'm late. I had a deadline to make." He approached the prosecutor and leaned close as if to tell a secret. She smelled like musty law books. "So many corrupt politicians to dethrone," he said loud enough for the jury to hear, "so little time."

The jurors laughed. His nerves began to ease.

The prosecutor backed away, yet her scowl relaxed. "Please be seated, Mr. Townsend." She pointed to the chair on her left.

As he sat at the conference table, Leo caught a blast of stale cigarette smoke radiating from the nearby court reporter. She gave him a yellow-toothed grin. A burly juror in the front row stood and introduced himself as the duly appointed foreman. Following his lead, Leo raised his right hand, stated his name as "Leonardo Salvatori Townsend," and agreed to tell the truth, the whole truth, and nothing but the truth. He ignored the phrase "So help me God." He was an atheist despite, or maybe because of, a childhood of Catholicism.

Anticipating a question, he glanced up at the prosecutor. Her cell phone was pressed to her ear. He couldn't believe it. He wanted to get through his testimony, be done with it and get back to investigating his current assignment. He shifted his chair closer to the table, making sure to scrape it on the tiled floor. The prosecutor turned her back on him and continued her conversation. He clenched his teeth. Several of the jurors stared at him. Avoiding their scrutiny, he looked down at his lap and realized he had rolled his jacket into a tangled ball.

"Mr. Townsend," the prosecutor finally began, turning off her phone, "I'm sorry. We're going to have to postpone your testimony until some-time next week."

His jaw relaxed, for the moment. A temporary reprieve, but like a root canal for a rotten tooth, he'd have to testify eventually. He'd rather get it over with. "Why?"

"Tomorrow's main witness has been called out of the country and has to leave as soon as possible. We need to juggle everyone's schedule to fit him in today. Please make sure you're available early next week."

Glaring at her, he stood, rumpled jacket in hand.

"I'm sorry for the inconvenience," she said then turned back to her phone.

Out in the hallway, Leo slumped against the dull grey wall and loosened his Jerry Garcia tie. His heartbeat had slowed and his hands no longer shook, but dread weighed him down. Sighing, he took out his cell phone. He pushed the number for his editor and started for the elevators.

"Nelson."

"Ted, it's Leo." Maneuvering around clusters of attorneys and clients, he sensed the stares of some of the women. He wished he could switch off his good looks when he didn't need them, when he wanted to be invisible.

"I thought you were testifying today," his editor said.

"I thought so too. They've postponed my testimony."

"Why?"

"Another witness has to leave the country so he's talking to the grand jury today." Leo passed the stairwell, deciding to take the elevator instead. Walking down sixteen flights was doable but he didn't have the energy. He stepped in front of one of the high-speed elevators and pushed the button, pressing his luck. "They've rearranged everyone's schedule," he told Ted.

"Too bad. I know you wanted to get it over with."

"Ah well, what the hell."

The doors opened revealing an empty elevator. At least something was going his way. He walked in, positioning himself to the left of the door where he could get out easily if people crowded in. The compartment's walls were a basket weave of shiny metal. Would he lose his phone signal?

A man in a business suit and a middle-aged couple in matching jean jackets entered the elevator while conversing in Spanish. The doors closed.

Leo lowered his voice. "Now I'm available to finish the sanitation workers' strike article. It'll be a winner." He swallowed twice to stabilize the build-up of pressure in his ears caused by the elevator's quick drop. "The union's leaders are fighting among themselves. There's been talk of lawsuits regarding lax safety regulations."

Silence. Had he lost the signal? "The shit's piling up."

Quiet.

Ted finally answered, "You're thinking about using that for the head-line, aren't you?"

"It's catchy, dontcha think?"

More silence from his editor, a man known for getting right to the point. Leo's feeling of dread intensified.

"I gave that assignment to Parker," Ted finally said.

"*What?*"

The other occupants of the elevator stopped speaking.

Leo turned his back on them. The Spanish resumed. "Why did you do that?" he asked Ted.

"I didn't know how long you'd be in court."

The elevator stopped on the tenth floor. The doors opened and three uniformed cops entered, their bulk filling up more than half the space. Leo wedged himself into the corner. His grip tightened on the phone.

"The union bosses scheduled an emergency meeting this morning," Ted continued. "Parker was available, you weren't. That's all there is to it."

Leo hoped this was true. "So put me back on it." He held his breath.

"Can't. Parker's wrapped up the story."

"Okay," he said trying to sound nonchalant.

The elevator stopped again, the opening doors revealing a loud group of women. They hesitated at the sight of the occupied compartment.

"Come on in," one of the cops, said waving his hand. "There's plenty of room."

The women shuffled in. An elbow jabbed Leo in the back. Someone stepped on his heel. His heart raced. He considered shouldering his way out, but then the doors closed. He concentrated on his phone conversation. "What else have you got for me?"

Ted cleared his throat. "Take a few days to regroup."

The women began flirting with the policemen. Leo covered his ear to hear Ted.

"… going to have to testify anyway, am I right?" Ted was saying. "I'd hate to give you another assignment and then have to pull you off it again."

Leo's phone began to slip out of his moist palm. He switched hands. "The prosecutor said they won't need me until next week. It's only Wednesday, plenty of time."

"To be honest, the work's starting to dry up for you. I'm sorry."

"What does that mean?"

"I don't have anything for you."

"ARE YOU FI—," he started to shout then realized the banter behind him stopped. "Are you firing me?" he asked in a hoarse whisper.

"Let's see how your testimony goes next week. We'll take it from there." The connection ended.

Leo stared at his phone, wondering if he could crush it with his bare hand. When the elevator doors opened on the ground floor, he fought the urge to shove everyone aside and get out. Instead he stayed put — polite society demanded it — and considered his options. Freelance for another paper? Teach a journalism course at his alma mater, the University of Chicago? Find a cheaper apartment?

With the elevator finally empty, Leo exited into the steely cold lobby, dragged himself past security, pushed through the revolving door, and stepped out onto the busy Chicago sidewalk. He bumped into a group of women waiting to enter and managed a "sorry."

"I'm not," one woman replied. The rest of the group laughed.

He ignored them. Shoving his phone in his pants' pocket, he zipped up his leather jacket and trudged the four blocks south on Dearborn toward Printers' Row. The temperature had dropped to what he suspected was a dismal forty degrees. The wind whipped specks of rain, or was it snow, against his face. He was actually glad for it. The weather would keep the neighbors inside, giving him a reprieve from small talk.

Trudging by Kasey's Tavern, his favorite watering hole, he wished he could pop in for a quick one. He reached for the cold brass handle but the door wouldn't budge. The bar wouldn't open for another hour. He jammed his hand back into his pocket and walked on.

Arriving at his building, Leo used his smartcard to enter. He checked his mailbox, *empty*, and then climbed the two flights of stairs to his studio apartment. Taking off his damp jacket and hanging it on a hook by the front door, he considered interviewing for the anchor job at WCH-TV. Ted always said Leo was too good looking to be sitting behind a computer. Yet the idea of reading the news rather than writing about it made him cringe.

Walking the few steps into the galley kitchen, he considered pouring himself a whiskey but looking at the clock, he thought better of it. It was barely ten a.m. Then he saw the note on the counter.

Leo. Thanks for the last couple of months. They were amazing! Charlie's back in town. I thought I was over him, but… Anyway, thanks — Cecile.

Great, just great.

He dug in his cabinets and grabbed a half-empty bottle of Jack Daniels. He opened it and began to pour when he remembered the rats.

Three weeks ago, he had awoken to the sound of chewing and the smell of rotting garbage. He found himself lying naked on a soiled mattress in a hellhole apartment in an unfamiliar part of Chicago. Rats gnawed on his Italian loafers. Empty liquor bottles and garbage were strewn everywhere. No one in the apartment but the rats. He kicked the bastards and grabbed his clothes, noticing that his wallet was missing. Head pounding, room spinning, mouth dry, he had staggered out, humiliated.

Leo poured the whiskey down the drain. He didn't want a repeat performance. Besides, getting drunk wouldn't bring Cecile back.

He trudged out of the kitchen into the living area, the heels of his Ferragamos scraping on the hardwood floors. He dropped onto the couch, kicked off the shoes and propped his feet up onto the glass table, inadvertently pushing an old Giordano's pizza box into an empty Goose Island beer bottle, tipping it over. Clinks echoed around the room. He shook out his damp hair. Ah hell, Cecile had never read a newspaper in her life, or anything else. She lacked a sense of humor and rooted for the White Sox. What had he been thinking?

More importantly, what was he going to do about his job? He was effectively fired. How would he afford rent? Make car payments? He hated the thought of losing his Mustang convertible even though he only drove it during the Chicago thaw. He loved that car.

Damn his editor. Damn *The Chicago Examiner*. *The Examiner*! He'd left his laptop at the paper. It was just the excuse he needed to go back and demand an assignment. Hell, he'd beg if he thought it'd work.

As he slipped his shoes back on, Bob Marley's *I Shot the Sheriff* rang out from his pocket. He grabbed his phone.

"I've got something for you," Ted said.

Leo slumped back onto the sofa and fought the urge to laugh with relief.

"Leo, you still with me?"

"Yeah, yeah, I'm here." He sat up, energized, though he wondered what had changed the editor's mind. "So what's the story? Does it involve government secrets, celebrity scandal, high crimes, espionage?"

"Possibly," Ted said without a trace of humor. "I don't want to discuss this over the phone. Come to the office. We'll talk when you get here. "

"I'm on my way," he said, getting up from the couch. "And Ted, thanks."


The sleet had stopped. Scattered sunlight melted ice patches on the sidewalk. Leo jogged back down Dearborn, passed the federal courthouse and turned right onto Adams Street toward Michigan Avenue. Holding the stitch in his side while swearing he'd get back to triathlon training, he almost hopped onto the Blue Line, but decided against it. He wanted to immerse himself in the city.

Reaching Michigan Avenue, he stopped to catch his breath and let a honking limousine drive past. The limo left behind a cloud of exhaust fumes. When mixed with cigarette smoke, deep dish pizza aromas and the fishy mist coming off Lake Michigan, the smell became what he liked to call "Chicago's perfume."

Heading up The Magnificent Mile, Leo darted around camera-toting tourists craning their heads to see the tops of skyscrapers. He dodged between clumps of perfumed businesswomen waiting for taxis, glad that he didn't have to wear suits and high heels to work. He jogged around students heading into the Art Institute with portfolios strapped to their backs, carrying Styrofoam coffee cups and bags of donuts. The smell of cinnamon trailed them. Leo's stomach growled reminding him he'd been too nervous to eat breakfast.

On East Wacker Drive, alongside the dark blue-green Chicago River, he accepted a flyer from protestors in matching tie-dyed shirts, always on the lookout for a good story. Then he sprinted the last hundred feet and pushed through *The Examiner's* front door.

"Marcus," he called to the security guard behind the front desk.

"Leo. How's it goin'?" the uniformed man replied.

"Couldn't be better." He shoved the flyer into his pocket and then swiped his identity card. "Cubs are headed to the World Series and I'm not goin' to jail. Yet."

Marcus laughed. "Glad to hear it. I'd hate it if you missed seeing the Cubbies win just cuz you were stuck behind bars."

Leo waved as he trotted down the hall toward the stairwell, but stopped as a group of Asian businessmen lined up to take the stairs. A tour group. He hustled over to an open elevator and then stood like an idiot in front of it as he debated wedging himself into the crowded compartment. He could wait for an empty one, but all the elevators would be packed until the building cleared out that night.

Just as the doors started to close, he stepped in. His heart kicked into overdrive. He stared at the teeth marks in his shoes and pictured himself rubbing polish into them. He had found that imaging small, repetitive tasks helped ease his fear of crowded places. This worked until the elevator jerked on the fifth floor, causing the men on either side to bump into him. He fought the urge to push them away as he pictured people panicking, stampeding, trampling. He wiped beads of sweat from his forehead.

The elevator stopped on each of the next five floors but no one got on; there wasn't room. Leo forced himself to stay put, though it was increasingly harder with each stop. He managed to distract himself by pulling the flyer out of his pocket. He looked at it but couldn't read it; his shaking hands blurred the words. Still, staring at the colors and images took his mind off the shifting, breathing, murmuring people pressing in on him.

When the elevator finally stopped on the eleventh floor, Leo shoved his way into the vacant hallway. He tossed the flyer in the trash then patted his jacket for the silver plated flask Cecile had bought him for his thirty-fifth birthday last May. The empty pocket reminded him that he'd buried the flask in his kitchen junk drawer after waking from that rat-

KRISTIN A. OAKLEY

infested bender. His last, he hoped.

Taking deep breaths, he walked down to the lunchroom for coffee. He settled on straight-up decaf and after a few gulps felt revitalized enough to flirt with a freshman copywriter. Pausing inside the newsroom doors, he glanced at the continuous stream of news on the overhead monitors, but saw nothing of interest. He wove his way to his cluttered desk and slung his jacket on the back of his chair. Collecting his reporter's notebook, he headed to Ted's glass-walled office.

"So what's this intriguing story you're willing to let me tackle?" Leo asked.

Ted rose from his swivel chair wearing his customary t-shirt and jeans. His black sports coat hung on the back of the chair, looking more dusty and wrinkled than ever. Ted preferred wearing just his message-laden shirts. This one read, "Those who would give up essential liberty to purchase a little temporary safety deserve neither liberty nor safety. Benjamin Franklin."

Ted wore the t-shirts to state his journalistic philosophies and to show off his scarred, muscular arms, souvenirs from covering Operation Desert Storm and the Rwandan and Sierra Leon civil wars. T-shirts were frowned upon at *The Examiner*, but because Ted had rescued two cameramen from machete-wielding soldiers, the managing editor looked the other way.

"There's this town that's somehow school-less," Ted said, walking around his paper strewn desk and leaning against it.

"School-less?" Leo asked, sitting on the lumpy coach that often doubled as Ted's bed.

"There isn't a single school within the town limits."

"Is that legal?"

"That's what I'd like you to find out." Ted crossed his massive arms.

"That's it?" He couldn't afford to be picky, but a town without schools? Who cared?

Ted scowled.

"I mean to say," Leo backpedaled, "I'm glad for the assignment, hell any assignment, though I would've guessed you'd give this one to Ferguson. Education is his beat."

"Ferguson was my first choice," Ted said. "But there's more to it. I just got off the phone with Raegan Colyer, you know, the governor's chief of staff?"

"Sure, I know her." He knew quite a lot about Raegan, including the shape of the mole on her left breast.

"She mentioned you. Liked your work. Anyway, we were discussing the governor's educational budget proposals when she brought up this town. Seems the governor's office is interested in finding out anything they can about it."

"Why is the governor interested?"

"Not sure."

Leo got up from the couch and began to pace the small room.

"Personally," Ted said, "the town's story doesn't interest me as much as the governor's involvement. Do you want the job?"

This was not the kind of assignment Leo would have agreed to a year ago when he would have had his pick of political corruption, conspiracies, murder. This story would be printed in the schools' section of *The Examiner*, not on the front page or even in the main news section. He swallowed. "Do I have a choice?"

"I'm not going to lie. If you don't take this story, I don't know what else will come your way. I'm not concerned about your writing skills, you're a natural. I am concerned about your reliability."

About to protest, Leo decided against it. Over the last couple of months, his work had been poorly researched, sloppy. Ted had covered for him while he struggled with his excessive drinking and his crowd phobia, but Ted had grown increasingly irritated with Leo's missed deadlines. Then his Smithson piece became a finalist for the Pulitzer Prize and Ted cut him some slack. But Leo couldn't rely on that achievement much longer. His drinking and poor work performance had damaged his reputation. He knew the newspaper was waiting to see if he'd divulge his source to the grand jury. If he did, the Pulitzer Prize nomination wouldn't be enough to save his job.

Ted went on, "It should take you a day or two to get all you need on the town. Plenty of time before you're called back to court."

Leo flipped open his notebook and pulled out a pen. "What's the name of this town?"

"Carpe Diem."

"Carpe Diem? Latin for 'live life'?"

"Actually, it's Latin for 'seize the day,' but you've got the drift. From what Colyer told me, a guy named John Holden founded the town about thirty years ago. Don't know if he's still around."

"John Holden, okay. Anything else?"

"Colyer mentioned the town's population has increased dramatically. In the nineteen eighties there were just a few residents. Today more than three thousand people live there. Colyer seemed bothered by this. She hinted it might be some sort of cult. Like that polygamist camp in Texas."

"A cult? Hmm, interesting. Still, why does the governor's office care? They've got more pressing matters."

"I have no idea."

"It doesn't make sense." Leo tapped his notebook with his pen. "I'll check around and get back to you."

At his desk, Leo jotted down questions, a list of people to interview, records to research, and several internet queries. He didn't think there was much to this story, but the governor's office had led him to the Smithson story and it had almost won him the Pulitzer.

Still that article had involved government corruption at the state's highest levels. A meaty story. Writing an article about homeschoolers wasn't anywhere near the same league. He could hear his longtime newsroom rival, Anders, telling his cronies how Townsend was demoted to writing about school crossing guards. It made Leo's stomach turn. He tried not to think about it and opened his computer.

Thirty minutes later, he overheard the words "Carpe Diem, Illinois." Surprised, he looked up at the nearest television monitor.

"—reporting a motorcycle collision with a sedan on Highway 20, five miles from the town. The accident is under investigation. A preliminary report suggests the bike crossed the center line. The unidentified driver of the motorcycle was thrown fifty feet and was taken by ambulance to the Carpe Diem Hospital. He is listed in critical condition. The driver of the car, Alexandra Shaw of Alanton, is the wife of state Senator Christopher Shaw. Mrs. Shaw is listed in serious but stable condition at the

Carpe Diem Hospital."

"Senator Shaw has some power in Springfield," Ted said, approaching Leo. "Made a few enemies."

"True," Leo said, wondering if the accident was in fact an accident. The story now had potential and, of course, a paycheck attached to it. "I'll grab lunch and head to Carpe Diem," he said.

# 3

Fifteen-year-old Tali Shaw listened to Kelly Clarkson sing *Since U Been Gone* on her iPod, plucked threads out of the hole in her jeans, and tried not to think of her mom in the operating room. Pushing her black woolen jacket off her hunched shoulders, she picked up a copy of *The Carpe Diem Daily News* from a nearby coffee table but couldn't focus on the headlines. She looked at the wall clock for the hundredth time, 10:35 a.m. They'd been in the hospital for more than nine hours.

She was not going to break down and cry, not in front of her dad. Her mom might die but instead of comforting her, he treated her like he'd rather have a different kid.

At least he was consistent. For years he had hired nannies to keep her out of the way. What was the last one's name? Rosita? Her mother fired the nanny for some unknown reason and refused to hire another one. Rosario? Rosalinda! The night Rosalinda left, her parents fought terribly but Alexandra didn't give in even after Christopher stopped coming home.

The third night without her dad, Tali picked at her pot roast, usually her favorite, thinking it would be better to just hire another nanny. Alexandra asked questions about school in a lame attempt to be chummy. Tali mumbled the answers.

Then Alexandra started to tell her a story. At first, Tali thought she had had too much wine and asked her what the frig she was talking about, but Alexandra ignored her. It was as if she had wanted to share this amazing tale for a long time and now was the only chance. Tali got caught up in the story, the pot roast and her absent father forgotten.

Christopher came home the next night, bringing flowers for Alexandra and a pat on the arm for her, though he rarely made it home for dinner after that. She didn't mind because there were fewer arguments and more storytelling, and finally a connection with her mother. When the story ended weeks later, Tali encouraged her mother to write it down. Alexandra then surprised her by signing up for a novel writing workshop in Chicago. They hoped the story would be published. At least that was the plan until the accident.

Tali sighed and glanced around the waiting room. She had the place memorized. Cushy chairs and couches, magazine covered tables, vases of fresh flowers, and walls of windows. It was a comfortable room but the last place in the world she wanted to be. A young couple sitting in the corner looked like they didn't want to be there either. The woman silently wept. The man made eye contact with Tali. She quickly looked at her father.

Usually, the great Senator Christopher Shaw looked amazing. But they'd been in a hurry to get to the hospital, so he had thrown on black jeans, a wrinkled yellow Izod shirt, and a brown woolen jacket. He had forgotten socks and had bed head. It was weird to see him like this. He was always totally put together, even at home.

It struck Tali how little she'd seen of him lately. He worked twelve hour days, traveled, and stayed for weeks at a time at his capitol office in Springfield. Not that she missed him. When he came home she avoided him. She'd rather message her friends or hang at the mall instead of listening to him go on about politics or argue with Alexandra. And her mom never told her stories when he was around. He didn't know about the novel or the Chicago workshop.

He was quiet now, probably playing solitaire on his laptop.

She looked at his computer to see if he was winning. Not solitaire, a long e-mail. She turned off her iPod.

"You're *working*?"

"Don't use that tone with me."

"It's, it's just… aren't you worried?"

"Yes," he replied, continuing to type.

She felt sick. Pulling away from him, she noticed a yellow stain on his fingers.

"What's with your hand—?"

"Senator Shaw?" A young uniformed police officer approached, the handcuffs on his belt clicking.

"Yes, I'm Christopher Shaw."

The officer nodded and looked at Tali. She examined the scuff mark on the top of her Uggs boot.

Christopher closed his laptop and set it aside. "This is my daughter, Natalia." She hated it when her parents called her by her full name.

The officer took his cap off and placed it under his arm. "I'm Officer Hank Dennison. I was the first to arrive at the scene of the accident. I'm sorry about Mrs. Shaw. I hope she'll be okay."

Christopher stood, shoving his stained left hand into his pocket before shaking the policeman's hand with his right. "She's in surgery but we're optimistic."

"Good," the cop said. "I have a few questions I'd like to ask you, if that's okay."

"Not at all. I have some things to ask you as well."

The cop sat across from Tali, set his hat aside, then pulled out a notepad and flipped through it. "Where was Mrs. Shaw headed?"

"To our home in Alanton," Christopher replied as he sat back down.

"And she was coming from…"

"Chicago. Most likely Michigan Avenue. She likes to shop."

Tali didn't correct him.

The officer looked back at his notes. "Your BMW M3, great car by-the-way, was in good shape? I mean, before the accident?"

"We take it in for maintenance every three thousand miles and recently replaced the tires."

Tali had gone with her mom to have the tires changed. She remembered how Alexandra complained about having to waste an hour there, but Tali loved being at the garage. Cars were awesome; besides, the mechanics were hot.

"Does Mrs. Shaw have any history of substance abuse?"

"Certainly not!" Christopher growled. Tali jerked more threads out of the hole in her jeans.

"I meant no offense. It's a standard question we have to ask." The officer waved the pad. "That's it. You have some questions?"

"What can you tell me about the accident?" Christopher asked. "The TV news reports mentioned something about a motorcycle."

"I guess I should have told you earlier. Sorry, I'm new to the job."

"Obviously."

Either the cop didn't hear him or decided to ignore the comment. "We don't have all the information yet. But what we do know is that at about ten o'clock last night, Mrs. Shaw was traveling west on Highway 20, near the town of Carpe Diem, when a motorcycle swerved into her lane."

"Ten o'clock?" Tali blurted out.

"Yes."

Tali felt sick. She had called her mom at ten. Had the ringing phone distracted her? Caused the accident?

"Why? Is there something important about the time?" the officer asked.

She hesitated and then shook her head, letting her blond bangs hide her eyes.

Officer Dennison paused, but when Tali offered nothing more he moved on, checking his pad. "Based on the lack of skid marks and the cycle's high rate of speed, we have reason to believe that the motorcycle driver may have intended to swerve into her lane."

"What do you mean?" Christopher asked.

"We can't officially say yet, but this may have been an attempted suicide."

Tali gasped, horrified. And relieved. Maybe she wasn't to blame.

"You've got to be kidding!" her dad raged. "Jesus, if he wanted to kill himself why not put a bullet in his head? Why try to take my wife with him?"

"Um, I don't know. We haven't talked to the motorcyclist yet. He's in a coma."

"Who is he?"

"Patrick Holden. He's from Carpe Diem."

"Patrick Holden? Forty-something hippie?" Christopher's voice trembled.

"I wouldn't call him a hippie, although he does have long hair."

"I saw him last night," Christopher said. "We had a late meeting. The guy's unhinged. He raved about individual freedoms, as if I need a lecture on that. Went off on children's rights of all things. Finally, I had had enough. When he wouldn't leave, I did. I have better things to do than listen to a lunatic."

All that time sitting in the waiting room and her father never mentioned his recent meeting with a crazy man. What else hadn't he told her?

"Did he seem suicidal to you?" the officer asked.

"Crazy yes, suicidal no. Oh my God, do you think he drove into my wife on purpose?" Christopher asked. "Somehow he knew it was her?"

"The odds are pretty slim." The policeman hesitated. "Unless you told him she'd be driving on Highway 20."

"I can assure you the location of my wife's whereabouts never came up."

"I didn't think so," the cop said. "It looks random. Patrick might have been looking for a truck or other large vehicle until your wife's car…"

"Hank, what the hell are you telling those people?" an old man shouted as he came into the room.

"John," Officer Dennison sputtered as the irate man limped to their group. "Um, this is the husband and daughter of Alexandra Shaw. Senator Christopher Shaw and Natalia."

"Tali," she corrected.

When she remained seated, her father said, "Natalia, for God's sake, stand up."

She stood.

"This is John Holden, Patrick's father," the cop said.

Mr. Holden had a mess of shocking white hair and smelled of earthy pine. His dark green pullover sweater was frayed around the cuffs and beneath faded jeans his toes peeked out of weathered leather sandals. At least he wasn't wearing socks.

"I'm sorry about Mrs. Shaw. I hope she'll be all right," Mr. Holden said. His deep voice was warm, soothing. His creased face softened until he rounded on the officer. "Hank, Patrick isn't suicidal."

"The evidence points to—"

"Damn the evidence. It was an accident!" The man waved his arms. "My son would never intentionally harm anyone, including himself. He's not capable."

"Mr. Holden," Tali's father interjected, quieting the man for the moment. "Your son came to my office last night. At one point he looked more than capable of hurting me."

"Impossible!"

"I had to leave the meeting."

"Patrick is passionate, particularly about educational freedom. Sometimes his passion is misinterpreted. Obviously, he didn't persuade you."

"No, of course not. As I said, I walked—"

"I told him he was wasting his time," Mr. Holden said. Christopher glared at the old man who ignored him and rounded on the officer. "Hank, it's irresponsible of the Carpe Diem Police Department to tell these people that Patrick is dangerous. I'm asking you to not say anything more until we've talked to him."

"Okay." Officer Dennison sighed then laid his hand on the man's shoulder. "How's Patrick doing?"

"He's in bad shape." Mr. Holden ran his fingers through his mop of hair. "Damn, I never could get him to wear a helmet."

"It's amazing he landed in a hayfield. Totally missed those trees," the cop said.

"Not amazing, just dumb luck," Mr. Holden replied.

"In Alexandra's case, extreme bad luck to be in your son's path!" Christopher yelled, clenching his fists.

Tali backed away. He looked like he was going to punch someone, though she couldn't blame him for being angry.

A tired doctor in a rumpled white coat approached them. "Senator Christopher Shaw?"

"Yes?"

"I'm Dr. Anderson," he said, shaking her dad's now unclenched hand and smiling at her. "Hi, Hank. Nice to see you, John," he said to the other two men.

Mr. Holden nodded to the doctor before saying, "I've gotta check on Patrick. Senator Shaw, Tali, I hope the best for Mrs. Shaw."

Tali watched him leave. He limped and he certainly wasn't big on personal hygiene, but even though he was upset he stopped to talk to the young couple. The woman wiped her tears. The man's anguished face relaxed.

"Overall the surgery went well," Dr. Anderson said. "We reset her various fractures and put a pin in her left thigh bone, which will be permanent. She may need several months of rehabilitation, but she's young. She should heal quickly." The doctor paused. "Unfortunately, we weren't able to save her spleen. It was severely damaged."

"What does the spleen do?" Christopher asked.

"The spleen is part of the body's immune system. It filters and regulates the amount of blood the body has, acting like a reservoir for when extra blood is needed, say in an injury. The spleen also eliminates old and damaged cells."

"And without her spleen?" Christopher asked.

"Your wife loses some of her ability to fight infections. We gave her a pneumonia vaccine and she'll have to have flu shots every year. We'll give her a national splenectomy card to carry with her at all times. Other than that, she should live a long and healthy life."

Tali felt weak with relief. She wanted to hug her dad, but she'd given up on seeking affection from him years ago.

"We're moving her from the recovery room into her own room. You can see her, but she's heavily sedated and won't wake up for quite some time. I'll talk to you once she does."

"Thank you," Christopher said right before the doctor was called away.

"I'm glad to hear Mrs. Shaw will be okay," Officer Dennison said.

Christopher nodded then turned to Tali. "After we see your mother, we'll get lunch and then check into a hotel."

"We're not big on hotels in Carpe Diem," the cop said. "Bed and breakfasts are more our speed. There's The Maple Tree Bed and Breakfast,

Austin Walker's place and the most popular one, The Bradbury Inn. It's on Countryside Lane not too far from here."

"Sounds good."

"I can call Mayor Evans for you. Tell her you'd like a room."

"No. If you could give me the Inn's number, I'll make the call. Wait, did you say *Mayor* Evans?"

"Yes. She owns The Bradbury Inn. Being mayor of a small town is a part-time job." He wrote the number down on his pad. "I almost forgot. Your wife's Beemer is impounded at the police station."

"You mean Bimmer," Christopher corrected. He was right, but Tali couldn't believe he'd care at a time like this.

"What?"

"Bimmer is the proper term for a BMW automobile."

"Huh, didn't know that. Anyway, we need to keep the car for a few days before you can claim it. Also, if you think of anything else that might help our investigation, please call me." He handed Christopher his card, started to leave, then stopped. "You said your wife had been shopping?"

"Yes. She goes into the city at least twice a month."

"Strange."

"What's strange?"

"There weren't any shopping bags in her car or alongside the road."

"I find that hard to believe. My wife's a shopaholic. Never leaves a store without buying something." He thought for a moment. "Maybe someone stole the packages."

"I doubt it. Not many people travel Highway 20 at that time of night. Huh," the officer scratched his ear. "Well, I've got to get back to the station. Call me if you think of anything else."

Christopher watched the police officer leave before turning on Tali. "Did your mother tell you where she was going?"

Tali concentrated on the toes of her boots.

"Answer me. Where did she go yesterday?"

"Chicago."

"I know that," he hissed. "She obviously didn't go shopping. What was she doing in the city?"

"I don't know."

Christopher stared at her for a moment then walked down the hallway.

She followed him into the intensive care unit, not taking her eyes from the backs of his brown loafers. When the loafers stopped beside a bed, she forced herself to look up.

Gauze strips covered her mother's head. Puffy purple skin pushed through the bandages in grotesque shapes. A breathing tube snaked out of her mouth. Other tubes connected her right hand, arm, and even her neck to beeping, glowing machines. Her left arm was in a cast, her swollen fingers sticking out like overstuffed sausages.

Tali's stomach churned. Her head spun. Then her cheek slapped the cool floor tiles right before the room went black.

# 4

*With her left hand in a cast, the right hand scratched and bleeding, she searched for the ringing phone, forgetting to steer the BMW. The car didn't veer from its course. A spotlight blinded her right eye; her left eye was swollen shut. The light didn't matter. Finding the ringing telephone mattered. A motorcycle was coming straight at her. Find the ringing phone. The cycle slammed into the side of her car, then into her ribcage. Find the phone!*

Tali jerked up, sweaty and shaking. Only a nightmare, but then why didn't she feel better now that she was awake? She looked at the canopy over her head, the landscape painting on the walls, the afternoon sunlight filtering through sheer curtains. No sports car mobile, Green Day posters, or navy blue shades. She smelled roses.

This wasn't her bedroom.

She massaged her throbbing right cheek. She had passed out because her mom… she swallowed back the lump in her throat. She remembered a nurse helping her out of the hospital and into her father's waiting car. After checking into this place, she had collapsed on the bed.

Pushing aside a small bowl of potpourri on the bedside table, she grabbed the clock. 2:50 p.m.

Tali fumbled in her jeans' pocket for her cell phone. Her boyfriend Tom had messaged her. His best friend Mike had been suspended for copying Emma's test. He said nothing about her mom. Typical. Noticing the low battery signal, she sent him a quick text, and then saw a message from her dad.

"M @ hospital."

She called him back and got his voice mail. Of course he'd leave her alone in an inn in a strange town with no way of getting to the hospital. She threw the phone on the bed. She wanted to see her mom, even with all the bandages and bruises. She'd be braver. She wouldn't pass out this time. Maybe Mom would be awake and she'd be able to talk to her, to apologize for the phone call.

Tali shoved a few annoying strands of blond hair out of her eyes. They felt slick, stringy. Disgusted, she wiped her fingers on her No Doubt sweatshirt. She needed a shower and clean clothes. She walked around the bed looking for her duffle bag then opened the closet door. It wasn't there. Dad must have left it in his room. Cursing him, she opened the bathroom door. Under the sink lay the bag.

Forgiving her dad for the moment, she took a long, hot shower, releasing some of the tension in her muscles and washing her greasy hair twice. She dried off then touched the charm dangling from her necklace.

Three years ago, her father had thrown out all of her *Car & Driver* magazines, torn down her Ferrari and Lamborghini posters and banned her from Grandpa Shaw's auto repair shop. He screamed that there was no way in hell his daughter would get sucked into that greasy lower class life. Her mother had just stood there.

A week later, her mom came home from a Chicago shopping trip with a small package for Tali. Inside the velvet box was a silver chain with a black 1957 Ford Thunderbird charm.

Now Tali kissed the miniature Thunderbird, threw on her baggy Alanton Tigers' sweatshirt, shrugged into her holey jeans and pulled on her Uggs. Too hyper to wait in her room, she decided to check out the Inn's main floor. At the bottom of the wooden staircase, she passed a tall, plain woman.

"You must be Natalia. I'm Mary Evans." She pushed her glasses up the bridge of her nose.

Not a very impressive mayor, Tali thought.

"I'm sorry I didn't meet you and your father earlier when you checked in," the mayor said. "Did you get a chance to sleep?"

Tali nodded, her hair falling across her face. She left it there.

"Are you hungry?"

Tali had skipped breakfast and lunch. She had been too upset and too tired to eat. Now her stomach growled.

The mayor smiled, making her look less plain. "I'll take that as a 'yes.' The kitchen stopped serving breakfast at eleven, but I'm sure Will can whip you up something."

Tali shook her head 'no.' She'd rather eat with her dad at the hospital than with strangers.

"Are you sure, because I think Will's trying out one of his new recipes. Do you like pasta?"

Tali nodded involuntarily. She adored pasta.

"Great. You'll like Pasta a la Will, or whatever he's calling it. Just go down the hall." The mayor pointed around the staircase. "The kitchen is at the end through the double doors."

Tali trudged down the long hallway. Photographs of sunflowers, star gazers and children in sandboxes covered the right-hand wall. Most were autographed *Q. A. Evans* although a few had *John Holden* scrawled on them.

Books were haphazardly stacked on shelves along the opposite wall. Tali recognized classics like *Moby Dick*, *The Martian Chronicles*, and *Pride and Prejudice*. She knew about these books but had never read them. No time. She had to read *The Lord of the Flies*, again. The school board had eliminated *The Lord of the Flies* from the junior high curriculum and made it required reading for senior high students even if they'd already read it. She was glad to see that Mayor Evans didn't have *The Lord of the Flies*.

Tali pushed open the kitchen door and smelled garlic, sautéed onions, and heavy cream. Across the room, an eleven or twelve-year-old boy stirred something in a copper kettle on a huge gas stove.

She cleared her throat. "Um, I'm looking for Will."

The boy turned around. He was short and chunky, though the chunkiness might have been because of his baggy jeans, bulky sweater and large apron. "You've found him. Are you Natalia?"

"Tali."

"Tali. Sorry 'bout your mom. I hope she'll be okay."

She nodded. "Wait, you're Will? The chef?"

"Yep, that's me. Though I'm not a full-fledged chef. Yet."

She studied his round baby face. "How old are you?"

"I'll be fourteen next month."

"Aren't you too young?"

"To be working? Nope, at least not in Carpe Diem. Mom doesn't pay me much, but I'm not complaining. I'd cook for free."

"Mom? Mayor Evans?"

"Yep." He grated fresh parmesan cheese into a saucepan on the stove. "I'm working on a new pasta recipe. Want some?"

She shrugged.

"It's not ready yet. How 'bout hanging out in the dining room?" Will pointed to a door on the far side of the kitchen. "I'll bring it out." He had his mom's smile.

Tali walked past the sizzling pan of sautéing onions and pushed open the door to the dining room. A fire in the stone hearth made the room's pale yellow walls glow. Pumpkins and maple leaves decorated the tables. Sheer curtains softened the large windows and more photographs and cluttered bookshelves covered the walls. She felt her knotted muscles relax. Happy to be the room's sole occupant, she pulled *To Kill a Mockingbird* off one of the shelves.

Will pushed the kitchen door open with his butt, his hands carrying two full plates. The room filled with a garlic and butter aroma, how Tali imagined Italy would smell.

"One of my favorites," he said pointing at the book with one of the plates.

"Never read it."

"Wanna borrow it?"

"No. It's required reading next year." She put the book back on the shelf.

"Huh, why wait? I read anything I want whenever I want to."

She didn't say anything. She only read good books in the summer.

During the school year, she was stuck reading whatever someone assigned her.

"Where d'ya wanna sit?"

She shrugged.

Will placed a large plate containing pasta with white sauce and a smaller plate heaped with salad onto a table next to the fireplace. "I put my homemade parmesan cheese in the sauce. The pasta is made from scratch using cake flour and extra egg yolks for richer noodles." He glanced up from the plate. "Oh, sorry, I always think people are as interested in cooking as me. What about a drink? Soda, juice, tea, coffee?"

"Diet Pepsi."

"Sure thing." He ducked back into the kitchen.

As Tali enjoyed her first delicious bite of pasta, a tall, black-haired teenage girl barged into the room. "Will!" she yelled. She stopped short when she notice Tali. "Oh, sorry, I didn't realize there were any diners. I'm Quinn. I'm looking for my brother. Have you seen him?"

"He's in the kitchen," Tali managed through a mouthful of noodles. "I'm Tali," she added.

Quinn was dressed in various shades of black with a diamond stud in her left nostril, a small silver hoop piercing her right eyebrow, jingling chain maille jewelry, and a black 35mm digital camera case slung over her left shoulder. She reminded Tali of the members of an Emo group at her school. Tali wouldn't be caught dead talking to them.

Will scooted into the room. "Here's your drink. Oh, Quinn. Did you meet Tali?"

"Yep. Look, you've got to clean up the kitchen. We've gotta get going."

"Right. Keep Tali company." He took off his apron as he left.

"You don't need to," Tali said quickly. What would Tom, her linebacker boyfriend, say if he knew she was talking to an Emo?

"Not a problem. Is it okay if I sit down?" Quinn motioned to a chair. When Tali shrugged and continued eating, Quinn sat. "I heard your mom was in a bad car accident. I'm so sorry. How's she doing?"

Tali pictured her mom's swollen face. "Okay."

"I'm sure she'll be fine. She's at one of the best hospitals in the state." Quinn eyed Tali's food. "What did Will make you?"

"Pasta." Obviously. She glanced at the grandfather clock in the corner. Three thirty. In Alanton, she'd still be on the school bus. "How old are you?"

"I'm seventeen. How old are you?"

"Almost sixteen. You must get out of school early."

"Will and I don't go to school."

Tali almost choked on a tomato. "You skip school?"

"We unschool."

"Natalia," Mayor Evans interrupted, entering the dining room.

"She likes to be called 'Tali'," Quinn said.

"Tali," the mayor corrected. "David, our concierge, told me your dad called the Inn a few minutes ago. He tried your cell phone but couldn't get through."

Tali pulled out her phone. Dead battery.

"He said your mother is awake."

"How is…"

"She's fine. I'd be happy to take you to the hospital. We could swing by on the way to my office."

Tali nodded.

"When you've finished eating, we'll go."

Tali ate the last forkful of pasta, and then tossed her napkin onto the table. "I'm done."

"Okay. Quinn, honey, you and Will should be home for dinner, right?"

"Yep. We shouldn't be more than a couple of hours. Wait, aren't you coming to the festival planning meeting?"

"Is that this afternoon? Oh shoot, I forgot! I've got a four o'clock interview with a *Chicago Examiner* reporter. He's doing a story on the festival. Can you run the meeting for me?"

"Me? No way! I'd rather die. Ask Will. He knows more about it than I do."

"Good idea."

"Interview?" Quinn said to her mother's back. "That explains the suit and high heels."

The mayor faced her daughter. "You're giving Tali the wrong impression." She smiled at Tali. "Don't listen to her. I'm always dressed to kill."

"Right, to kill chickens out back." Quinn leaned closer to Tali. "She lives in sweat shirts and jeans."

The mayor waved her hand dismissively as she went into the kitchen. A moment later, she came back. "Will jumped at the chance to run the meeting."

"Good. Hey, ask the reporter if *The Examiner* is looking for photographers." Quinn held up her camera case, her chain maille jingling.

"You bet. Okay, Tali, let's get going. My SUV's out front."


Tali trudged through the intensive care unit, past rooms with curtains for doors which failed at hiding beds filled with lifeless bodies. She made it to her mother's room and pushed aside the curtain. Alexandra was propped up on pillows, listening to Christopher ramble on about something. The breathing tube was gone and she didn't appear as puffy, though her left eye was still swollen shut. Sitting up, she looked stronger.

"Natalia," her mom managed to croak.

Starting to cry, Tali ran to the bed, hesitated, and then gave her mother a gentle hug. She glanced at her father lounging in a chair and then confided to her mom, "I'm sorry. My fault," she sobbed. "I shouldn't... have ... called you."

"What are you talking about?" Christopher demanded.

She shivered in her mom's arms. "I called Mom right before the accident."

Alexandra slowly shook her head.

"It was stupid to call her," her father said. "And so late on a school night." He relaxed back into the chair. "But your mother's right, you're not to blame. The motorcyclist ran into her. The accident was unavoidable."

She wanted to believe that. Maybe it was true? She hoped so. She did feel relieved now that she had told her mother. She wiped her eyes, hugged her mom again and kissed her on an unbruised spot of cheek. "I'm glad you're going to be okay."

"Careful with our patient," Dr. Anderson chuckled as he walked into

KRISTIN A. OAKLEY

the room. "How are you doing, Mrs. Shaw?"

Alexandra nodded.

Tali moved out of the doctor's way, walked around the bed and leaned against the windowsill.

"You'll be with us awhile I'm afraid."

"How long?" Christopher asked.

"As long as your vital signs remain stable, Mrs. Shaw, we'll move you out of the intensive care unit tomorrow morning. After that, you'll be with us seven to nine days. Maybe longer." His pager beeped. "If you have any additional questions, be sure to have the nurse page me."

After the doctor left, Christopher said, "You'll be here seven to nine days? I'll have to hire a cook and a maid."

"Wait, we're leaving? No, we're staying with Mom."

Alexandra mouthed the word *no*.

"I have work and you can't miss school," her father said.

"I couldn't give a crap about school."

Christopher stood up. "You'd better take school more seriously young lady, if you plan on going to college."

She looked at the tiled floor through blond strands of hair.

"You're coming home with me," he said.

She noticed specks of pink in the grey tiles.

"Look at me when I'm talking to you."

Tali peeked at him through her hair and noticed how good it smelled. Lilacs? She'd have to check out the name of the shampoo when she got back to the Inn.

"You're coming home with me," Christopher repeated.

Sighing, she nodded.

"Good."

She pictured being home alone while her dad attended endless meetings. After school, she'd enter an empty house with no "how was your day?" Instead of Mom's dinnertime stories over pot roast, she'd eat TV dinners in front of television reality shows. The worst part would be not being there for her mom. She looked at Alexandra, who attempted a smile but grimaced instead.

"No," Tali began in a whisper, "I'm staying."

"What did you say?" Christopher asked.

She cleared her throat. "I'm staying. I'll call Tom. He can get my assignments. Bring me my textbooks and my bike." Her words ran together. "I'll ride it to the hospital. It's not far."

Her father walked around the bed to her.

She shrank back but didn't drop her eyes.

"You'll fall behind in your work which is not acceptable," he said exhaling stale coffee fumes. "High school is very important. You're coming home with me."

"No."

He leaned closer. "What did you say?"

"I can manage my school work." Her voice quivered, yet somehow the words came out. "Tom will keep me up-to-date. I'll e-mail my completed assignments to my teachers. Finals aren't until mid-December."

"Soccer?" her mom struggled to say, pulling their attention.

"I'm the newbie on the soccer team," Tali answered, walking around her dad and over to the bed. "I won't play. And our team sucks. We'll lose right away. Anyway, it doesn't matter." She touched her mother's hand. "I'm staying here."

Alexandra held her gaze. Tali thought she saw a hint of pride.

"It's not a good idea," Christopher said.

"Please, Daddy." She only used "Daddy" when she was desperate.

He glared at her. "What the hell. I have meetings in Springfield and won't be able to babysit you anyway. You can stay—"

She nodded, ignoring the babysitting crack.

"—only if you keep up with your homework. I'll check with the Inn to see if you can keep your room there." He sat back down in the chair and crossed his arms. "I'll be leaving in the morning."

"*Tomorrow morning?*" Tali looked at her mom who stared at the cast on her arm.

"I have several important meetings in Alanton tomorrow and I've got to get back to Springfield on Friday. I'm working on getting a few bills through committee. There's one bill in particular which will help to ensure—"

"Whatever. I can't believe you're leaving tomorrow." She looked at her mother's closed eyes and watched as a small tear ran down her cheek.

# 5

Wednesday afternoon, Leo pulled his Mustang convertible over for gas in the unincorporated town of Elon. The gas station was equipped with two pumps, a cracked picture window, and a scrawny mutt who eyed him suspiciously from atop a pile of dusty grain sacks.

Ignoring the dog, he filled the car's tank and rubbed a smudge on the red fender, relieved it wasn't a scratch. He glanced down Elon's Prospect Street at the boarded up store fronts and crumbling brick façades. Dried flower beds were occupied with litter until gusts of wind blew the trash across the empty street. A rusty pickup truck sat in front of Carl's Tavern. Leo and the dog were the only living things in sight and the dog was questionable.

Leo walked past the bored animal and into the station. Musty staleness hit him. A teenaged attendant, skinny as the mutt, balanced against a wall in a dented metal chair. Surrounded by cigarette cartons, the kid argued into a cell phone with someone named Josie.

"Hey, kid." Leo rapped his knuckles on the stainless steel counter.

The kid called Josie a whore.

"Kid!" Still nothing. "Oh hell, here's the money for the gas." Leo tossed a wad of crumpled bills at the cash register then walked out.

He climbed into his convertible, started the engine, and lowered the top, hoping the crisp autumn air would lift his mood. He dreaded spending the next couple of days in a godforsaken little town like Elon, interviewing people who kept their kids chained to the kitchen table while making them recite their multiplication tables.

He restrained himself from racing out of the dreary village, anticipating a speed trap, but as soon as the speed limit allowed he gunned it. Through the rush of air he heard his cell phone play *I Shot the Sheriff*.

"Townsend," he answered as he put on his Bluetooth headset.

"It's Beth. I've got the research you asked for. I've uncovered some interesting stuff."

"Great. Go ahead." Leo pictured the young *Examiner* intern huddled in her cluttered cubicle, her eyes glued to her Post-It-Note covered computer.

"Carpe Diem began as an intentional community," Beth said.

"A what?"

"An intentional community, IC. A group of people who decide to live together because of shared interests."

"You mean a commune?"

"A commune can be an intentional community but not all ICs are communes. More typically, people live in their own houses next to each other. If they are organic vegetarians, they may group their homes around a common garden. Think of it as a suburban commune."

"So there are other towns like Carpe Diem?"

"No. While there are a lot of intentional communities around the country, Carpe Diem is unusual because it's based on homeschooling. Some of the communities I discovered homeschool their children, but it's never their main reason for forming. They're interested in simple living or they care about the environment. What makes Carpe Diem even more unusual is its size. It's the largest intentional community by far that I found. The next largest group has only one hundred and fifty people."

"Christ!"

"What?"

"Sorry, I'm stuck behind a school bus letting kids off." Leo watched as a young boy jumped off the bus and then tipped backward, almost falling over, his arms flaying. "Look at that little guy struggling with a huge backpack. Is that necessary?"

"So you didn't read my article about back problems in the average nine year old."

"You're kidding, right?"

"Nope," Beth replied.

"Good."

"Good?"

"The bus is turning."

"Getting back to Carpe Diem," Beth continued, "The town is the home of a well-respected hospital which serves several communities."

"A town of three thousand people has a hospital?"

"Carpe Diem's founder, John Holden, has a noted Chicago surgeon for a brother. The brother led a successful campaign to build a county hospital on the edge of Carpe Diem."

"Which provides a major industry for the community."

"Exactly."

"Anything else?"

"Just this. John Holden was a school teacher in Chicago's inner city schools. A pretty damn good one, too. He won Teacher of the Year awards, both locally and nationally. But the year he won his third national award he quit teaching and disappeared. No one knew what happened to him. Until now."

"Sounds like I'll be making a visit to Mr. Holden after my meeting with the mayor."

"Speaking of the mayor, how did you get the interview? What did you tell her?"

"That I was doing a piece on small towns. She didn't seem to care. She agreed to the interview right away. It was almost too easy."

"Small town mayor, maybe she's bored."

"Probably. Still, I was intentionally vague. I want her to be open about homeschooling. I'm afraid if I tell her that's the thrust of my story, I might get a sugar-coated version. Anyway, I'm hoping to come up with a better cover once I get there."

"Flash her your dimpled grin and she'll forget you're a reporter, let alone why you're there."

"I only use that as a last resort."

Beth laughed.

"Thanks for all the info."

"No problem. Just put a word in to the managing editor and maybe he'll hire me permanently."

"Will do. I'll be in touch." He took off the ear piece then pushed an Eric Clapton CD into the car's player.

Fifteen minutes later, he sped past the sign for Carpe Diem. Cursing, he slowed down to make an illegal U-turn onto the two-lane road that led to the town. The road wound through a pine forest dampened by a recent rain. Inhaling the earthy evergreen smell, he felt lucky to have missed the downpour; his soft-sided overnight bag and computer case lay unprotected on the back seat.

The forest gave way to perfect rows of dried cornstalks and fruit-laden apple trees on one side of the road. On the other side, sodden sheep and cows lumbered alongside a fast-flowing creek. Leo assumed an Amish family owned the tidy farm until he noticed a girl dressed in overalls, splashing in puddles with her yellow rubber boots near the front porch of a stately home. Hearing his car, she waved. He honked and waved back.

Passing the farm's pumpkin patch, he entered a saturated tunnel of colorful maples. An occasional drop of water splashed onto the car's upholstery or onto his head, shockingly cold. As Leo exited the tunnel, Eric Clapton finished singing *Sweet Home Chicago*. A damp banner proclaiming "Carpe Diem Fall Festival" hung from a tree's branch. An abandoned ladder stood propped against the tree.

Further into town, Leo passed American Craftsmen-style houses with wide front porches and idle porch swings. A few of the antique lamps lining the streets were decorated with hanging baskets of yellow and orange mums; more baskets lay at the base of other lamps. Flats of unplanted flowers sat neglected next to damp sidewalks. Beautiful little town, but where were the residents? Had the rain had driven them inside? This picturesque town had something in common with the town of Elon; the streets were empty.

He entered the town square and slowed to let a black cat saunter across the cobblestone street, then spotted the ivy-covered Town Hall. He found several available parking spots near the building's entrance.

Leo checked the Mustang's dashboard clock: 3:15 p.m. Even though the school bus slowed him down and he missed the turnoff, he was early. Plenty of time to grab a cup of coffee and talk to the locals. If he could find any.

He raised the top on the convertible, finger combed his damp and windblown hair and then locked the car door. Probably unnecessary in such a small town but coming from Chicago, locking the door was a habit.

Leo walked down the wet brick sidewalk along Main Street, passing by the Carpe Diem Public Library, Keagan's Irish Pub and several shops. All were closed, though not boarded-up like the businesses in Elon. Glancing into Miss Simms' Dance Studio, he saw a polished wooden dance floor surrounded by mirrors and next door at the Fair Goods Trading Center, pottery and woven blankets covered the shelves.

At the corner of Main and Summerhill, he smelled vanilla through the open doorway of Joan and Dan's Diner. He entered the restaurant and wound his way around vacant oak tables to the back of the restaurant, where a young clerk sat behind the long chrome counter.

"Hello," said the teenager, putting down his battered paperback copy of *Fahrenheit 451*. "How can I help you?"

"I'd like a large black coffee to go."

"Any particular flavor? Today's special is French Vanilla Bean."

"Sounds great." Leo sat on the nearest stool. Cellos played *Let It Be* through the HD sound system. He watched the young man pour coffee into a large blue thermal cup with the words 'Carpe Diem, Every Day' scrolled on it. "I wanted the coffee to go."

"We're not crazy about Styrofoam so we use these. No extra charge."

"Thanks." Leo took the coffee and handed money to the clerk. "Sure is quiet around here."

"Most everyone's at the Community Center for the town meeting."

"Town meeting?" Leo tasted the coffee. Smooth.

"They're finalizing plans for next week's Fall Festival." The clerk sat back down. "This band will be performing," he said referring to the bluegrass music coming through the speakers.

"They're good."

The clerk smiled. "I'm the one on the fiddle."

As if on cue, they heard a fiddle solo with fast-paced fingering.

"Impressive."

The young man tilted his head, acknowledging the compliment.

"I'm Leo Townsend." Leo held out his hand.

"Brendan Miller."

"This festival, is it a big deal?"

"People come from all over the Midwest."

"With music like this, I'm not surprised."

"Some say the barbeque cook-off, pumpkin carving contest, and corn stalk labyrinth are better than the music."

"Hard to believe," Leo said. "Wait, don't you mean 'corn stalk maze'?"

"No. It's much more than a maze. It takes an hour to get through, on average. Guides are posted in strategic places so we don't lose anyone."

Leo laughed. "Sounds great." After another sip of coffee, he asked, "Isn't it early for a town meeting? Don't folks work?"

"Most people in town have their own businesses. They set their own hours."

"What about school? Aren't the kids just getting home?"

"There aren't any schools in Carpe Diem. We unschool. "

"Unschool? What's that?"

"Brendan," a deep voice interrupted from a doorway behind the counter, "could you help me with these boxes? It looks like we got a double shipment. I can't make out what you wrote on the order forms."

"Be right there." Brendan looked at Leo apologetically.

Leo rose from the stool. "I'll let you go. Thanks for the coffee."

"You're welcome. Come back anytime."

Leo stepped out of the warmth of the diner into the damp October afternoon thinking he should have Beth research unschooling. He began to pull his cell phone out of his pocket when he heard someone yell.

Across Main Street, about a half block away, five teenage boys stood in a circle surrounding something on the sidewalk. Between their skinny adolescent legs, Leo could make out a young child sitting on the curb with his face in his hands, rocking back and forth. The little boy was crying. The older boys were shouting. One, holding the black cat, began laughing. The others joined in. The little boy's crying intensified.

Leo hesitated for an instant, then took off for the gang.

# 6

As Leo stepped off the curb, someone behind him said, "Mr. Townsend?" He turned to see a tall woman in a conservative blue suit and heels. "Yes?"

She offered her hand. "I'm Mayor Mary Evans." Her lifeless brown hair grazed the top of her pressed white blouse. Several limp strands were tucked behind her ears that were pierced by simple gold studs. Tortoise shell glasses did a good job of hiding her eyes. Her nose and mouth blended into the rest of her forgettable face.

"It's a pleasure to meet you," he said stepping back onto the curb. Her firm grip surprised him. He caught whiff of lavender.

"I hope you found Carpe Diem easily enough," she said.

"Yes, I did. It's a beautiful town."

"Thank you. We think so too. Why don't we go to my office?" She gestured toward the Town Hall. Her pleasant smile added character to her plain features.

Leo looked across the street. The boys had disappeared. The mayor's presence probably scared them away. "Sure," he replied.

Entering the three-story building, they passed brick walls similar to those in his Chicago apartment. Artificial gas lamps lighting the long hallway and wooden signs over doors labeled town clerk, treasurer, and

KRISTIN A. OAKLEY

engineer simulated a main street at the turn of the twentieth century. Mayor Evans' heels clicked on the cobble stone floor.

At the end of the hall, wrought iron elevator doors opened to reveal a disheveled, white-haired man in his seventies reading a newspaper. The mayor abruptly suggested they take the stairs instead of the elevator, commenting that she preferred the exercise. Leo agreed, but he wondered if she was avoiding the old gentleman and why. As they started up the stairs, he looked back to see the man arguing with his newspaper.

Leo followed the mayor up three flights, through a reception area devoid of a receptionist, and into a small, efficient office.

"Have a seat," the mayor said, catching her breath, indicating the blue guest chair opposite her desk. She kicked off her high heels, reducing her formidable height by several inches.

"Thank you." Leo placed his coffee cup on her wooden desk next to a portrait of the mayor with two teenagers. An attractive girl, despite black attire and multiple piercings, stood behind a younger, stocky boy.

"My children, Quinn and Will," the mayor said, noticing his interest in the photo.

The rest of the office contained little else: an empty in-box, an old desk-top computer and a metal file cabinet. One large corner window allowed in natural light, yet the absence of curtains made the office feel temporary.

"How long have you been mayor of Carpe Diem?" Leo asked.

"Five years. This is my second term."

He tried not to look surprised. He placed his computer bag on the tan carpeting then dug through it to find his notebook and a pen.

"I see you've already visited Joan and Dan's Diner. Can I get you a refill?" she asked, gesturing to his coffee mug.

"No thanks. I'm set."

She slid into her leather swivel chair then pushed her glasses up the bridge of her nose. "On the phone you said you're doing a piece on small towns in Illinois."

"I'm specifically interested in their festivals. You're having your Fall Festival next week, right?"

"Yes, we are. What would you like to know?"

"Let's start with the itinerary."

Once she finished giving him the details, he asked, "Is there anything unique about Carpe Diem's festival?"

She frowned.

"Don't get me wrong. It all sounds great. I'm just wondering if there is something extra which might attract people from Chicago."

"I see what you mean." She adjusted her glasses. "Every local business has a booth. We have quite a lot of artisans in town so there'll be pottery, paintings, stained glass, sculptures, photography, jewelry, fabric arts, those types of things."

Leo wasn't impressed though he tried not to show it. He had grown up in a small town and had been to his share of fairs. Every one offered Ferris wheels, goat auctions, or craft booths. Sometimes all three. This was nothing new. He had assumed that a town that rejected conventional schooling would be nonconformist in other ways, too.

"Is there anything else you'd like to know?" Mayor Evans asked.

He looked over his notes. "No, I think that should cover it."

She stared at him. "I'm wondering Mr. Townsend—"

"Call me Leo."

"Leo. I'm wondering why you drove all the way from Chicago to interview me about the festival." She leaned forward, settling her elbows on the desk. "We could have done this over the phone."

He rubbed the stubble on his jaw and flashed what he knew was a convincing smile. "Well, Mayor Evans—"

"You can call me Mary."

"Mary," he continued, "my piece is, in fact, about more than just festivals. I'm interested in small town life. What makes the people here different than their city counterparts? Visiting the towns was imperative. I'll e-mail the paper the festival information you've given me," he shook his notepad, "so they can include it in the Events section. After that, I plan on staying a few days to get a feel for Carpe Diem."

Mary eased back into her chair. "Well then, we should head over to the Community Center."

"Is that where the festival planning meeting? Brendan, the kid in the diner, mentioned it."

"Yes."

Leo hesitated. The last thing he wanted to do was enter a room full of people but he couldn't think of a way out of it. "Great, let's go," he managed, hoping the false enthusiasm camouflaged his fear. He shoved his gear into his computer bag then grabbed his empty coffee mug while Mary slipped her shoes back on.

Once outside, she said, "I almost forgot. My daughter, Quinn, was hoping *The Examiner* might want some photos for your story. She's an accomplished photographer."

"That would be great." It would give him a terrific opportunity to ask the girl about unschooling. "*The Examiner* wouldn't pay her for her time, just for any pictures it uses."

"I'll check with Quinn, but I'm sure she'd just appreciate the opportunity to work with you."

As they crossed Main Street, Mary's cell phone rang out the theme to *Mission Impossible*. "Excuse me," she said as she took the phone from her jacket pocket. They continued onto the paved path leading into the town square.

"Hello?" She paused.

Leo could hear a loud, harried voice.

"David, calm down. We have plenty of room for the Orlander and Riverdale parties."

Trying not to eavesdrop, Leo paid particular attention to the surroundings. The footpath led them through a wildflower garden crowded with monarch butterflies. He spotted a black squirrel behind a yellow flower. A black-eyed Susan?

"No, the Moores can't make it this year. Their daughter is expecting a baby. Right. The Riverdales can take their suite."

The path took them over a hill which sloped down to a sizable pond surrounded by willow trees. A breeze swayed the long branches.

"No, no, it's good you called. I'll see you later." She clicked her phone off and shoved it back into her pocket. "I'm sorry. I usually don't take calls when I'm with someone, but this is a busy time for us at the Inn."

"You manage an inn and run this town?"

"Actually, I own the Bradbury Inn. Running the town is a part-time job."

"You wouldn't happen to have a spare room available for the next few days?"

"I think we can squeeze you in," she said as they passed a large white gazebo.

"There's something I'd like to ask you. Brendan mentioned Carpe Diem doesn't have any schools. Everyone unschools. What is *unschooling*?"

The mayor hesitated then adjusted her glasses. "Unschooling is a method of homeschooling that is child-led."

Child-led? This didn't gel with Leo's perception of homeschooling. "I picture homeschooled kids sitting at the kitchen table while their mom lectures and hands out assignments and tests. Isn't that what schooling's about?"

"Schooling, yes, education, no. School boards and teachers see their role as filling children with information," Mary said. "They choose what children are going to learn and decide how to present it, generally using textbooks, workbooks, and tests."

"And unschooling?"

"Unschooling is the opposite of schooling. The children determine what they need to learn, when they will learn it, and how they go about it. Unschoolers learn through real-life experiences. For example, instead of reading about spelunking, they would actually explore a cave."

"What about a child who decides he doesn't want to learn something like math?"

"Math is all around us in games, cooking, crafts, music, everywhere. It's unavoidable. Simply by living, the average child learns the basics. And unschoolers are big believers in self-motivation. Even if the child isn't interested in exploring math beyond the basics now, someday, inevitably, he will be. It could be a computer program he wants to try and needs to understand algebra first or a tree house she wants to build and realizes a background in geometry would be helpful."

They exited the town square, crossed Mulberry Street and followed the sidewalk to the entrance of a single story, modern building decorated with geometric shapes. It was painted in varying shades of greens, blues, and yellows. The building looked like a cross between Frank Lloyd

Wright and Dr. Seuss.

Mary opened the triangular doors revealing a large, bright lobby covered with artwork. Their footsteps echoed on tiles which spelled out "Carpe Diem."

Leo heard a rumble of voices and pictured a large crowd. His heart raced. Stalling, he asked "How successful is unschooling?"

Mary hesitated, then whispered, "Just between you and me, unschooling isn't successful. Picture a town where everyone does what they want, whenever they want. Nothing gets done, particularly those things no one wants to do. Math is the least of our worries." She reached for the door, adding, "It's a nightmare to govern."

What? Had she really said that? And if that was true, why would she admit such a thing? If it wasn't true, why would she say this? Leo started to ask her if he'd heard her right, when she pulled open the door. The crowd noise hit him. He forced his feet to move, to follow her into the immense auditorium crammed with people. Stay in the back of the room. It'll be fine.

Groups of people sat in chairs or stood next to long rectangular tables posted with signs that read, "Volunteer Sheets," "Booth Map Sign-Up," "Talent Show Sign-Up," "Contest Committee," "Labyrinth Organizers," "Food Committee." They talked, laughed, mingled.

Leo felt his chest tighten, the first sign of a panic attack. He concentrated on breathing. He turned his attention to the few people standing on the stage at the other end of the auditorium. Mary's teenage son, Will, leaned against the podium. Leo recognized him from the photograph in the mayor's office. The boy covered a microphone with his hand while he talked to several adults and teens. A short, overweight, red-haired woman waved her arms as she talked while the others seemed to ignore her. To Leo, the scene appeared chaotic. He looked at Mary who gave him a see I-told-you-so look.

Her expression became professional as she introduced him to two women nearby, Charlotte Jansen, the owner of the Fair Goods Trading Center, and Kate Dodds, a book critic. Both women took in Leo's height and build. He was used to women ogling him, but found it annoying. Thankfully his annoyance replaced some of his anxiety.

"Mr. Townsend, I believe we're coworkers," Kate finally said. Her green turtleneck sweater and khakis accentuated her short coppery hair, pale, freckled skin and shapeless figure.

"Coworkers?"

"I'm a theatre critic for *The Chicago Examiner*."

"Oh, sure, *that* Kate Dodds. I enjoy reading your reviews, even when I disagree with them."

The women laughed a little too enthusiastically. Charlotte tossed her long, white-blond hair which swayed across the words "Viva La Fair Trade Revolution" on her blue t-shirt. The shirt in combination with her snug jeans complimented her curves.

Leo motioned to the stage. "What's going on?"

"The meeting's almost over," Charlotte replied. "All the committee leaders gave their reports. Everything was set until Thelma appeared. They're letting her have her say."

"Always a good thing to do," Kate added.

"Thelma Garrison is our town busybody," Charlotte explained. "She has to have a hand in everything."

"And," Mary added, "sometimes she comes up with great ideas. I think this festival was originally her idea."

"Right, I'd forgotten that," Charlotte said. "So now they're deciding how many food booths to have and whether alcohol should be sold."

"Mary, it looks like your son is about to wrap things up," Kate pointed out.

"Can I have your attention please?" the boy asked into the microphone. It took a few minutes for the room to quiet down. "We have the menus for the food booth."

"The kids run the three food booths," Mary interjected.

"You're kidding," Leo said.

She shook her head.

Will continued, "One booth will have fair food like mac and cheese, chicken nuggets, hot dogs, and pizza. The second booth will serve soup and sandwiches. The third will be vegetarian. Oh, and the festival will be alcohol-free." This comment elicited groans.

Thelma Garrison moved toward the microphone. Will waved her

away. "We know an alcohol-free festival won't bring in as much money, but it just makes sense. It's a family event."

"I disagree, Will," a crusty old gentleman at the front of the auditorium interjected. Leo recognized him as the man at the Town Hall who had argued with his newspaper. Probably the town drunk. "The festival takes place in the heart of downtown near our restaurants. Are you going to ask those businesses to—"

*I Shot the Sheriff* rang out from Leo's pocket. "Excuse me," he said to the women. He walked out of the auditorium into the vacant lobby, glad to be away from the crowd but sorry to miss the rest of the debate.

"Hey, Ted."

"I heard Beth did some research for you."

"She's been a big help."

"I've told her you're on your own on this one. She's got enough on her plate."

*Damn!* Was this more punishment for his transgressions? He had taken the intern under his wing with Ted's blessing. Her research skills were terrific. Now he'd have to find a Wi-Fi connection and do the unschooling research himself.

"Sure, I understand," he managed.

"How's the story going?"

"This place is odd. It has me a little spooked."

"Oh yeah, in what way?"

"Don't get me wrong, the town is beautifully kept. The people I've met are very friendly."

"So what is it?"

"It's the kids. A teenage kid served me coffee at the local diner, at a time of day when he should have been in school. Then I saw teenagers bullying a small child. Now I'm at a town meeting led by adolescents who've decided to ban liquor from an upcoming festival. It's like they run the place."

"Fascinating."

"You don't know the half of it. They don't just homeschool in Carpe Diem. Kids are 'unschooled' which means they do whatever they damn well please. That's straight from Mayor Evans' mouth."

"You're kidding!"

"No, I'm not. She actually told me Carpe Diem is a nightmare to govern because there's no discipline."

"Why would she say that?"

"I was wondering the same thing." Leo hesitated. "Also, I'm e-mailing Terrence a piece about Carpe Diem's Fall Festival. I mentioned to the mayor I was here to report on the festival so I'm hoping he'll have room for it in the Events section."

"Good luck with that. Terrance hates last minute additions."

"I'll throw in a couple of tickets to a Bear's game."

Ted chuckled. "That outta do it."

The auditorium doors burst open. People filed into the lobby. Leo backed away from the growing crowd. "Gotta go."

"Keep me posted."

"Will do." He shoved his phone back into his pocket and rubbed the scar on his jaw as the crowd engulfed him.

# 7

Leo fought the urge to flee. He reminded himself that the mass of people would be gone soon. He closed his eyes and pictured driving down Chicago's Lake Shore Drive with the Mustang's top down.

Feeling calmer, he slowly opened his eyes and began to search for the mayor. She would be easy to find; she was almost as tall as he was. He spied a mousey brown-haired woman and walked toward her until she turned her head, revealing stunning green eyes unfettered by glasses. Definitely not Mary.

Someone tapped him on the shoulder.

"Who ya looking for?" Charlotte Jansen asked in a silvery voice.

"The mayor."

Charlotte crossed her arms. "Check the auditorium." Her tone had tarnished.

"Thanks."

Mary was on the opposite side of the auditorium talking to the town drunk. Or rather Mary waved her arms while the old guy shook his head. Leo quickened his pace, hoping to catch some of their conversation.

"Don't blame Patrick!" she shouted. "And don't you dare blame yourself."

The man looked at his watch. "I have to go. We'll talk about it when

I get back."

Mary started to say something but hugged him instead. She followed him to the doorway then noticed Leo. "Was there something else you needed?" she asked.

"What was that all about?"

"Mayoral business."

He studied her face, the bland glasses framing her brown eyes. "I wanted to ask you more about unschooling."

Her face remained expressionless.

"I'm confused by your comment that it doesn't work."

She glanced around the now empty room, but said nothing.

"How about discussing it over dinner?" He rambled on, "My treat. Actually, *The Examiner's* treat."

"Thanks. I can't," she finally answered. "With the festival coming up, I'm pretty busy. I really don't have the time." She walked away toward the lobby where a few people lingered.

Had she just turned him down? Had that ever happened to him before? Leo watched her leave then realized he should try again. "You still have to eat," he called.

She continued through the lobby and out onto the sidewalk.

He followed. "Look, it's only quarter to six," he said catching up to her. "If we pick a nearby restaurant, you'll be back to the Inn by seven. Seven thirty at the latest."

Mary slowed down as she tried to navigate the cobblestone street in high heels.

"I'll help you change sheets at the Inn," he continued, offering his arm which she waved away. "Wash windows, scrub chamber pots."

A sly smile crept across her face. "O-kay. I suppose I have time for a quick dinner at Dan and Joan's."

They took the path through the vacant town square. Since no one was around, he asked, "If unschooling's not successful, why do you do it?"

"I thought you were only interested in small town festivals. Why the sudden interest in education?"

"I'm curious about all aspects of small towns."

"I imagine curiosity is essential for a journalist."

"Yes it is. So unschooling—"

Mary stumbled. He grabbed her around the waist, stopping her fall. She was ballerina thin, simultaneously strong and fragile.

"Thanks." Her face reddened. "My shoe got caught. I'm not a fan of high heels."

"Are you all right?"

"Fine, thanks." She pulled away and continued down the path at a slower pace. "How long have you been a journalist?"

"Since I was twelve."

She stopped to look at him. "Seriously?"

He nodded. "My small-town paper paid me a penny a word."

"Excellent." She started walking again. "What town is that?"

"Endeavor, Wisconsin. About three hours north of here."

"Funny," she said as they crossed Main Street. This time she took his arm for support.

"What's funny?"

"I pictured you as a city guy."

"I am. Left the family farm for Chicago at seventeen. I've lived there ever since."

Entering the diner, Leo smelled fresh bread and warm apple pie. They grabbed a candlelit table by a window that was hand painted with maple leaves. The light created a stained glass effect. Leo hung his computer bag and jacket on the back of a wooden chair.

"Family farm?" Mary asked once they were settled.

"Yep. Been in my family for generations. As the oldest son, I was expected to take over, but I never liked being friendly with my food before I ate it." He pushed his sleeves up. "To be honest, I never could drive a tractor straight. I'd get caught up reading the book in my lap before I realized I'd driven into the neighbor's field."

Mary laughed. "Don't tell me. You were reading *The Good Earth*."

"*Animal Farm*."

"Of course." Her smile illuminated her face. "You're the oldest of how many?"

"Two. I have a younger brother."

"Who, at age twelve, ran a successful business and opened a shop on

Main Street," she suggested.

"No, he founded his own chain of fast food stores. Burger something or other, I always forget the name."

"Uh huh."

"Actually, he farmed with my dad for many years. Now he's a graphic designer."

"Didn't like the farming life either?"

"No, he—" Leo touched his scar. The last thing we wanted to do was talk about his brother's accident. Thankfully Brendan arrived with two glasses of water.

"Hi Mr. Townsend. Mary. I heard Will ran a successful town meeting." Brendan handed them the menus.

"He did," Mary said.

"I think it's great that you let—"

"What's today's special?" Mary asked, interrupting him.

Brendan stared at her for a second as if shocked she'd interrupt him, then replied, "Lamb meatballs with lemon-braised collards, rice pilaf and a yogurt cucumber salad. It goes great with cabernet sauvignon."

"What, no meatloaf, mashed potatoes, and Budweiser?" Leo asked.

Brendan chuckled. "Once in a while Mom'll make that sort of thing, but she's a gourmet who likes to experiment with ingredients from the farm. She describes today's special as 'eclectic but very homey'."

"Sounds great," Mary said.

"I'll give it a try," Leo agreed. He'd prefer deep dish pizza and beer, but he was curious. He knew he probably should avoid the wine, but didn't see the harm in one glass.

After Brendan took their orders and retreated to the kitchen, Leo asked, "The farm?"

"Carpe Diem has a farm. You passed it on your way into town. We raise cows, chickens, sheep, a few pigs, and have an apple orchard and several vegetable gardens. Everyone who pitches in gets some of the harvest. Quinn could take you over there for a tour if you'd like."

"I don't know if I'll have time." He fiddled with this fork. The last thing he wanted to do was slop through cow shit. He hated everything about farms: the filth, the smell, the brain-numbing chores. He looked up from his silverware. "So, tell me about unschooling."

"What do you want to know?"

He looked around the crowded restaurant and lowered his voice. "You said it isn't successful. If that's the case, why be mayor of an unschooling town?"

The mayor clasped her hands and set them on the table. One ring on her small finger decorated her left hand, no rings on her right. She didn't wear fingernail polish but there appeared to be dried paint under her nails. "Years ago, unschooling made sense to me. It sounded like a good theory." She took off her glasses and wiped them on her napkin.

"And now?"

Replacing her glasses, she remained quiet as Brendan put a basket of crusty bread and two wine glasses on the table. He poured the cabernet then left the bottle with them.

"And now," the mayor continued once they were alone, "I have my doubts."

"And what would those be?"

She studied him before answering, "I think all mayors have doubts about their community. It goes with the job." She picked up the bottle of wine and handed it to him. "The wine is excellent. Brendan's father makes it. They have a small vineyard on their property not too far out of town."

The label was a creative knock off of Edward Hopper's painting *Nighthawks*. The restaurant illustrated on the label looked the same as Hopper's diner, although apple trees and a distant cornfield replaced Hopper's cityscape. The wine was called *Piquant*.

"I designed the label," Mary said.

"You run a town and an inn and in your spare time you design wine labels?"

"I studied art before I entered politics. I find I still need a creative outlet."

Leo set the bottle down. "What made you switch to politics?" He sampled the wine. Biting and interesting, like its name.

"Actually, being an art major was the switch. I've always been passionate about government. My dad practiced law. He wanted me, his only child, to follow in his footsteps, to join his firm in Springfield."

She rubbed the bridge of her nose under her glasses. Leo wondered why she didn't wear contacts. "He pressured me. I rebelled and enrolled in the University of Illinois as an art major. He wasn't pleased. He threatened to disown me until my mother calmed him down."

"You eventually buckled under his pressure?"

"Not his pressure, my own. I've always been a political animal. I realized it during my freshman year when the Gulf War broke out. I wondered about the global consequences while my classmates worried about color schemes." She took a piece of bread. "Still, I didn't change my major until my junior year. Too stubborn. When I finally told my father I had switched to political science he wisely kept his cool. My mother told me later she caught him dancing a jig in his study."

"What does he think now that you're mayor?"

"He died before I moved to Carpe Diem."

"I'm sorry."

Mary set the bread down. "A drunk driver swerved into their lane. Killed both my parents instantly."

"Oh my God, that's terrible."

"Yes." Mary sighed, drank from her water glass and then continued, "With my parents gone, I decided to move to Carpe Diem. Later I ran for mayor. I think my father would have had mixed feelings about me being a mayor. He loved the law, though like most people, he didn't have a lot of respect for politicians."

"Don't tell me, he was raised in Chicago."

"Springfield."

"Ah, the birthplace of corrupt governors."

"The capitol of the land of greased palms." Mary winked. "I'm sure your father couldn't have been too pleased with your decision to leave the farm."

"No. In fact, we haven't spoken in years, at least not civilly."

"I'm sorry."

"It's not a big deal. We never talked much anyway. Nothing to say." Leo finished the wine in his glass. "I read all the time. He's never picked up a book, or newspaper for that matter. Once, I was excited to see him paging through a magazine until I discovered it was a grain catalog." He poured wine into her glass and refilled his own. "My dad viewed reading as a waste of time, especially when the goats needed milking or the corn needed harvesting."

The food arrived. It smelled of garlic and exotic spices. Leo took a bite. "This is amazing."

"Joan's an incredible chef." Mary cut into a meatball. "Her knowledge of seasonings is extraordinary. She's teaching Will. He can learn a lot from her, although most of her knowledge is intuitive. It's not something you can teach."

Leo sampled the collards and found he liked their mild flavor.

"Will's our chef at the Inn," Mary continued. "He'd eventually like to study at a culinary institute."

"How old is he?"

"He'll be fourteen in a few weeks."

"Isn't he too young to be a chef?"

"Not at all." They ate in silence for a moment and then she added, "In Carpe Diem we don't pigeonhole people by age. If a person wants to become proficient at something their age shouldn't matter. For instance, I teach water color painting to Hilda Gutherson who celebrated her eighty-fifth birthday last week."

"No kidding?"

Brendan returned as they finished their entrées, suggesting the chocolate mousse drizzled with raspberry sauce for dessert.

"This diner puts most four-star Chicago restaurants to shame," Leo said tasting the mousse moments later.

"Joan's from Chicago. Rumor has it she could have been head chef at any number of restaurants. But she prefers the country, which is lucky for us." Mary checked her watch. "I should be going."

"Not before we finish the wine," Leo said, pouring the last of it into their glasses.

"Fine," she agreed, "but I have to get back to the Inn soon or my concierge will never let me hear the end of it."

Later that night in his room at the Inn, Leo unpacked his things and debated raiding the minibar. He decided against it. He had research to do and an article rough draft to outline. Unlike Hemingway, he wrote better sober.

He considered the day's events, particularly his conversation with the mayor. Mary was an interesting woman. She ran a town, owned an inn and taught painting on the side. Probably read the paper, too.

Picturing her smile, he grabbed his toiletries out of his duffle bag then stopped short on the way to the bathroom. *I'll be damned. I never did get a straight answer from her about unschooling.*

# 8

Illinois Governor Michael Thomas looked up from his speech notes as Raegan Colyer, his chief of staff, glided into his office. He straightened his hunched shoulders and adjusted his tie.

Raegan's low cut blouses and tight skirts always made his pulse race. When they first met twenty years ago, he tried to grab her ass. She nearly broke his hand. He never made a pass again. Now in her mid-fifties, she either had amazing genes or a great plastic surgeon.

"Raegan, what's happening in the trenches?"

"Where to start? Disgruntled staff, obnoxious lobbyists, dissatisfied constituents." She slid into one of two stiff floral chairs in front of his enormous cherry wood desk.

"You're here to blow off some steam?" He glanced at his Rolex. "Is it cocktail hour yet?" He rolled his sleeves down and began buttoning the cuffs.

"Soon."

He stopped buttoning.

"What are you working on?" she asked.

He sighed. He wanted to kick back with a drink. He rested his beefy hands on his enormous gut then picked a piece of dried spaghetti sauce off his shirt, a remnant from lunch. "I'm looking over my speech to the

Illinois Federation of Teachers."

"*Your* speech?" Raegan raised an eyebrow.

"*Talbot's* speech. I've got to hand it to him, he sure knows how to make me sound eloquent and knowledgeable about teachers' pensions." He chuckled.

"Which reminds me, have you looked over the report I gave you about that town—"

"Carson Day?"

"Carpe Diem."

"Yeah, I did." He eased back into his leather chair, making it groan. He took note of Raegan's immaculate Armani suit, which appeared freshly pressed even this late in the day. Not many civil servants on a government salary would flaunt their extracurricular wealth so brazenly. He also noticed stress didn't seem to affect her. Every strand of the woman's thick black hair was in place and her make-up was flawless.

Michael wondered why, for the hundredth time, she didn't run for office. No one else would stand a chance against her, including himself. Thank God she put all her efforts into getting him elected.

"I don't think the town's a big threat," he said. "We've got high unemployment, crumbling roads, a rise in inner-city crime and the sanitation workers' strike to deal with. I don't see why we should give a damn about some hick school-less town."

"You're right. Carpe Diem's not a *major* issue." Raegan inspected her manicured fingernails. "It simply reminded me of your campaign promise last year to reform Illinois schools."

"What about it?"

"You can't reform the Carpe Diem schools," she said. "There aren't any."

"So?"

"As you've read in my report," she continued, "the town has expanded to over three thousand residents. It could easily support an elementary school, a middle school and a senior high. Yet it doesn't have any schools, public or private."

"You're concerned about a few hundred uneducated brats?"

Raegan raised an eyebrow again.

He tried a different tack. "Is it revenue? Are we losing cash because of this town?"

"Definitely. We're not getting federal school funding. And Carpe Diem doesn't provide income for school personnel. But there's more."

Michael watched his chief of staff stand, brush an imaginary crease out of her skirt, then drift over to the wall-to-wall bookcases that brimmed with legal books and portraits of the Thomas family. He took note of her black high heels and shapely calves that were surprisingly free of spider veins.

"If this town is a success," Raegan began, "which can be argued it already is, and word gets out, what will stop other towns from closing their schools?"

"You're exaggerating."

"I don't think I am. People all over the state are dissatisfied. They have good reason to be, what with low test scores, high dropout rates, gang violence, and illegal drug use, not to mention many schools claim to be going bankrupt." Her dark eyes narrowed. "There are even reports of teachers sexually abusing their students."

"All true." Michael pictured the inner-city Chicago school he had visited the previous week. Tattooed gangbangers leaning against graffitied, crumbling walls while inside the classrooms, chaos reigned. "So you're predicting a full-scale revolt against traditional education?"

Raegan smiled. "I wouldn't go that far, but I think Carpe Diem is a real threat to our public schools."

"I still think you're making a big deal out of nothing."

She picked up a photograph, the one of sixteen-year-old Cameron Thomas sitting proudly behind the wheel of his brand new, powder blue Corvette. She studied the picture for a moment and then said in a steely voice, "Do I have to remind you that the Illinois Federation of Teachers was your biggest contributor during the last election?"

This surprised him. She never used her knowledge of the payoffs as leverage to get what she wanted. "I'm well aware of that," he spat, his hands shaking. Why had he ever confided in her? "Sit down."

Raegan stared at him, then drifted back to her chair.

He pulled out his bottom desk drawer, took out two highball glasses and a full bottle of scotch, placed them on top of his forgotten speech and began to pour. He pushed a filled glass to her before taking a gulp from his own. The familiar burning sensation quelled the tremors in his hands. "Maybe we should stop the potential problem before it becomes a real one," he conceded.

Raegan didn't reach for the liquor. "What do you have in mind?"

"What if we simply make the Carpe Diem kids go to the nearest schools? Isn't that the law?"

"Truancy laws give an exemption for homeschooling," she said. "I suppose the town is using it as a loophole."

"Don't the statutes require towns to provide public schooling?"

"I don't think there is such a requirement although I'll ask my staff to research it if you'd like."

"Yes, look into it. That may be the best way to—"

"However," Raegan tapped her fingers together, "even if there is a law or precedent, it seems Carpe Diem may already have circumvented it by building its neighborhood center and community college. Most property taxes collected appear to go to those two entities."

Having emptied his glass, Michael hoisted his three-hundred-pound frame out of his chair. "Okay, how about another angle?" He huffed, slightly out of breath. "So we want Carpe Diem to open some schools. No way will they do that voluntarily; we'll need to force their hand. How about playing hardball, digging up some dirt on the town?"

"Dirt?"

"Are the kids educated at all?" Michael continued. "Without school buildings and teachers, they probably don't know shit. Can we prove that the kids are illiterate?"

"Perhaps."

"What about, what's it called," he stopped his pacing, "socialization? They must be odd. How do they do once they're out in the real world? There must be a study or news report."

"No. Nothing. In Carpe Diem they purposely avoid testing their children except when applying to colleges. And college entrance scores are inaccessible."

Michael lowered himself back into his chair. "Okay, let's do this." He

KRISTIN A. OAKLEY

slapped his beefy hands together. He loved taking charge. It made him feel essential. "Keep working on the legal end while sending in a reporter."

"I'm a step ahead of you. I called Ted Nelson at *The Chicago Examiner.* I asked him to assign Leo Townsend to the story."

"You've already..." Michael felt deflated. He poured more booze into his glass. "Hold on. Leo Townsend?" He spilled some of the precious liquid. "Why? He's a mess." He blotted the liquor with his rumpled shirt sleeve.

"Exactly."

"Now you've lost me."

"Not too long ago he was the best. Remember?"

"Sure, he's got terrific instincts," Michael said, leaning back in his chair, glass in hand. "And a talent for coaxing anyone into his confidence. Most of his sources aren't aware he's a reporter until they read their name in his column. But he's gotten lazy. I heard *The Examiner* almost fired him until he became a Pulitzer Prize nominee, making him one lucky son-of-a-bitch."

"He only came close to winning the Pulitzer Prize because of information you provided him," Raegan interjected. "He owes you."

"Actually, Raegan, you're the one who did the providing." He chuckled. "But that story's gone sour. When the prosecutor asks Townsend to divulge his source to the grand jury, the odds are he'll comply. *The Examiner* will fire him for sure." He took a long pull from his glass. "Are you suggesting that because Townsend is desperate to redeem himself that he'll be easy for us manipulate?"

"I'm simply assuming he'll be happy to get any story."

For some reason, Michael didn't believe her, but he let it go. Instead he inhaled the rest of his scotch, acutely aware that only a small amount of the golden liquid remained in the bottle. "Sounds like you've got it taken care of. I'm done with my speech. Why don't we head to Marley's?"

"I'm sorry, I've got plans."

"Oh?"

"The secretary of state is in town. He's taking me to the opera." Raegan rose.

Disappointed, he poured the rest of the alcohol into his empty glass. "Isn't he married?"

"Not when he's in Chicago." They both laughed.

"Which reminds me," she said. "Do you remember state Senator Christopher Shaw's aide who disappeared about fifteen years ago? It was rumored they were having an affair."

"Tall, gorgeous blond?" Michael whistled.

"She's resurfaced. In Carpe Diem." Raegan pulled out a folded sheet of paper from her breast pocket. "You might find this interesting." She placed it on top of Michael's full glass. Without another word, she glided out of the room.

He watched the heavy door close, then picked up the paper. As he finished reading, he smiled, toasted himself then drained his glass.

He fumbled in his wrinkled pants' pocket for his private cell phone. "Tommy, it's Michael. Hey, what ever happened to that gorgeous broad who worked in Senator Shaw's office years ago? You know, the one he was boinking, who then disappeared."

As he listened, Michael noticed Raegan's untouched glass. He downed it. Raegan never touched the liquor he offered her which suited them both just fine.

# 9

On Thursday morning, Tali slouched in the dining room chair and fingered her peach-colored napkin. The George Winston piano music floating through the Bradbury Inn's sound system didn't calm her. "I can't believe you're leaving. It's only been two days since the accident," she mumbled.

"What?" her father asked glancing up from the documents piled next to his plate.

"It's just, I don't know. What if questions come up about Mom's care?"

"Call me on my cell phone." He bit into his marmalade-topped English muffin. "I'm needed in Springfield more than I am here. Your mother's going to be fine. She just needs time to recover. Sitting around watching her get better isn't necessary. The doctors have assured me they'll take good care of her. There's no reason why I have to stay by her bedside." He shoved the last of the muffin into his mouth and returned his attention to his paperwork.

Tali pushed the hair out of her damp eyes then took a gulp of her apple juice. "I'll do more than sit around. I'll read to her, get her stuff, keep her mind off the pain." She took a warm blueberry muffin from a basket in the center of their table and broke it in half, releasing berry-scented steam. "Being here for Mom is more important than any *job*," she said to the muffin.

Christopher slapped his hand on his papers, causing fresh-squeezed orange juice to slosh out of his glass. Tali flinched. "Someday, Natalia Leigh Shaw, you'll understand there are issues, larger and more important than those affecting our family, which have to be addressed. That's what I try to do in my *job*." His eyes narrowed and a vein bulged on his forehead. He swore as he wiped juice off the top document.

Hoping his precious papers were ruined, Tali noticed the stain on his fingers. "What's with your fingers?"

"What?"

"They're yellow and peeling." She pointed to the first two fingers on his left hand.

He rubbed them. "Something got on my scarf. Burned a hole right through it. I must have dropped it in antifreeze in the garage at the office. Stung like hell when I touched it."

"Good morning, Tali," Will said, stopping by their table with a basket of hot croissants. "Hello, Senator Shaw. How's breakfast?"

"Terrific," Christopher grunted.

Tali attempted a smile. The food looked terrific, but she couldn't eat anything.

"Excellent. Would you like a fresh croissant?"

"No, thank you," Christopher said digging into the scrambled eggs on his plate.

Tali held up the two halves of the muffin and shook her head.

"Anything else? More coffee, Senator?"

"We're fine."

"Okay. Enjoy your breakfast," Will said, then headed over to the man at the next table.

Tali set the muffin pieces on her plate. "What issues?"

"What?" Christopher grumbled through a mouthful of eggs.

"You said there are issues more important than our family. *What issues?*"

He dabbed his mouth with his napkin. "Poverty, health care, the economy. The issue I'm dealing with currently is homeschool—" His cell phone rang. He checked the number. "Speak of the devil."

Tali sighed and picked at her muffin.

"Yes, Adam, that's right. No, no. Let's make it more precise. How about, 'Parents who homeschool their children in this state and throughout the country pretend to be experts when it comes to schooling even though they may only have an eighth-grade education.' Yes, it does the trick. Add: 'Generally they know little about chemistry, geometry, or how our government is run, yet they still assume they can teach these subjects.'"

Tali sat up straighter in her chair. She had never really thought about homeschooling. How did parents teach subjects they didn't know?

"Yes, you can talk about religion without offending anyone. Something like, 'Worse still, they isolate their children from society, indoctrinating them according to their religious beliefs. Children aren't exposed to other points of view or other ways of life." Christopher took a swig of coffee. "Sounds good." He set the cup down. "You'll get a final copy to me today? I should be in the office in a few hours. I'll see you then." He set down his phone. "What was I saying?"

"You were talking about homeschooling. Who's Adam?"

"You know Adam. He's my administrative assistant."

"I've never been to your office. I've never met—"

"Oh well, that doesn't matter," Christopher said waving his hand. "Anyway, you heard what I said, so you can understand that outlawing homeschooling is paramount."

"I think homeschooling would suck." Tali spotted Will coming through the kitchen door, balancing a basket filled with muffins. "I wonder how Will stands it."

"Who's Will?"

"Our waiter."

"A waiter. Talk about lack of ambition," Christopher said.

"He's the chef here and he's only thirteen."

He gave her a blank stare. "So he spends his days scrambling eggs? Think of the things he's missing by not being in school."

"It'd be weird not going to school," Tali agreed. "Not seeing my friends all day, no dances, having Mom for my teacher."

"What you're talking about is socialization and you're right, home-schooled kids are stuck with their mom or dad all day. How will these kids do once they're out in the real world? It's not right for them to be isolated, for them to learn little or nothing at all. These are some of the reasons why I'm pushing to make homeschooling illegal."

Christopher took a final sip of his coffee. "After finishing a few things in Alanton, I have to get to Springfield to push my bill through the Senate's Education Committee. Monday is the full Senate vote. If we miss the deadline, it might be years before we get this chance again."

Tali nodded. She understood, but didn't agree. Mom's health was more important than some homeschooling law. "Next *Monday*? Today is Thursday. You won't come back until Tuesday?"

"Probably not until Wednesday," He gathered his papers.

"That's almost a week!"

"Yes, and I still don't think you should miss that much school. Your education is more important than playing nursemaid to your mother." He picked up his leather briefcase from the floor and shoved the documents into it.

Tali crushed her napkin into a ball. "Tom's coming with my assignments this afternoon. I'll e-mail my homework to my teachers. I can keep up with my classes."

"You'd better." Christopher reached into his pants' pocket for his leather wallet. "We'll stop by the front desk to reserve the room for you for the next week. Here's two hundred dollars for meals." He tossed the money on the table. "You've got your debit card if you need more. When my schedule frees up, I'll come get you. Hopefully your mother will be discharged by then."

He looked at his watch then gestured at her plate and the untouched muffins. "I have to get back to Alanton. Are you ready to go? "

She nodded.

"I'll drop you at the hospital."

Starting to rise, she stopped. "You're not going to say goodbye to Mom?"

"No time. You do it for me."

"Unbelievable," she muttered though not loud enough for him to hear.

Pushing her chair from the table, Tali noticed the thick, tousled brown hair of the man sitting at a neighboring table. Walking past, she pulled

KRISTIN A. OAKLEY

her eyes away from his chiseled cheekbones and dimpled chin to sneak a glance at his computer screen and read, 'How will these kids do once they're out in the real world?' It was her father's comment, word-for-word.

# 10

*Despite Carpe Diem's beauty, or maybe because of it, you get the feeling that you're in a Stephen King novel. Something is just not right. Across the picturesque Main Street under a canopy of glowing sugar maples, five bored teenagers bully a small boy. Why aren't these kids in school, you wonder? Then you remember. Carpe Diem has no schools.*

Bob Marley sang out from Leo's jeans' pocket interrupting his typing at a table in the Inn's otherwise deserted dining room.

He checked the number on his cell phone and the time, 9:30 a.m. "Hi Ted, what's up?"

"This thing's heating up. To be honest, I thought I gave you a fluff piece. Now I'm not so sure."

"Hang on." Leo dug around in his computer bag for his Bluetooth headset and clipped it to his ear. "What's happened?"

"*The L.A. Times* has a lead story on homeschooling. The California Court of Appeals found yesterday that parents do not have a constitutional right to homeschool their children."

Leo whistled.

Ted continued, "It also ruled that parents without teaching credentials cannot legally teach their children. This effectively makes homeschooling illegal in California."

"Wow."

"It's not just *The Times*. *The Wall Street Journal, New York Times, Washington Post*—all our competitors are jumping on the story today. Homeschooling is a hot topic. I've sent Barnes to California."

"Lucky Barnes."

"Not as lucky as you. You've got an exclusive which, by the way, you need."

Leo winced. He wondered how long it would take before Ted stopped reminding him of his mistakes.

"I want your article on Carpe Diem before everyone discovers there's a whole town in Illinois that unschools."

Leo skimmed his article on his laptop. "I'm working on a rough draft. State Senator Christopher Shaw is pushing a bill to make homeschooling illegal in Illinois."

"Incredible! You've interviewed him?"

"Well, actually…" He massaged his temple. "I overheard his conversation."

"You don't have a direct quote?"

"Not yet. He left before I could ask for an interview. To be honest, I didn't want to talk to him about it here. It's surprising he wasn't more discrete. I wonder if he knows Carpe Diem is a homeschooling town." He Googled *Senator Christopher Shaw*. "But I've got his contact information. I'll call him this morning."

"Good."

"Shaw wants the Senate to vote on the legislation next week."

"Great! The timing couldn't be better."

Leo took a sip of his cooling coffee. "I also want to talk to John Holden, the founder of Carpe Diem, but I haven't been able to reach him. His son, Patrick, is the one who drove his motorcycle into Alexandra Shaw's car. Rumor has it he was trying to kill himself."

"Jesus! That's terrible. Do you think his suicide attempt had anything to do with homeschooling?"

"I doubt it. The son is almost forty."

"Never mind. We don't have time to track down Holden," Ted said. "Get me a final draft without his interview."

"It would make a better article with it."

"I need this today."

"Okay, I may have enough, even without Holden. I've spoken with the mayor and am touring the town today with her teenage daughter. I'm hoping to get the kid's perspective in addition to interviews with some other townspeople. It should give the piece balance. Right now it's pretty anti-homeschooling. I'll try to get it to you by nine o'clock tonight, in time for the second edition."

"Well, if that's the best you can do. We'll hold off on printing Barnes' piece on the California case until then. Send it earlier if you can."

Leo noticed Mary and Quinn standing near the buffet table, looking in his direction. Closing his laptop, he wondered how long they had been there.

"Gotta go Ted. My tour guide's here."

"Get me the article tonight."

He turned off his ear piece and shoved it back into his bag as Mary approached.

"Leo, this is my daughter Quinn."

He got up from the dining room chair to shake her hand. Her multiple silver bracelets jingled. "Nice to meet you, Quinn."

"Hi, Mr. Townsend."

"Leo."

"Leo." She was decorated in black from her fingernails, eyeliner, hair and lipstick to her down jacket, jeans, and high top sneakers. A black camera bag was slung over one shoulder. She had her mother's smile. At least her teeth weren't black.

"I wanted to thank you for your marvelous article about our Fall Festival," Mary said, holding *The Chicago Examiner* in her hand. Her gold knit sweater and cream colored slacks complemented her ordinary features. "Several tourists called saying they read your column and wanted more information. It's been a great advertisement."

"Glad I could help." He turned to her daughter. "So Quinn, are you ready to give me the grand tour of Carpe Diem?"

"Sure. We'll visit some local businesses, the library, community college, that sort of thing. While we're out, I'll get a few shots of the town's architecture and landscaping." She fingered her camera case. "The morning light will be great."

"Sounds good. Just give me a minute to take my computer up to my room and make a quick phone call. Then I'll be ready to go." He shut down the laptop and packed it away.

"I've got to get going, too," Mary said. "Lots of festival permits to issue at City Hall. Take good care of Leo, sweetie." She kissed her daughter on the cheek and, with a smile to Leo, left the room.

Upstairs, Leo turned on his laptop. It took several minutes for the outdated and unreliable computer to warm up. But he couldn't bring himself to replace it even though *The Examiner* offered to provide him with a new one.

Leo touched the dull gold nameplate on the corner of his computer. 'To Leo, let your fingers take flight, love Penman." His grandfather, Sawyer Addison Townsend, nicknamed Penman, had given Leo this computer even though he claimed that the incessant machines diluted the creative process. When Penman handed Leo the laptop, he said, "Maybe I was wrong about the dilution part. I've seen your fingers fly across the keys." A week after Leo became a finalist for the Pulitzer Prize for the Smithson piece, Penman had succumbed to cancer.

Finally, the computer screen lit up with Senator Shaw's website and contact information. Leo placed the call.

"Senator Christopher Shaw's office," a soft, female voice answered.

"This is Leo Townsend of *The Chicago Examiner*. I'd like to speak to the senator."

"Senator Shaw is unavailable at the moment. Do you have a number where he can reach you?"

He gave her his information. "Tell the senator I'm reporting on his homeschooling legislation and would like a direct quote. With yesterday's court ruling in California, it's a hot topic."

"I'll be sure to pass that along."

Leo shoved his phone into his jeans' pocket and walked across the hardwood floors to the armoire to retrieve his leather jacket. As he slipped it on, a muffled *I Shot the Sheriff* rang from his pocket.

"Leo Townsend."

"Mr. Townsend, Senator Christopher Shaw."

Leo walked back over to his computer and pulled up a blank screen. "Yes, Senator. Thank you for getting back to me so quickly."

"I've got a long drive so I have time to talk. I understand you'd like to discuss my homeschooling bill?"

"Yes. What is the purpose of your bill? What are you trying to accomplish?"

"As you're probably aware, homeschooling is currently legal in Illinois. Homeschools are considered private schools and fall under those regulations which require privately educated children to attend school from the ages of seven to seventeen. They must be taught in English and study the same subjects as those taught in public schools.

"But there are no testing, registration, or curriculum requirements. Truancy is a factor only if someone reports a family and even then parents are rarely held accountable."

"Do they need to be held accountable?" Leo asked. "How well do these children do in the real world?"

"Well, I don't think I'm going out on a limb to say it's obvious they don't do well, not well at all," the senator replied. "Picture a parent, typically a fundamentally religious mother with barely a high school education, standing at the kitchen table attempting to teach calculus to her teenager while keeping two or three younger children preoccupied with math problems." The senator's phone crackled. "How can she, without the professional training of a teacher, possibly cover subjects as diverse as biology, chemistry, civics, English literature, and foreign languages?"

"Aren't there any statistics showing how well they do?"

"Not in Illinois, though nationwide there have been tests." There was a pause as the senator's phone cut out. "—do show favorable results for homeschoolers, but those are only the homeschoolers who have agreed to the tests. You can assume that—"

"Only those homeschoolers who are doing well submit their test scores."

"Exactly."

"How would your bill—"

A knock on the half-opened bedroom door interrupted his question.

Quinn peeked into the room. "Leo, are you ready to go?"

He hunched over his computer. "—hold people accountable?"

More crackling. "I'm losing the connection. It always happens driving through this section of the state."

"Can you e-mail me a copy of the bill? My address is leotownsend@ chicagoexaminer.com."

"Yes." The line went dead.

"I'm sorry," Quinn said. Her bracelets clinked as she adjusted the camera bag on her shoulder. "I didn't mean to interrupt. But we do have a lot of ground to cover…"

"Not a problem. I lost the connection anyway." Leo saved his notes, shut off his computer and shoved it in its bag. He left the bag leaning against the desk and locked the door on his way out.

# 11

Leo and Quinn left the Bradbury Inn, drove past other Victorian homes with wide verandas and entered the center of Carpe Diem. In the town square, people were busy planting the mums Leo had noticed when he first came to town. Grandmas helped muddy toddlers arrange flowers along the sidewalks. Agile teenagers climbed ladders to hang baskets from lampposts.

"Wow, this is a big production," he said.

"Yep, and we do this twice a year," Quinn said. "In the spring we plant impatiens. Usually the fall planting party is on the second weekend in October, but we got caught in a rainstorm, so we postponed it. Now we're working like crazy to get it done in time for the festival."

Leo parked along the tree-lined Main Street, behind a car overflowing with flats of flowers. When they exited his Mustang, he locked the doors. Quinn gave him a look which said *you've got to be kidding.* He shrugged.

As they walked down the sidewalk, Quinn talked to some of the gardeners then took pictures of the leaves painted on the diner's windows. A little boy with a black cat skipped by.

Leo called to the kid, "Hey buddy, how are you?"

The boy stopped. "Good."

"I was worried. I saw some kids picking on you yesterday."

The boy frowned and hugged his cat. "Nobody picked on me."

"I'm sure it was you. Yesterday afternoon. You sat on the curb over there." He pointed across the street. "A teenager held your cat and laughed. You were crying."

Quinn stopped taking pictures. "Is that true, Jimmy?"

The child stroked the purring cat for a moment. "Oh, I remember." He looked at Leo. "They weren't picking on me. They were laughing cuz Billy found Puck. I was so happy, I cried." Jimmy blushed.

"You mean those kids aren't bullies?"

"No. Johnny's my big brother. Steve and Andrew are my cousins. And Billy and Dylan have been my friends forever." He played with Puck's front paw, making it wave. "Bye!" He scooted off down the street.

Leo and Quinn continued up Main Street.

"We don't have bullies in Carpe Diem," Quinn said. "There aren't any schools to produce them."

"You believe schools produce bullies?"

"It's a theory of mine."

"I'd love to hear it."

"Okay," Quinn said. "I was curious when I noticed lots of news reports about teenagers committing suicide because they'd been bullied. I discovered it's a major problem in schools. I didn't know much about bullies, or how they operated, so I did some research. I visited a few public schools and shadowed my friends throughout their day."

"School friends? I thought Carpe Diem didn't have schools."

"It doesn't. But Will and I met some great school kids, like my best friend Gina, at the American Players Theatre acting camp in Wisconsin. I also worked at the Heifer Ranch in Arkansas two summers ago with school kids down there. And I'm the art teacher's aide at the Elon Middle School."

This didn't fit Leo's image of homeschooled kids staying at home all day. "I assumed because you homeschooled you'd be—"

"Isolated? It's a common misconception."

"What did you find when you visited the public schools?"

"The administrators and teachers have an amazing amount of power over students. Administrators pick the curriculum. Students can't choose what to study. For instance, they're told sophomore year they'll study geometry and biology. Teachers determine the study methods; this typically means lectures and government-approved textbooks. Hands-on experiences are rare. One school I went to eliminated their biology lab; students had to read about dissection."

Quinn snapped a few pictures of a mother with her three children discovering a worm in the mums. She lowered her camera. "And teachers have control over the most basic human needs. Kids have to ask for a pass to go to the bathroom. Even worse, teachers try to control students' thoughts."

Leo laughed. "You're exaggerating."

"Am I? When the bell rang, it didn't matter if they were deeply involved in a subject, students had to move on to the next class. One friend told me about being punished for daydreaming in class while another friend received a failing grade for voicing political ideas their teacher didn't agree with."

They walked closer to the curb to let a raucous group of women pass. The women headed into The Booksellers' Shop. Immediately, the noise level dropped yet whiffs of perfume remained.

"Now that you mention it," Leo said. "I remember a high school teacher giving me a C on a paper. He said it was well-written though he disagreed with my premise." Quinn gave him a 'see I-told-you-so' smile reminiscent of the one her mother had given him yesterday. "But how does this result in bullying?"

"In my research, I discovered a psychological term called 'identification with the aggressor.' It means that children mimic someone in power — in this case school officials — to gain control over a frightening situation. My guess is that's what school bullies are doing." She stopped to take a picture of a teenager handing a basketful of mums to another teenager perched halfway up a ladder.

"School officials do have a lot of power over students," Leo agreed. "But that's necessary power. And schools aren't frightening places."

"I disagree about the necessity of power, and maybe after you've been in Carpe Diem a while you'll agree with me." She gave him a sly grin. "But schools are definitely frightening. Picture a typical five-year-old

KRISTIN A. OAKLEY

going to school on his first day. Chances are, he's crying."

"It's a new experience. Okay, that might be scary. But that doesn't last. Once he gets used to the place, he'll be fine."

"It's not just the younger kids though. My high school friends are afraid of giving speeches, afraid of failing grades, afraid of not fitting in. They even have nightmares about it."

"I still have nightmares about walking into a classroom where everyone is completing a test that I didn't even know was scheduled," he admitted.

Quinn nodded. "School can be a scary place and the students don't have control. But most of the kids, like you and my mom, just chill. They figure school's their job. Something they have to do." She snapped photographs of the ivy-covered public library down the street, her voice muffled by her hands holding the camera. "Other kids become bullies. It's their way of trying to manage a scary situation; they mimic the school officials."

Leo still wasn't fully convinced. "I think parents have more influence over children than the schools do. If a parent is a bully, the kid learns that behavior from the parent."

Quinn studied him. "Where did the parents learn it? Don't forget, they also went to school."

"Hmm…"

"Look, all I'm saying is there aren't any schools, grades or domineering school officials in Carpe Diem. And as far as I know there aren't any bullies—"

A short blast from a car horn interrupted her. A blue Honda Civic pulled up alongside the curb. Quinn walked over to the vehicle and squatted beside the open passenger window, resting her camera in her lap. "Hey Billy, what's up?" Leaning across the front seat was the teenager Leo had seen holding Jimmy's cat and laughing while the little boy cried. He had a brown crew cut and wore a Chicago Bears jacket, quite a contrast to Quinn's Goth look.

"The newspaper committee is meeting at my house tonight at seven. We need to come up with a few more activities for the festival. Can you come?" He shouted over the idling car engine. "We're planning on having the usual stuff, running the printing press, making invitations and designing posters. I want to add some short writing activities this year. Maybe the participants could interview your mom or Chief Billiot like a reporter."

"Speaking of a reporter, I've got one right here." Quinn beckoned Leo to the car. "Billy Turner, this is Leo Townsend of *The Chicago Examiner*."

"Nice to meet you, Mr. Townsend."

"You too," Leo agreed as he reached into the car to shake the young man's hand.

"Billy's the assistant editor of the *Carpe Diem Daily News*," Quinn said. "He writes intense editorials."

"I only write the truth." Billy winked at Quinn. "Mr. Townsend, are you going to be in town for the festival?"

"No, I've got to get back to Chicago."

"Too bad, I would have recruited you for our newspaper booth."

Leo wiped his brow in mocked relief.

Billy laughed. He looked at Quinn. "We could also offer journaling or story writing. Is that too much? See, I need your help. Can ya come?"

"Sure, I'll come. You'll owe me though." She grinned at him.

"Owe you?"

"I need someone to help me with the photography booth since John's in Chicago and probably won't be back in time for the festival. I can run the portable darkroom by myself, but someone will have to demonstrate how to make the pinhole cameras."

"I forgot John won't be here. Helping's not a problem if the two booths are next to each other like they were last year."

"That's the plan."

"Good. A couple of other newspaper people could help out, too."

"Cool. See you tonight."

"See ya." Billy waved to them before driving off. Quinn stood up, re-adjusting her camera.

"Not much of a bully," Leo commented. He began to second-guess what he'd seen the day before. He might have to change the beginning of his article.

KRISTIN A. OAKLEY

"Nope. Billy's a sweetie," Quinn said. They walked to the library.

"And he's a Carpe Diem native?"

"No. He was eight when he moved here with his family. When he was six, his public school diagnosed him with ADHD and wanted to put him on Ritalin. His mom refused and unschooled him. His symptoms disappeared."

"Disappeared?"

"I guess it happens a lot. With unschooling you're free to explore your interests in the way that works best for you. Billy likes to solve math problems by pacing around the kitchen table. He says he thinks better when he's moving. At school, they forced him to sit still all day so he acted out. They punished him, oh sorry, 'took disciplinary action,' and isolated him from the other students. He withdrew and became depressed."

When they reached the bottom of the library steps, Quinn stopped and turned to Leo. "Unschooling turned Billy back into a happy, easygoing kid. A few months later, his family heard about Carpe Diem. They visited and fell in love with the town."

"And now he's assistant editor of the paper?"

"Yep and he's only seventeen."

Leo whistled. "His newspaper booth sounds terrific. It's a bit unusual for a community festival."

"Not at our festival. All the booths have hands-on activities."

They climbed the library steps. Her black high tops and his leather loafers scraped the worn stones.

"Huh. Your mom didn't mention it."

Quinn stopped. "Really? She probably just forgot."

"Maybe." Leo found this odd. He had specifically asked Mary if the Carpe Diem festival was unusual, but she had failed to tell him about running printing presses and portable darkrooms.

Quinn continued up the steps. "How about we check the town's historical records in the library? You've got to meet our librarian, Peyton Blaney, she's awesome."

"Sounds good."

"Once we're finished here we can stop by some shops, get lunch at the Thai Hut, and then hit the community college."

"Works for me. To the library it is."

After Leo and Quinn visited the library, they entered Charlotte Jansen's Fair Goods Trading Center. They were immediately hit with the smell of incense and coffee. Leo ducked under hanging baskets and sidestepped crates overflowing with brightly colored wool blankets.

"Hi Quinn, Leo," Charlotte Jansen said. "The bracelet you ordered is in, Quinn. I'll get it for you." She pushed through a beaded doorway to a room in the back, making the beads clatter.

"Let me guess, it's black," Leo teased.

"What else?" Quinn said, unabashed.

Charlotte returned. "Here it is." She handed Quinn the open box. "Black onyx from South Africa."

Quinn set her camera on the counter then slid the bracelet on. "It's beautiful. How much do I owe you?"

"Even with the cost of this bracelet, I think I still owe you for my elephant photograph." She pointed to a framed picture of a large grey elephant trailed by a calf as they waded through tall, straw-colored grasses. Mount Kilimanjaro loomed behind them.

"Why don't we call it a 'fair trade'?" Quinn suggested.

Charlotte laughed. "You've got a deal."

As they left the store, Leo welcomed the fresh air. The incense had given him a headache. He noticed that the gardeners had finished planting their flowers. Gold, crimson, orange, and white mums were everywhere. The effect was sublime.

"When did you go to Africa?" he asked Quinn.

"Two years ago. Several Carpe Diem families went together. I had an excellent—"

"PUCK!" A boy shouted.

Tires screeched. There was a sickening thud.

"JIMMY!" Quinn screamed.

# 12

Tali's day had started out horribly. Her father dropped her at the hospital's entrance and drove off without a backward glance. She flipped him
the bird and then slipped into the nearest bathroom to calm down before
facing the cold intensive care unit. She trudged up two flights of stairs to
the ICU, shuffled past rooms filled with comatose patients, and drifted
into her mother's room.

The bed was empty.

She shot into the hallway and banged into an overstuffed supply cart.
Boxes of latex gloves, rolls of gauze, and dozens of bottles, plastic thank
God, went flying as the cart crashed to the floor. A nurse rushed over to
help her pick up. She told Tali they had moved her mother out of the
ICU to a room on the fourth floor.

Alexandra's new room had an actual wooden door, fewer machines, a
small closet, and a bathroom with a shower stall. On either side of the
room's large window, two lavender recliners doubled as beds and on
the table between them, a clay pot held what Tali recognized as yellow
freesia. Their sweet fragrance masked the smell of rubbing alcohol.

Yet underneath the pretty floral bedspread lay her mom, all bandaged
and, well, crumpled. Dr. Anderson said that she would make a full, but
slow, recovery. Still…

Tali had spent the morning not looking at her sleeping mom's bruised face. Instead she watched lame TV talk shows with the volume turned down while playing games on her phone. When lunchtime came, she ate a pretty decent cheeseburger, a milkshake and salty fries in the hospital cafeteria.

In the afternoon, Alexandra continued to sleep, so Tali went back to channel surfing. After watching one rerun of *Seinfeld*, she found nothing of interest. Bored and restless, she went downstairs to investigate the gift shop. There she had bought a few magazines and a colorful get well balloon and then made a detour back to the cafeteria for a large Diet Pepsi.

Tali drank the last sip of her soda and paged through Modern Women magazine. *Fix You* by Coldplay echoed through her iPod ear buds as she looked at pictures of gorgeous women and read about how they struggled to take their last ten pounds off. She glanced at her mom who was just as beautiful, until the accident. A few brown strands of hair were stuck to Alexandra's purple, blotchy forehead; the rest of her head wrapped in gauze. The swelling around her left eye had gone down, though the bruises still made her look like a raccoon.

Alexandra opened her eyes and smiled, creating tiny middle-aged wrinkles.

Tali turned off her music, pulled out her ear buds and shoved an annoying piece of blond hair out of her face. "How're you feeling?" She tried to control her shaky voice.

"A little thirsty," her mother whispered dryly.

Glad to be able to help, Tali grabbed the cup and pitcher from the bedside table and began to pour. "What'll it be? A Cosmopolitan? A Margarita?"

"No Bloody Marys," Alexandra croaked, then winced.

"Definitely not. I'm out of Tabasco sauce anyway." She pushed a button to raise the top of the bed, adjusted the pillows and gave Alexandra the cup to hold in her cast-free hand.

"Do you need anything else? Should I turn on the TV?"

"Mirror."

Tali had expected this and shook her head. She grabbed the magazine. "I could read to you. There's important stuff about how celery helps you lose weight and which lip gloss makes you more kissable."

Alexandra chuckled. It was rough and shaky, but a definite chuckle.

"Super, you're awake," a nurse said entering the room. Broken conversations and mechanical beeps came in from the hall. "I'm Denise. I'll be checking your vital signs."

The nurse, who wasn't much older than Tali, wore a stethoscope, a multi-colored smock, and crisp white pants. She smelled of Dove soap and baby shampoo. She looked at Tali. "Are you Mrs. Shaw's daughter?"

Tali nodded, then looked at the piping around the toes of her Uggs and said, "Tali."

"Nice to meet you," Denise said.

"Aren't you too young to be a nurse?" She couldn't help asking.

"I'm not a full-fledged nurse yet. I'm a nurse's assistant." Denise took the empty cup from Alexandra and then wrapped the blood pressure band around her arm. "I'm saving up to go to nursing school at the University of Illinois at Chicago."

"Aren't you in high school?"

"No. I'm too busy working and taking nursing courses at the Carpe Diem Community College." Denise noted the blood pressure reading. "Your vital signs are normal, Mrs. Shaw. How are you feeling?"

"Achy."

"Not surprising with what you've been through. We've got you on a morphine drip." Denise handed Alexandra a small controller device attached to an IV. "You push this button to release more morphine as needed. Don't worry, you can't overdue it, there's a maximum setting. If the pain gets more intense, be sure to call me. Is there anything else I can get you?"

"A mirror."

"Why don't you wait a day or two until the swelling goes down?" Denise said in a rush. "Dr. Anderson will be stopping by later this evening to see you. And don't forget to use your call button if you need me." She left the room.

"I look that bad?" Tali's mother croaked.

"You're just bruised. You'll be back to your beautiful self in a couple of days." Tali gave her mom a gentle hug. Alexandra looked away. "So.

Denise. She must've graduated early. I wouldn't like that. Think of the things I'd miss."

Alexandra didn't respond.

"'Course I wouldn't miss the stupid homework."

"Natalia."

Tali glanced at the wall clock. "No, I mean it. Tom'll be by soon with my assignments. I'll probably have to do a lame research paper on the life cycle of a fruit fly or something. Who cares about that crap anyway?"

"Scientists."

She rolled her eyes.

"Exposes you to more than reality TV," her mother managed.

"I like more stuff than just TV," Tali protested. "I bet Denise doesn't waste her time writing useless papers."

"You hate school?"

"School's definitely boring, but I don't *hate* it. Britney Crandall and her crowd are lame and I could drop kick Missus Turner with her old person smell. But I'd die if I couldn't hang with my friends and," she pointed to her sweatshirt, "cheer for the Tigers. Imagine not going to homecoming!"

"Who's not going to homecoming?" A large, teenage boy barged into the hospital room. Tali's overstuffed backpack hung from his right shoulder and he gripped her red overnight bag and computer case in his enormous left hand.

"Tom!" She ran to hug her boyfriend.

"Wait." He tossed the bags in the direction of the closet then hugged her. "I brought all your junk, including your bike. It's chained to the rack outside the hospital entrance." Well over six feet tall, with short blond hair, he filled out his orange Alanton Tigers football jersey, number 23. His torn Gap jeans dragged on the floor but couldn't cover his huge untied Nikes.

"Thanks. You must've skipped out of school early. It's not even four o'clock."

"Yeah, blew off Spanish. I won't miss anything. It's a month into school and Mizz James is still going over the syllabus."

Behind them, the door opened. "Excuse me, Tali," Denise interrupted. "Who's your visitor?"

"This is my boyfriend, Tom."

"And captain of the high school football team," Tom added while checking the nurse out. "Yo, Denise. What you doin' after work?"

"Tom!" Tali said, giving him a shove.

"What, I'm kidding."

"Um," Denise began, "Dr. Anderson wants to limit visitors to family only. At least for the next few days."

"That's just great," Tom said. "I drove for two friggin' hours. Now you tell me to get lost?" His anger increased his size.

"No, you're welcome to stay in the building as long as you'd like," Denise replied, her voice steady. "We have a wonderful cafeteria, a coffee shop,—"

"I—"

"—and a comfortable lounge in the atrium."

"Come on Tom," Tali grabbed his arm and her backpack, "let's go to cafeteria."

"Not the cafeteria. If we go anywhere, it'll be the coffee shop."

She nodded. "Mom, is that okay?"

"Yes."

Customers filled the coffee shop, many toting get well balloons or stuffed animals. Three doctors were hunched over paperwork at a corner table, arguing. Tali overheard them say "impossible" and "unbelievable" and wondered what they were talking about.

At the next table a young family and an old guy in a wheelchair laughed; apparently Grandpa was going to be okay. Two businesswomen relaxed in chairs near a fireplace; a waitress brought them muffins and steaming coffee in huge, yellow mugs. The smell of vanilla made Tali's mouth water. She wished she had brought her purse.

"Let's crash here," Tom said as he took the backpack from her and plopped it in a booth near the entrance.

"Thanks for coming." She slid into the seat across from him. "You're totally awesome."

"No problem. Anything for my girl." He leaned in for a quick kiss. "Danielle says 'hi.' She had to work tonight. She's hoping to get here soon."

"Yeah, she texted me. Tell your sister to stop working so much and have some fun."

"It's never gonna happen. The girl's determined to make enough money to buy her own car. She doesn't have rich parents like yours who'll give her one for her sixteenth birthday."

"Or the chance to make the all-state football team so her dad will buy her a Camaro," she said under her breath.

"Used Camaro," Tom corrected. He opened up her backpack and pulled out notebooks, textbooks, and assignment sheets. He shoved the books toward her. "I brought all your crap for the next week. You won't miss much except for Monday's—"

His cell phone rang. He took it out of his back pocket, assignment sheets still in his other hand.

"Joe, whaz up?" Laughter. "No shit!" Pause. "No way." He leaned back in the booth, wedging the phone between his shoulder and ear. "Hey man, I'm really not surprised. That chick's messed up." He crossed his arms, crumpling the papers in his hand. "Yeah, you can tell her I said that."

Tali sighed.

Tom noticed. "Gotta go. See ya."

She frowned.

He shrugged. "Where was I?"

"Monday's assignment?"

"Oh yeah, the Civil War quiz. Mizz Doherty says you can take it later. The biology paper's due Tuesday." He handed her a wrinkled sheet of paper.

"Research the life cycle of the North American white-tailed deer. Great." She dropped her elbows onto the table and rested her chin in her hands.

A waitress stopped by. "Can I get you anything?"

"Nope," Tom answered for both of them. "Don't sweat the paper," he reassured Tali, ignoring the surprised, retreating server. "Mr. Westcott was cool with giving you another week."

She nodded.

"Here's your Algebra II quiz. We both aced it, thanks to you."

Tali shifted uncomfortably. She didn't like helping him cheat, but if she didn't he wouldn't even think about going out with her.

At Alanton High, a football star like Tom dated a cheerleader, the homecoming queen, or the class president. She was a plain old girl. Nothing special. She did play for the soccer team, but mostly sat on the bench. And she wasn't even pretty, what with hunched shoulders and dull, dirty blond hair hanging in her face.

"There's a shit load of reading. Here's the list." His phone rang again. "Mike, my man, where you been? No, not tonight. I'm in some pissant town with Tali."

Tom leaned back in the booth, oblivious to her glare. "Who's gonna be there?" He sat up straighter. "No shittin'?" He looked at Tali like he wanted to ask a question then decided against it. "No, can't do it tonight. How about tomorrow night? Really? Oh, too bad. Sure, go ahead, I've got time."

Tali yanked the sheet of paper out of his grip. He still ignored her. Fuming, she scanned the paper then saw movement out of the corner of her eye. Officer Dennison.

"Miss Shaw," the officer said. Dressed in full uniform, he held his hat in one hand and her mother's purse in the other. "Your mother's nurse said I'd find you here."

Freaked, she dropped the list and started sliding out of the booth.

"Wait, there's nothing wrong," the cop said.

Relieved, she slid back.

Tom kept talking on his phone.

"I've got your mother's purse from the car. Normally, we don't deliver stuff. But I just got off duty and stopped by to visit my girlfriend, she's a pediatric nurse. The chief suggested I bring it. Anyway, your mother was asleep, so I thought maybe you'd like it. Her nurse told me you'd be here." He handed her the black leather bag.

She nodded and unhooked the purse's silver chain. Checking inside, she spotted her mother's wallet. *I can buy a blueberry muffin.*

Tom erupted with laughter at something Mike said.

The cop glanced at Tom, then said, "I'm sorry to say, her car's in pretty bad shape."

Tali pictured twisted metal and shivered.

"If you'd like to take a look at it, you can. It's at the police station's impound lot."

The thought horrified her. She shook her head. Blond strands fell across her face.

"Sure, I understand. Some people are curious. Don't worry about it. Your insurance company will contact your folks if they haven't already. Anyway, have your mother check through her purse. If there's anything missing, or if she did have shopping bags or anything else in the car that we didn't find, have her call me. You've got my card."

Tali shook her head again.

"I've got plenty." He took a business card from his front shirt pocket and passed it to her. "Okay, well, I should go. Take care."

She pushed her hair aside to watch him leave and then looked down at the business card with its official police seal. Tucking it into her mom's purse, she noticed an old slip of paper with *Chris and Mary Tomlinson?* scrawled on it. People Mom met at the writers' workshop?

"God, I don't want to miss that!" Tom exclaimed. "I know, I know. I'll talk to her. Yep. I'll call ya back." He shut off his phone and continued to look at it. "Um, what did the cop want?"

"He dropped off Mom's purse."

"Great," he said without interest. "Well, I should go."

"What? You just got here."

"Hey, don't get your panties in a twist. Mike's having this party tonight. The quarterback and three other players from last year's team are coming. I haven't seen those guys since they graduated. I wouldn't miss it for anything."

"Not even for me?"

"Look, I skipped football practice to drive all this way with your stuff, what more do you want?"

"How about dinner? I'm all alone here. I can't believe you're bailing on me." But she wasn't surprised. Tom had been spending more and more time with the guys even before the accident. "You're just like my dad," she said in a small voice.

"Don't give me that crap. I'm around a lot more than your old man."

"Right."

"I *was* planning on coming back on Sunday, but not if you're going to be a bitch." He shot out of the booth.

"Me?!"

"Forget it. I'm gone." He left.

Tali pulled her necklace out of her sweatshirt and fingered the car charm, then put her face in her hands and cried.

# 13

"Tali, are you okay?"

Tali looked up to see blurry images of Quinn and a tall, gorgeous, vaguely familiar guy. She wiped her eyes on the sleeve of her sweatshirt and nodded. She felt herself blushing, embarrassed that they had seen her crying.

Quinn slid into the booth. Her black down jacket shushed against the red cushions.

Tali slunk back against the booth, pulling away from Quinn, worried that Tom might come back and see her sitting with this Emo girl.

"Tali, this is Leo Townsend."

"Hi, Tali," Leo said.

She nodded.

"I'll get us a couple of hot chocolates," he suggested and left for the coffee shop counter.

"What's wrong?' Quinn asked. "Is it your mom?"

She shook her head.

"She's going to be okay?"

Tali nodded.

Quinn stared at her for a moment. "Look, I know you don't know me very well, but I'd like to help."

Tali considered this, then realized she needed someone to talk to. She took a deep, shuddering breath. "My boyfriend left."

"Was he the big guy who nearly knocked Leo over as we came in?"

"Probably. He brought me my things."

"That was nice," Quinn prompted.

Tali shrugged and looked down at the purse in her lap. "I thought he'd stay longer. Take me out to dinner."

"So where did he go?"

"Home for some party," she mumbled, still not looking at Quinn.

Quinn crossed her arms. "He sounds like a total jerk."

Tali lifted her head. Blond hair fell across her face. "He's not. He's a sweetheart."

"The sweethearts I know don't leave their girlfriends when their mothers are in the hospital and they need their support." Quinn pushed aside the biology textbook then drummed her black fingernails on the table. "You can tell a lot about someone by how he handles a crisis—or avoids it."

Tali glared at Quinn's brown eyes, as dark as her own, then softened, realizing Quinn was right. If Tom really cared about her, he would have stayed. He wouldn't even think about leaving. Her next words poured out.

"That's not all. A cop dropped off my mom's purse." She touched the bag's soft leather. "He told me the car's totaled." Her voice decreased to a whisper. "My mom could've died."

Leo arrived with three mugs of hot cocoa topped with whipped cream. Deep chocolate smells warmed the booth. He set napkins and cups on the table next to Tali's books and papers and slid beside Quinn.

"Is everything all right?" he asked, his eyes intense and full of concern. Neither Tom nor her dad ever looked at her that way. In fact, they hardly ever looked at her at all.

Tali shook her head, too upset to answer him. She sipped the rich cocoa and felt it warm her throat. The muscles in her face relaxed. She licked cream from her upper lip.

Quinn answered for her, "Tali's mom was in a car accident."

"That's awful. How is she doing?"

"Okay," Tali managed.

Quinn continued, "Tali's staying in Carpe Diem until her mom recovers. The big guy who crashed into you is her boyfriend. He dropped off her stuff then abandoned her to go to a party."

"I'm sure he had his reasons." Leo took a hefty gulp of cocoa and cream.

"Really? Tali's pretty upset. She needs him. At least he could have taken her out to dinner."

"It does seem insensitive." He looked again at Tali.

She peeked at his pale green eyes through strands of her hair.

"Why don't you come to dinner with us?" Leo offered.

"Great idea." Quinn flashed him a smile.

Tali shook her head. Talking to Quinn was one thing, but going out to dinner with her and a strange man? "I don't think so," she muttered.

"It'll be fun," Quinn told her. "We're heading over to the photography studio where I work. I'd love to show you my stuff. After that, we're going to check out the community college and then go to Sapori D'Italia for pasta."

"I shouldn't leave my mom."

"We'll stop by her room so you can check in with her. She probably needs sleep more than anything. And this town is small, we won't be far."

She liked the idea of getting out of the hospital for a while even if it was with Quinn. Heck, it's not like anyone she knew would see them having dinner. Tom was long gone. But she would definitely check with her mom first. If her mother okayed it, then she would go. She nodded.

"Great!" Quinn said.

After drinking a bit more, Tali lifted the mug. "Thanks, Mr. Townsend."

"You're more than welcome, but call me Leo."

"Leo." Tali checked him out. With his thick brown hair, chiseled cheek bones, and dimpled chin, he was hot, for an old guy. Suddenly she realized where she had seen him before. "Are you staying at the Bradbury Inn?"

"Yes." He brought his mug to his lips.

"You sat at the table next to my dad and me at breakfast this morning." She put down her mug and blurted out, "You typed what we said on your laptop."

"*What?*" Quinn shot at Leo.

"Why would I do that?" He sounded calm, but cocoa spilled out of his mug as he set it down. "What were you talking about?"

"Homeschooling."

"That explains it. It was a coincidence," Quinn said. "Leo's a reporter for *The Chicago Examiner*. He's writing a book about small towns. Of course he'd mention homeschooling when describing Carpe Diem. The whole town unschools."

"Exactly," Leo said.

Tali stared at him. She was sure that he had typed her dad's exact words. Then he shot her an amazing smile and she knew she'd pretty much believe anything he said.

They finished their drinks, shoved the books and papers into her bag and left the coffee shop. Back in Alexandra's room, Tali left her pack on one of the recliners while her groggy mom insisted she go out to dinner. She propped up her mother's pillows, tucked in the sheets, filled her water glass and started to tidy the room.

"Go, Natalia," Alexandra said, "I'll be fine."

"Are you sure? I'm okay with staying."

"Go."

She gave her mom a gentle hug then joined Leo and Quinn outside the room. While they walked down the hallway, she asked, "Hey, why are you guys here, at the hospital?"

"We brought Jimmy Edwards in," Leo replied.

"A little boy who lives near me," Quinn explained as she stepped out of the way of two nurses wheeling a patient on a gurney. "We saw him, um, get hit by a car today."

Tali gasped.

"He's going to be okay," Leo added as he passed three uniformed policemen. "Thankfully the car had slowed down to avoid Jimmy's cat, Puck. When Jimmy ran in front of the car to rescue Puck, it simply pushed him to the ground. He's got a broken arm and a few cuts and bruises but he'll be fine."

"It was scary." Quinn shuddered.

As they walked across the parking lot toward a red Mustang, Leo fumbled in his jacket pocket for his keys.

"This is *your* car?" Tali said. "A 2006 Ford Mustang GT Convertible?" She couldn't believe she'd get a chance to ride in one of these.

"Yes, it is," he replied. "You know cars."

She kicked a pebble with her boot and nodded.

"Why don't you ride in the front?" Quinn suggested.

Maybe this day wouldn't be so horrible after all.


The clock on the Mustang's dashboard read 6:30 p.m. when they left the community college and drove by the police station on their way to the restaurant. As they rounded the corner, Tali looked back and spotted a familiar silver BMW in the parking lot behind the station.

"Stop!"

"What's wrong?" Leo asked swerving to the curb.

"That's our car." She pointed to the BMW. Despite her earlier doubts, Tali suddenly had an intense desire to check out the damage. "Can we see it?"

"Are you sure?" Quinn asked.

She nodded.

"I don't think we have time." Leo checked his watch. "We still have to eat and I have an article to write and submit."

He glanced at her. Her pleading look must have worked because he added, "Oh, what the hell. A few more minutes won't make much of a difference. Besides, cranking out last minute stories is a specialty of mine."

He turned the car around and pulled into the police station. Following the *impound* signs, Leo drove down a short blacktopped driveway to the back of the building. In a far opposite corner of the lot sat the mangled BMW.

As Tali climbed out of the sports car, she felt both excited and nauseous. She'd get to see the inner workings of the car, but she worried about seeing the damage. As they reached the sedan, she wondered if this was a good idea. The roof was caved in and the windshield looked like a giant spider web. The flattened left front tire bent at a weird angle. The caved-in driver's side looked like a large "V."

Leo let out a low whistle.

Tali fingered the tiny car charm on the end of her necklace. She remembered her first driving lesson in the BMW. Surprised at how easy the car handled, she pulled too fast into the garage, cutting an ugly gash above the left front tire. She figured her driving days were over. Then her mom pointed out a second, older dent near the bumper. It was the result, Alexandra said, of drinking too much coffee. Those 'war wounds,' as her mom had called them, were now twisted into the crumpled metal.

Tali heard a clicking noise. She backed away from the car. Quinn walked by with her camera snapping away.

"Quinn!"

Quinn shoved the camera back into its bag. "Sorry," she said. "It's a bad habit."

"Why is the side crushed in like that?" Leo asked.

"A motorcycle plowed into her car," Tali answered.

"Jesus!" He ran his hand through his hair. "I think I heard about this on the news. Is your father Christopher Shaw, the state senator?"

She nodded, not taking her eyes off the car, though there was something in his voice that made her think he already knew this.

"Which explains the homeschooling discussion. He isn't a fan, is he?" Leo asked.

Quinn's head snapped around to Tali.

Too busy wondering about the stain on the dashboard, she ignored Quinn. *Is that blood?* She felt weak. Her legs gave out. Leo grabbed her. The musky smell of his cologne cleared her head.

"Thanks," she said feeling better.

"You don't have to do this." Leo squeezed her arm.

"Can I help you?" A mechanic came out of the garage. "Oh, hi Quinn."

"Hi, Josh. This is Tali Shaw and Leo Townsend. Guys, this is Josh Brody."

Josh Brody saluted and then noticed his greasy hand. He wiped it on a grimy blue towel tied to the belt on his work pants.

"Tali wanted to take a look at her mom's car. Is that okay?"

"Sure. How's your mom doing?" Josh asked her.

"Okay," Tali answered. He was almost as tall as her boyfriend though his blue work shirt hung loosely; Tom's muscles pulled his football jersey taut. Josh's wavy hair, the color of black motor oil, matched the grit under his fingernails and the grease smeared on his cheek. A few days' growth on his face added to his grungy appearance. His eyes were an unusual blue-green color.

"I'm glad to hear it."

"We should get going," Leo said, glancing at his watch.

As they headed back to the Mustang, they passed by the open garage door and saw bits and pieces of metal and two flat tires lying on a blue tarp.

"Is that what's left of the motorcycle?" Leo asked.

"Yes. I'm trying to see what I can save," Josh answered. Thunder rumbled nearby as if telling Josh that saving anything was a lost cause.

"Do you mind if I have a look?" Leo asked. "I'm not a mechanic though I once built a dirt bike from scratch. Used to write for *Mechanics Magazine*."

"Sure, come on in." When they entered the garage, the smell of rubber mixed with oil hit them. Quinn wrinkled her nose. Tali liked the smell. It made her think of Maseratis and Lamborghinis.

"Josh, have you ever been to school?" Leo asked. "I know Quinn hasn't."

"I take classes at the Carpe Diem Community College." He paused during a louder burst of thunder, then continued, "But other than that, no."

"You're taking auto mechanics at the college?"

"No. French, computer graphics, and a chemistry lab."

"I assumed you'd be studying to become a certified mechanic. You're what, seventeen?"

"Yep, but I passed my certification exam two years ago."

"At fifteen? That's pretty young to take mechanics courses."

"Maybe, but I never took any classes." They stopped in front of the motorcycle pieces.

"*Really?*" Tali couldn't believe it.

Josh explained, "When I was seven, I took apart my mom's vacuum cleaner. Boy was she mad until I rebuilt it and it ran better. So she took me to the library where I checked out all their books on machines. Every birthday and Christmas, I asked for models. On my twelfth birthday, my dad arranged for me to help out at the local garage. I've been working there ever since. And a couple of nights a week I work here at the police station."

"It's what I've been telling you Leo," Quinn said. "Unschooling gives you the freedom to follow your passions. If you're interested, learning comes naturally. Learning by doing works best of all."

This was a new idea to Tali. She assumed she had to go to school, complete assignments and take tests to learn anything.

But Quinn talked about interesting stuff, which had to be different. The boring stuff, stuff everyone told you you needed to learn, like geometry, well that, Tali was sure, you'd still have to learn in school.

When they got to the blue tarp, Leo picked up the motorcycle's handle bars, keeping them away from his designer jeans.

Seeing the scattered remains of the motorcycle reminded Tali of what Office Dennison had said about Patrick Holden. Her hands tightened into fists. "The police think the driver tried to kill himself," she spat.

"Yes," Josh answered. "The road conditions were fine and there were no skid marks." His voice rose over the rain now beating on the garage roof. "No indication of breaking and I haven't been able to find anything mechanically wrong with the motorcycle. Patrick loved his bike. Kept it in good shape."

"Why would a man who loves his bike want to destroy it?" Leo replaced the handlebars and crouched beside the tires.

"People say he wanted them to 'die' together. I don't buy it though."

"Why not?" Leo asked.

"Patrick is passionate about a lot of things, but he's most passionate about life," Josh answered. "Most people are all talk, he's action. He never backs away from a fight. I admit, he pisses people off and tends to lose his cool. He argues a lot with his dad. But giving up, killing himself, and hurting someone else. I don't buy it."

Leo examined one tire, looked at the second tire and then back at the first. "Maybe you're right. Maybe this wasn't a suicide attempt," he said.

"What do you mean?"

"This is the front tire, right?"

"Right."

"Take a closer look."

Josh inspected the tire. "It's flat, so?"

"Look at the steel rim."

"There's a black spot," Quinn said.

"It's nothing," Josh explained. "Just brake dust."

"Look closer," Leo told him. Josh crouched down and wiped the smudge with his rag.

"No way!" Josh exclaimed.

"*What?*" Quinn asked.

"It's melted." Josh pointed to an inch of steel.

"Definitely," Leo said. "The accident didn't cause this. Something dissolved it. I'd guess some sort of acid."

"Acid from the engine?" Tali asked.

"No." Josh shook his head. "How did I miss it?"

"You weren't looking for this," Leo said.

"What? Wait, it wasn't suicide?" Quinn asked. "Did the bike malfunction?"

"No," Leo answered. "This bike's been sabotaged."

# 14

"It definitely looks like Patrick's motorcycle has been sabotaged," Leo repeated. So much for his deadline, but this was turning into a much bigger story.

"Sabotage? Are you sure?" Quinn asked while she photographed the deflated tire.

"I'm no expert, but that's what it looks like."

"There's probably some kind of test," Josh said, rising from his crouched position. "Our police department has a chemistry expert. I'll get Chief Billiot." He bolted for the station's door. "Don't touch anything," he yelled over his shoulder.

"You bet," Leo called back, standing.

Quinn stopped taking close-ups of the front tire. "Why would someone sabotage Patrick's bike?"

"I have no idea. Does Patrick have any enemies?"

"Wait," Tali interrupted. "Did someone try to hurt my mom?" Her lip quivered.

"I doubt it." Leo wanted to reassure her. The poor kid had been through enough. "My guess is it would be difficult to know exactly when the tire would give out. If someone wanted to hurt your mom, there are easier ways of doing it."

Tali nodded and wiped her eyes with the sleeve of her sweatshirt.

"What's going on here?" a gruff voice shouted over the thunderstorm.

Josh and two police officers strode toward Leo and the girls. Based upon the older officer's purposeful stride, Leo guessed that he was Police Chief Billiot. His brown skin, plaited black hair, broad face, high cheek bones, and hawk feather earring didn't make him a stereotypical police chief.

The younger officer had freckled skin and short red hair, the chief's polar opposite. He carried a camera bag and what looked like a doctor's kit.

"Chief Keme Billiot, this is Leo Townsend from *The Chicago Examiner* and Tali Shaw," Quinn said.

"I heard a reporter from *The Examiner* was in town. Glad to meet you." The chief had a crushing handshake. "Miss Shaw, how's your mother doing?"

"Okay," Tali answered, staring at the ground.

"That's good news. This is Officer Charles Ellery. He dabbles in chemistry," Billiot said, slapping the young man on the back. Officer Ellery winced. "We're not big enough to have our own lab. But for most things, Chuck can get the job done." The chief raised an eyebrow. "So, Mr. Townsend, this sabotage theory isn't some sensational story idea you're dying to write, is it?"

"Not at all." The accusation didn't bother Leo. As a veteran journalist he had been accused of worse, but even in his most drunken state he never considered fabricating anything. "Though it looks like I happened upon quite a story. We were heading out to dinner when Tali spotted her mother's car and wanted to take a look. I noticed the motorcycle pieces—"

"I told him he could have a look," Josh interrupted. "He knows about bikes and saw this." He pointed to the jagged, black edge of rim that had pulled away from the tire.

Chief Billiot eyed Leo a bit longer before looking at the tire. "Does look odd. Okay Chuck, check it out."

The young officer opened his bag and pulled out a camera. He photographed the tire from all angles. Once satisfied, he set the camera aside and began sifting through his kit.

"Why would anyone sabotage Patrick's bike?" Quinn asked the chief.

"Hang on a minute. I'm not convinced it was sabotage. Let's give Officer Ellery a chance."

Leo watched the officer pull on a pair of latex gloves and remove cotton swabs and a plastic bag from his kit. Instantly, Leo thought of a dozen questions he wanted to ask, but decided not to interrupt Ellery's work.

As the officer wiped the blackened area, Billiot said, "This might take awhile. Since you haven't eaten, why don't you get dinner?"

"Good idea," Leo said.

"But come back," the chief added. "I may have more questions for you."

"And we'll want to know what your findings are," Leo added.

Billiot didn't reply.

Leo drove down the damp, tree-lined streets. Light from antique street lamps reflected in puddles. Shops were closed for the night. At the edge of town, Quinn directed him down a long winding drive leading to an intimate Italian restaurant.

When they entered Sapori D'Italia, a large woman in a red-checked dress and vibrant red heels gave Quinn a bear hug. "Come siete il mio caro?"

"Buoni, buoni Francesca. Questi sono i miei amici, Tali Shaw e Leo Townsend." Quinn answered.

"Welcome, Quinn's friends. I hope you're hungry." Francesca said rolling her r's.

"Estremamente," Leo answered.

"Buoni. You speak Italian, Signore Townsend." Francesca laughed.

"Some. My mother is from Italy. A small town called Norcia southeast of Florence."

"Si, si. Their ham and sausages, norcineria, are fantastico. You are extremely hungry, si? You have come to the right place. We have plenty for you to eat." She led them through a small red and gold dining room with

Sicilian landscapes, Roman columns, grape vines, and enticing smells of garlic. The room reminded Leo of his mother's kitchen. The rest of their home was pure Midwestern farmhouse, but his mother had insisted on having an Italian kitchen.

Couples and families occupied several of the dozen tables and chatted over plates of antipasto and marinara-covered pasta. Francesca seated Leo and the girls at a corner table. "I hope you enjoy your dinner." She handed them the menus.

"Grazie Francesca," Quinn said.

As Francesca glided out of the room, Tali asked Quinn, "You speak Italian?"

"A little, though I'd like to become fluent."

"Sounds like you're fluent, senorita." Tali gave Quinn the slightest grin, the first hint of a smile Leo had seen.

Quinn laughed. "'Senorita' is Spanish, you mean signorina."

Tali shrugged, still grinning. "Close."

"What kind of language program are you using Quinn?" Leo asked. "Or are you taking classes at the community college?"

"Neither. Francesca and her husband, Anthony, are teaching me. On Mondays and Fridays, my brother Will comes here to learn authentic Italian cooking. I tag along. When they get the chance, the Scallinis help me with my Italian." Her new onyx bracelet clinked against her skull and crossbones watch as she picked up a menu. "In return, I pitch in by waitressing, bussing tables, whatever they need."

"I'd like to learn French," Tali said to the laminated card listing the daily specials. "My great-grandma was French, but my high school only has Spanish. It's required. I suck at it."

"With the exception of senorita," Leo teased.

A swarthy waitress with a Scallini family resemblance set crusty bread and water on the table, took their orders, and gave Leo a wink.

"Maybe you need some motivation to learn Spanish, Tali," he suggested, slathering butter on a chunk of bread. "Working in Chicago, I realized speaking Spanish would be a great advantage so I took an immersion class offered at the paper. That did the trick."

"And while I don't need Italian for any job, yet," Quinn sipped her water, leaving black lipstick prints on the glass, "it certainly helps with my classical singing."

"Classical?" Leo asked. "I pictured you singing screamo, especially after you saw Jimmy's accident."

Tali stifled a laugh and pushed a few strands of hair away from her eyes. Quinn scowled.

"Classical, definitely classical," he amended. Quinn's scowl softened.

"I'd like to take voice lessons," Tali said, "and try out for the varsity choir."

"At least your school has choirs." Quinn tore off a slice of bread and brushed the crumbs off her black jeans. "I've read that some of the Chicago schools got rid of their music departments because of budget cuts."

"I suppose your options are limited too, Quinn, without any schools in Carpe Diem," Leo said.

"Actually, there are several terrific community choirs in Carpe Diem. I'm in two. The madrigal singers, we're big at Christmastime, and the Carpe Diem Choir. The choir went to Washington, D.C. last month and sang for the president."

"No kidding." Leo was impressed.

Quinn continued. "Plus, our community theatre does a couple of musicals a year. I'm trying out for *The Sound of Music* at the end of this month." She finished buttering her piece of bread. "The Italian will really be useful next summer. With Will's work at the Inn and my job at the studio, we're hoping to raise enough money to go to Italy."

"Cool," Tali said.

"Hey Tali, I have an idea. Why don't you come with me to my Italian lesson tomorrow?" Quinn suggested as the waitress placed a Caesar salad in front of her. "There's always good food."

"Maybe, if Mom's okay."

After crunching a crouton, Leo asked Quinn, "How do you do it?"

"Do what?"

"Have two jobs, here and in the photography studio, sing in two choirs and possibly a musical and still find time to get your school work done."

"I don't do school work, at least not in the conventional sense. Unschoolers don't sit at desks filling out workbooks, completing assignments. Some homeschoolers do that but Will and I don't."

"What do you do?"

"I learn through living. When I discuss European politics with Francesca in Italian, I'm doing what you'd call 'school work'." She speared a tomato with her fork.

"What about grades?" Tali asked.

"No grades, no tests."

"How do you know if you're learning anything?" Tali took a bite of her salad.

Before Quinn could answer, Francesca, carrying her coat and purse, appeared at their table. She spoke to Quinn in Italian and with a wave, left.

"Francesca's done for the night. She told me she'd see me at our regular time tomorrow," Quinn said.

"I think Quinn just answered your question, Tali," Leo said.

The waitress brought steaming plates of pasta. As Leo dug into his fettuccini, he asked, "Do you know Patrick Holden, Quinn?"

"Yes, but I know his dad, John, better since he owns the photography studio. You could say he's my mentor." Quinn ate a piece of bread before she continued, "John said he and Patrick argued the day of the accident. Something about a meeting."

"Oh my God!" Tali nearly spilled her Diet Pepsi. "Patrick went to see my dad. Dad said their meeting didn't go well." Her eyes widened. "You don't think my dad—"

"Had something to do with this?" Leo's forkful of noodles stopped midway to his mouth. "Could he do something like that?"

"No," she replied, though she didn't sound convincing.

"How did your dad react to the accident?" he asked.

"Freaked out." Tali played with her knife. "He didn't know that Patrick drove the motorcycle until Officer Dennison told him. Then he was pissed."

"Did he say anything?"

"He said Patrick was a lunatic. He wondered if Patrick plowed into Mom on purpose to get back at him."

"To get back at him for what?"

"Something to do with the meeting, I guess."

"John mentioned Patrick wanted to stop passage of an anti-home-schooling bill," Quinn said as she wiped a bit of marinara sauce from the corner of her mouth. "Maybe that was it."

Tali nodded and fingered her necklace. Her hair fell across her face.

Quinn touched Tali's shoulder. Tali looked surprised and a bit uncomfortable, but she didn't pull away.

"Let's finish eating and get back to the station," Leo suggested and then waved to the waitress for the check.

Leo smelled the acrid odor of new carpeting as he entered the quiet police station. He missed the craziness of the Chicago Police Department. Just walking across the lobby of police headquarters, a reporter could pick up a story or two. Good stories. Here the headliner would be the carpet installation.

He walked up to the empty desk and looked for a bell. The phone rang. Someone down the hall yelled, "Sarge!" There were footsteps and a muffled conversation.

Chief Billiot, Officer Ellery, a third officer and Josh appeared around the corner. The chief introduced the third officer as Hank Dennison and then led them down a short hall into a medium-sized conference room.

Everyone except Josh took seats around the table. He stood behind Quinn. "I'm a bit greasy," he explained in a choked voice, clearly upset about something.

"I'm afraid I have some bad news," Chief Billiot said, his booming voice softening. "We just got word. Patrick Holden died earlier today."

"No!" Quinn cried.

Tali looked pale.

"I'm afraid so. We heard he was doing better, but apparently he took a turn for the worse. They couldn't save him."

"That's terrible," Leo said.

"How is John doing?" Quinn whispered.

"I'd say he's in shock. I didn't tell him what we've discovered about the motorcycle. I think he's had enough for one day."

"What did you discover?" Leo asked.

"What I'm about to say must be held in the strictest confidence until we have more evidence," Chief Billiot said. "This is off the record, Mr. Townsend. Normally I wouldn't be telling you this, but I realize Miss Shaw is concerned about her mother, so I'm making an exception. Ellery—"

Officer Ellery cleared his throat. "We've discovered traces of nitric acid on the rim which dissolved a small area of the steel. Nitric acid is nasty stuff. It can turn skin yellow and cause it to peel."

Tali gasped.

Ellery nodded. "Like I said, 'nasty stuff.' Anyway, when the rim dissolved it pulled away from the tire causing a flat."

"A motorcycle with a flat front tire is uncontrollable," Leo said.

"Definitely," the chief agreed. "And forensics estimated the speed of the motorcycle to be eighty miles an hour. He didn't have a chance."

"Wouldn't the acid have caused a flat immediately?" Leo asked.

"No, the acid was diluted," Josh answered.

"By a ratio of three to one," Ellery said. "This slowed the dissolution until half an hour or more after someone poured it onto the tire. It was well planned."

Chief Billiot leaned back in his chair and crossed his arms. "Looks like John Holden is right. His son didn't attempt suicide."

"Who sabotaged his bike? Who killed him?" Quinn asked.

"It may take days or weeks before we even have a suspect. At this point, I don't have a lot more to tell you."

"Is my dad a suspect?" Tali's voice shook.

"You mean because they argued?" Officer Dennison asked.

Tali hesitated. She mumbled something about fingers, shook her head, and then nodded.

"No," the chief replied. "His angry reaction to the suicide theory proved to me he didn't know about the sabotage. However, I'll send a detective to his office. Maybe someone saw something suspicious."

Leo glanced at the teens. Quinn cried silently. Josh put his arm around her, forgetting about the grease. Tali looked sick. "I think we'd better get going," he said, rising from his chair.

"Fine, but leave me a number where I can reach you."

While Leo gave the chief his phone number, Josh hugged Quinn and then Leo and the girls left the police station. Sliding behind the Mustang's steering wheel, Leo turned around to Quinn and told her how sorry he was.

"It's hard to believe he's dead. That someone killed him," Quinn said.

"It's awful," Tali agreed.

Leo took his keys and cell phone out of his pocket and checked the time. "Shit! It's almost nine o'clock."

Another missed deadline, but the story now involved sabotaged bikes, even murder. He was sure Ted would understand. "I've got to call my editor."

"The newspaper meeting at Billy's!" Quinn exclaimed.

"I wonder how Mom is," Tali added.

Both girls pulled out their cell phones as Leo exited the car.

"Ted, I'm sorry I didn't make the deadline. There've been some major developments. I'd like to work on the story a while longer—"

"Whadya mean? I received your article hours ago. It's great."

"What article?"

"The homeschooling article. Geez, Leo what other article are you—"

"I never sent it."

"Sure you did. We got it to press."

"You've printed it? It'll be in tomorrow's paper?"

"Yep."

"Oh, Christ."

"Leo, what the hell's going on? Have you been drinking? The article came from your e-mail with your byline on it. Just before the first edition deadline I might add, much to my surprise."

"I didn't even finish the article, let alone send it. I don't know what's going on. Look, I'm heading back to the Inn. I'll check my computer, then call you back."

"Sure, but it's a done deal."

# 15

In the hospital parking lot, Leo dug around in his trunk. He pushed aside a beat up duffle bag and a pile of old newspapers and found his rusty bike rack under a stadium blanket. He fit the frame into the hitch of the Mustang and strapped Tali's bike to it as Quinn asked, "Could you drop me at Billy's? It's not far from the Inn. I'd like to tell him about Patrick in person."

"Sure," Leo agreed, but he wasn't happy about it. Now he'd have to make another stop before he could sort this thing out.

"Mom's doing well," Tali called as she came out of the hospital and into the parking lot. "Her voice was stronger and she ate some Jell-O."

"Excellent, we need some good news," Quinn replied.

"She might even be up for a short ride in a wheelchair tomorrow," Tali added as she and Quinn piled back into the car.

Pulling out of the lot, Leo tried to reconstruct the morning's events. He knew he hadn't sent the article. He was sure of it. Even if his work had been sent, it wouldn't be a full column, just bits and pieces of information and his impressions of the town. Why would Ted like it?

Leo remembered saving his work after talking to Senator Shaw, powering down his laptop, and then packing it up while Quinn watched. He pictured setting the bag on the floor, and visualized leaning the computer against the desk so that it wouldn't fall over. He even remembered looking back at it as he left the room.

"Slow down," Quinn said. "Billy's house is the next one on the right."

Pulling into the driveway, his mind went over the morning's events yet again. He was vaguely aware of Tali leaving the car to let Quinn out of the back seat. He managed to say goodbye to Quinn and thank her for the tour of the town.

Neither Leo nor Tali made any attempt at conversation as he drove the few blocks to the Bradbury Inn. After unloading Tali's bike, he said a hasty goodnight. Inside the Inn, he climbed the carpeted stairs two at a time.

Checking his pockets for the room key, he came up empty. Cursing, he ran back outside to the car, searched the interior and found it on the floor under the driver's seat. He reached his room and fumbled with the errant key. Taking a steadying breath, he slowly inserted it into the key-hole. He heard the satisfying "click." He shoved open the door.

The computer case sat on the floor exactly where he thought he had left it. He looked around the room. The bed was neatly made and the room smelled of lemon cleaner. A small, gold box of chocolates sat on the bedside table but his computer and overflowing duffle bag appeared untouched. He closed the door, tossed his jacket on the bed, and strode over to the desk.

He grabbed his computer, placed it on the work space, plugged it in, and turned it on. While waiting for it to boot up, he checked his phone for messages. Ted had received the article and loved it and Barnes had updated him about the situation in California. He made a mental note to call Barnes back in the morning.

He looked at the computer. The screen remained black. Dammit! What the hell is wrong with this computer? No fan noises, no clicking, no little blue light. He checked all the connections, took the battery out, tried and retried everything. Nothing. He barely restrained himself from throwing the damned thing across the room.

He called Ted, hoping to find him at *The Examiner*. His boss often worked late and camped out at the office, either because he loved his job or wanted to avoid his dull wife. Numerous phone calls later, Leo still couldn't locate Ted. He finally reached Carmen, a layout editor who stayed late to check the news wires.

Carmen reminded him about *The Examiner's* annual board meeting. These yearly showdowns were notorious for running all night. At Leo's insistence, she tried tracking Ted down. She discovered the board was convening over a late dinner at an undisclosed restaurant instead of in the conference room. Carmen assured him that once the meeting ended, Ted would check his messages and get back to him.

Eleven o'clock, several more calls, no Ted, dead computer. Leo lost it. Three beers and a shot of whiskey from the minibar couldn't calm him. He threw his toiletries and assorted clothes into his overnight bag, packed up the useless computer, and grabbed his leather jacket. Leaving some cash, enough to cover the cost of the room and the alcohol, he left.

He stole out the Inn's front door, relieved not to run into the mayor, Quinn, or Tali. He didn't want to explain his hasty retreat. He'd call them in the morning. Of course, by then they would have read the paper. Explaining the article would be tough. He tried to recall what he had written, but the alcohol and the chaos of the day fogged his brain.

Tossing his bags into his car, he jumped in and drove off.

From her darkened bedroom window above the Inn's entrance, Mary watched Leo leave. She turned on her cell phone.

"He's gone… just now. Yes, I already told you I sent it. What? NO, I WON'T. Absolutely not. I did what you asked. I'm done." Mary shut off her phone and flung it onto the bed.

She stared at it for a moment while hugging her body, trying to stop the shivering. She pictured Leo's green eyes tinged with sadness, the faint scar on his jaw, and the way he ran his hand through his wavy brown hair as he thought of something clever to say. Miserable, she trudged into the bathroom for a long, hot shower.

Pulling out onto the two-lane country highway, Leo flipped on the wipers to clear rain off the windshield. Half an hour later, he slowed the Mustang through Elon past Carl's Tavern. Several men sat on their motorcycles drinking beer under the awning.

Leaving Elon, he sped up to seventy then soon slowed down to enter yet another sad rural town. Frustrated, he stopped to let a man stagger across the street to a pickup truck. Another man ran to catch up. An argument ensued.

Finally leaving the towns behind, Leo drove past endless, monotonous farmland. The gentle rain became a downpour and the roads became waterlogged. Christ, what else could possibly go wrong?

As he slowed his vehicle around a curve, an oncoming black SUV veered into his lane. He jerked the wheel onto the shoulder. Mud and gravel sprayed as he struggled to maintain control. The SUV barely missed him, sailing past without stopping. Swearing, he managed to steer the Mustang back onto the road, his hands shaking.

Twenty minutes later, as he slowed down for the last town before the exit to Interstate 90, he heard the siren. Flashing blue lights reflected in his rearview mirror. *This is a nightmare!* Remembering the beers and the whiskey, he popped a piece of gum into his mouth as he pulled over to the side of the road.

The policeman approached and shined a flashlight directly into his eyes. Leo rolled the window down. Rain struck his face. "Hello, officer." He tried not to sound exasperated and forced a grin.

"License and registration." The policeman stood at six feet six or seven. A plastic slip covered his cap and drops of rainwater dripped from the brim on to the tip of his nose. He didn't flinch. Under his clear slicker he wore a full uniform, complete with a gun.

Leo handed over his documents. "What seems to be the problem?"

"A check of your plates shows an outstanding warrant for fifteen traffic violations."

"That can't be right. I don't have any—"

"Sir, please step out of the vehicle." The cop opened the front of his slicker, shoved Leo's license and registration in his shirt pocket and backed away from the car.

Leo had been pulled over before. His right foot was often heavier than he realized. But the police never pocketed his papers and never asked him to get out of his car.

"Sir, step out of the vehicle," the officer repeated.

Leo complied.

"Turn around and put your hands on the roof of the car."

"You've got to be kidding."

The cop grabbed Leo by the shoulder, whipped him around and shoved him against the wet Mustang. He slapped on a pair of handcuffs. Pain shot up Leo's wrists. The officer gripped Leo's forearm and pulled him along. When Leo slipped in the roadside mud and landed hard on the pavement, the peace officer dragged him the rest of the way, then pitched him into the back of the idling squad car.

# 16

A stale smell permeated the Senate conference room, matching Christopher Shaw's mood. The room was littered with the trash of eleven members of the Illinois State Senate's Education Committee, who had been butting heads for two hours. Used muffin wrappers, stained coffee mugs, crumpled napkins, and piles of legal documents spilled across the large oval table. Jackets and sweaters were draped haphazardly over the leather chairs.

"Chris, what's with this homeschooling obsession? We have a hell of a lot more pressing matters to deal with." Senator Jason Peabody argued as he tossed his copy of the anti-homeschooling *Education for All Bill*, onto the table. Muffin crumbs scattered.

"Like revising the thirty-year old school code," Senator Barbara Fritz interjected, pushing the sleeves of her blouse up to her elbows. Other committee members murmured their agreement.

Christopher couldn't believe his ears. He had pushed for tougher homeschooling laws for almost two decades without making any headway. Putting together this particular bill outlawing homeschooling had taken over a year. It finally looked like he might get it passed until this resistance just days before the Senate vote. He had thought the bill would fly through the Education Committee. Now he wasn't sure.

Christopher leaned forward, resting his elbows on the walnut conference table. He pressed his fingers together and tried to keep his temper in check. "It's our duty, our elected duty, to ensure that every child in Illinois gets a decent education. Homeschooling does not ensure this. It should not be an option—"

Senator Julie North coughed.

He glared at her. "What?"

"Irate homeschoolers are clogging my phone lines. I've had to borrow aides from other senators to answer the phones."

"I'm getting calls, too," Senator Fritz chimed in. "My constituents are not comfortable with this bill. As their representative, neither am I."

"Look, I can appreciate the pressure from constituents," Christopher said. "I feel it too."

"These parents are relentless," Senator North said.

"People with extremist views often are," Christopher said. "Yet we can't allow children to be neglected because their parents can get away with calling truancy 'homeschooling.' We have to stick to our guns."

Senator Fritz reached for her coffee mug. "I can deal with the angry phone calls as long as what we're doing is constitutional."

"It is," Christopher assured her. "We've been over this before. The constitution secures the right to life, liberty, and the pursuit of happiness. Education is essential for all three. Therefore, constitutionally, our state government is bound to provide schooling for all of its citizens." He noticed Senator Fritz smile slightly as she made a note. He had her, but he went on.

"Also, as Thomas Jefferson argued, our society would fail without an educated electorate." Christopher stood and walked around the table. His footsteps were muffled by the plush carpeting. "There's no way of knowing if homeschooled children, future members of the electorate, are receiving an adequate education."

"Whaddya mean?" shot Albert Jones, a veteran senator and the only person in the room who hadn't removed any clothing or loosened his tie. His balding head glistened with sweat.

"In Illinois there's no testing, certification, teacher review, or registration for homeschoolers. No accountability whatsoever." Christopher stopped in front of the large windows where he knew the sunlight would create a halo effect around his slim figure. "We're neglecting our constitutional duty by allowing this travesty to continue."

"We could require mandatory testing," Senator Jones suggested, wiping his temple with an embroidered handkerchief.

Christopher faced the old man. "That would be like placing a Band-Aid on an eviscerated body." His hand slashed through the air. The senior statesman turned red. Christopher attempted to appease him by holding both hands out, palms raised. "Albert, what about social development and accessibility to diversity? Homeschooled children are isolated by people who often have extreme religious beliefs and refuse to expose them to opposing ideas."

"So pass a law requiring teacher review of curriculum, activities," Jones argued, still red-faced. "Instead of outlawing homeschooling."

Christopher started to pace again. He knew if he looked at the man one more minute he would want to shake him until his shriveled old brains rattled. "Testing and teacher review laws are ineffectual," Christopher said. "In states where there are such requirements, parents often circumvent the law by ignoring it or going underground." Everyone murmured their agreement except Jones and Senator Doug Fleming.

Christopher directed his next point at Fleming, a socialist. "Public education is the means by which students learn patriotism and come to understand the importance of community and working together for the greater good." The leftist looked at Christopher, one black furry eyebrow raised. "Additionally, public education means equality. It's not fair that homeschooling kids don't have the advantages of chemistry labs, school orchestras, and football teams."

"Many of our public schools don't have those things," Fleming argued.

"Exactly. The amendment would guarantee these amenities and more for all schools. When homeschoolers enroll in public institutions, we'll receive additional federal money to fund those improvements."

Fleming's eyes widened, both eyebrows now raised.

"Look, I've spoken with the governor on this," Christopher said. "He's backing the bill one hundred percent."

"Why?" Fritz asked.

"He's concerned about the state missing out on federal school funding. But it's really Raegan Colyer, the Governor's chief of staff, who's pushing this."

"Well, that makes sense," Fleming spoke up. "Were you quoting Colyer when you mentioned patriotism and community?"

"Yes, to some extent, although I agree with her."

"She's not a woman to trifle with. I understand she's in line for a cabinet seat in the new presidential administration," Fritz said in a loud whisper to Jones.

Christopher ignored this. "Unity, working for the greater good, this is what holds this country together. What would happen if we became a nation of individuals who were all taught different things and who were all led to believe our interests were more important than the interests of the country?"

"Now, you sound like me." Fleming smiled.

Christopher continued, "Maintaining our common bond is one argument among many that homeschooling should be eradicated."

"Senator, there's something else to consider," his assistant, Adam Gallagher, remarked from a corner of the conference room.

"Later," Christopher snapped. He didn't want his momentum to be stalled.

"There's a new threat to public education that you might not be aware of," Adam persisted.

"Fine." He would reprimand him later. "What is it?"

Instead of answering, Adam handed each senator a sheet of paper.

"What's this?" Christopher said under his breath. He could feel his blood pressure rising.

"It's the silver bullet," Adam whispered back.

## A HEDONISTIC SCHOOL-LESS SOCIETY
*By Leo Townsend*
*Tucked away in a secluded region of northwest Illinois is the pretty, seemingly-idyllic town of Carpe Diem.*

"Carpe Diem?" Christopher whispered in Adam's ear. "Where Alexandra and Natalia are?

"Yes, Senator," Adam replied.

Christopher sat down and continued to read.


*Despite Carpe Diem's beauty, or maybe because of it, you get the feeling that you're in a Stephen King novel. Something is just not right. Across the picturesque Main Street, under a canopy of glowing sugar maples, five bored teenagers bully a small boy. Why aren't these kids in school, you wonder? Then you remember that Carpe Diem has no schools.*

*Here, children aren't in a classroom learning socialization skills and the three Rs. Instead, they roam the streets or pour coffee in a diner for minimum wage.*

*According to Peyton Blaney, town librarian and archivist, Carpe Diem was founded in 1979 by John Holden, his wife Suzanne, and twenty-five friends and relatives. It is an intentional community, a suburban commune, founded around an extreme homeschooling movement called "unschooling."*

*Unschooling is the belief that children should control their own education. Some unschooling parents even let their children determine their own bedtime, what to eat and when and what, if any, chores to do. They leave education totally up to the child. Not surprisingly, many unschooled children don't learn to read until they're teenagers.*

*"In my opinion, unschooling isn't successful," Carpe Diem Mayor Mary Evans confesses. "Picture a town where everyone does what they want, whenever they want. Nothing gets done, particularly those things no one wants to do. It's a nightmare to govern."*

*Homeschooling, including unschooling, has been legal in Illinois since 1950 when the Illinois Supreme Court ruled homeschools are private institutions. State Senator Christopher Shaw is trying to change that by making homeschooling illegal in our state.*

*According to Senator Shaw, "Under current Illinois statutes, privately educated children must attend school from the ages of 7 to 17 and be taught, in English, the same subjects as those taught in public schools. But there are no testing, registration, or curriculum requirements. Truancy is a factor only if someone reports a family, and parents are rarely held accountable. How will these kids do once they're out in the real world?"*

Christopher looked up at Adam and mouthed, "I'm quoted." Adam nodded.

*It could be argued that in Carpe Diem every child is truant. Visit the town during normal school hours you'll find children hanging out on street corners and loitering in convenience stores. One dictatorial 13-year-old came in off the streets to run a town meeting. As chairman, he took great delight in determining when and where the adults could enjoy a beer.*

*Perhaps the most surprising and alarming fact about Carpe Diem is its growing population of 3,000 residents. Apparently, a hedonistic lifestyle is popular.*

*Nearby towns are considering the elimination of public education as well. "Our town is slowly going bankrupt," Bill Curtis, the mayor of Elon, admitted. "We can't afford to heat the school buildings, let alone pay the teachers a decent wage. Parents have expressed an interest in pulling their kids out of our crumbling schools."*

*What kind of society will we have if we discard public schooling and allow our children to run wild like the children of Carpe Diem?*

The conference room erupted with angry shouts. "Now do you understand my obsession?" Christopher yelled above the fray. He waived the article in his hand. "Other communities are thinking of following Carpe Diem's lead. We need to stop this movement now. We're running out of time!"

Fifteen minutes later, Christopher sat behind his desk holding a copy of the anti-homeschooling bill. On it were the signatures of every member of the Senate Education Committee. With those signatures and *The Examiner* article in his arsenal, next Wednesday's vote would be a piece of cake.

Christopher considered getting Vicky, his secretary, to frame the bill and looked through his door to where she sat at her desk. He stopped gloating. Two state troopers appeared to be questioning her. He couldn't make out what they were saying.

Must be lunchtime, he thought as he slipped out the back door.

# 17

Early Friday morning, Tali zipped up her orange Alanton Tigers sweat-shirt, stepped into the hallway at the Bradbury Inn, and smelled pancakes and bacon. She was hungry but she couldn't stop thinking about her father's yellowed fingers and that made her queasy. Officer Ellery had said someone had used nitric acid, which turned skin yellow, to mess with Patrick Holden's motorcycle. Her father had the chance and a scary temper, but murder? She touched her necklace.

Should she tell the police?

But he didn't hide his fingers from her and his explanation about dropping his scarf in antifreeze made sense—

"*I can't believe you said that!*" Quinn shouted from the lobby.

Tali hurried down the stairs.

Quinn stood in the middle of the reception area, face-to-face with her mother, ignoring the guests standing by the front door. She didn't have on her inky make-up and her damp, jet black hair had lost its spikiness. Barefoot, the black polish on her toes chipped, she wore a bulky black sweater over her skinny black jeans. She looked younger, innocent, and mad as hell. "'In my opinion, unschooling isn't successful'," she said in her mother's voice as she read out loud from a newspaper she held in her shaking, ring-covered hand.

"Honey, keep it down, you're disturbing the guests." Mayor Evans tilted her head in the direction of the middle-aged couple who then bolted out the door. Dull strands of hair hung in the mayor's red face. Her grey suit needed pressing. Her glasses were smudged. "I never said that." She grabbed her daughter's arm. "You *know* I'd never say that."

"What's going on?" Tali asked.

Quinn shook herself free from her mother's grip. "Mom's a traitor."

"*What?*"

Quinn handed her the newspaper.

Tali read it while mother and daughter glared at each other. "Kids don't roam the streets. My dad *is* quoted. Leo lied to us." She continued to read. "Dad didn't say this. And who's this 'dictatorial teenager'?" She gasped. "*Will?*" She looked at Quinn who continued to glare at her mother. Tali finished reading. "I can't believe Leo wrote this. He seemed like such a nice guy."

"He was jerking us around," Quinn seethed.

"Did you ask him about the article?" Tali couldn't believe that the man who had invited her to dinner when Tom abandoned her, who held her when she felt dizzy, and who figured out the truth about her mother's accident, could do such a thing.

"The coward left before the paper arrived," the mayor said.

"Left?"

"Once I read his article, I went straight to his room. He didn't answer, so I unlocked the door and went in. There was no sign of him except for the money he left to pay for the room and the booze he raided from the mini bar."

"I can't believe…" Tali's voice trailed off as she looked at Quinn.

Quinn ignored her. "Did I tell you Brendan called me this morning, Mother?"

"Brendan Miller? Dan and Joan's son?"

"Yep, he called me from their diner right after he read the article. Apparently, he met Leo Townsend."

"Yes, Leo told me that himself—"

"Brendan wanted to know why you'd give such a shitty interview."

"I didn't—"

"I defended you. I told him Leo came to Carpe Diem to talk to you about the Fall Festival, not about homeschooling. Brendan said that couldn't be. He said Leo hadn't heard about the festival."

"Yes, he had."

"No, Mom. Brendan said Leo asked him where all the townspeople were so he mentioned the Fall Festival planning meeting. Leo didn't know a thing about the festival so Brendan filled him in."

The mayor's face went pale. She backed into one of the lobby's tall chairs.

"This is a small article," Tali insisted, shaking the page. "No one will read it. No one will care."

"Ha!" Quinn spat. "Mom just got back from her office at the Town Hall. The phones are ringing like crazy. CBS, *People Magazine*, *The New York Times*, you name it. They're all on their way."

"So?" she shrugged. "They'll see how great Carpe Diem is. What's the big deal?"

"Wow, you really don't know shit about what homeschoolers have to put up with, do you?"

"Hey, don't get pissed at me. I didn't write the damn article."

"Don't take this out on Tali," the mayor snapped.

"You're right. I'm sorry, Tali."

Tali nodded. She handed the article back to the mayor.

"Quinn, honey, please believe me. I didn't say these things." The mayor reached out her hand. "I could never say these things. You know I love this town."

"Yeah, I guess," Quinn replied and took her mother's hand.

"Why don't you and Tali get something to eat?" The mayor stood up. "I need to figure out how to handle this."

"Mom, how *will* you handle this?"

"First, I'm getting a retraction from Mr. Townsend." She walked to the front desk, tossing the article aside. She grabbed a pen and paper. "I should probably call a town meeting and talk to John..." Her voice trailed off as she wrote things down.

"How's John doing?" Quinn asked.

"I don't know. Nobody's been able to reach him," the mayor replied, picking up the phone.

"Come on Quinn," Tali said, nudging her. "Let's get breakfast. I'd like to hear all about the crap homeschoolers have to put up with."

After breakfast, Tali steered her mountain bike down the Inn's driveway and thought about what homeschoolers went through. Imagine having to hear, "No school today?" whenever you left Carpe Diem and having to explain that you don't know what grade you're in not because you're stupid, but because your life isn't divided into grades.

Quinn had told her that when she traveled outside of Carpe Diem, she carried a homeschool ID card to avoid being taken away by a truant officer. She said that in Rockford, the public was urged to report any child not in school. And that was in Illinois, where the laws were favorable to homeschoolers.

Not too long ago, Iowa homeschoolers could have their kids taken away from them if they refused to send them to school. The parents actually set up an underground railroad to smuggle children out of the state. Tali couldn't understand how this could happen in the 'land of the free.'

She rounded the corner onto Main Street, slowing down to sneak a peek at the police station garage. She saw a mechanic and pulled to the curb.

Even from this distance she knew it was Josh. She recognized his black hair, grungy work clothes, and his confident walk as he carried his metal tool kit to a cop car parked in the lot. Reaching the front of the car, he set the box down then opened the cruiser's hood. She watched as he grabbed an oil-soaked cloth from the loop on his blackened overalls.

Tali considered joining him. It would be interesting to hear his take on homeschooling. She played with her necklace, rubbing the smooth car charm between her fingers and thumb. She looked up the maple-lined street blazing with color.

At home, her father had ordered all the maple trees chopped down and replaced with pine trees. For him, leafy trees were a big mess. Tali had wondered why he cared. The gardener did all the raking.

A sudden gust of wind tossed the tree limbs, creating a shower of leaves and releasing the crisp, earthy scent of fall. She zipped up her jacket. A black cat, Puck?, sauntered up the concrete steps of the post office. It hopped onto a large blue mailbox then stretched out in a patch of sunlight.

She glanced back at Josh. He picked up a tool, probably a combination end wrench, attached it to something under the hood then cranked on it.

She pictured herself standing next to him as he named car parts and explained how they worked. He'd be surprised when she'd interrupt him and finish his explanation. She checked the time on her cell phone. It was 8:57 a.m., still early. She had told her mom she'd be at the hospital sometime around ten. Plenty of time. Then she pictured Tom freaking if he caught her talking to the hot mechanic.

Feeling guilty, she grabbed her bike's handle bars. She looked one last time at Josh. He spotted her and waved. She waved back. God he was cute. And Tom hadn't called her since he walked out yesterday…

Tucking a bit of hair behind one ear, she peddled into the police station's driveway.

"You're just in time," Josh said. "How about helping me install a few spark plugs?"

Geez, his eyes were amazing. Tali nodded and parked her bike near the police cruiser.

Josh started to explain how carburetors operated and laughed when she completed his sentence. "Heck, let me get out of your way," he teased as he backed away from the car.

Tali shook her head. "I hung out at my grandpa's garage. But no one let me touch anything."

"Well, let me demonstrate." He showed her how to replace a spark plug and handed her the next one. She hesitated then bent over to work on the car. A curtain of blonde hair blocked her view. Josh found a clean black rubber o-ring in his tool box and gave it to her. "It'll help keep the hair out of your eyes," he said.

Tali tied her hair up, feeling naked.

He stared at her. "Sorry, it's just, I mean, um…"

She yanked the o-ring out of her hair. "I look stupid."

"No, not at all. Actually, you're really pretty." He blushed.

"Oh." No one had ever said that to her before. She stared at her boots, strands of hair falling in her face. She slowly pulled them into a pony tail and secured it with the o-ring. "Thanks," she said and then leaned over the automobile.

Before she knew it, she had replaced her first spark plug. "I've always wanted to work on cars," she admitted.

"Why don't you?" Josh handed her another spark plug. "Don't they have an auto mechanics class in your school?"

"They do," she replied from underneath the hood. "But only boys and butch girls take it. And it's a joke. By the end of the semester the only thing they've learned is how to change the oil."

"Well, come over whenever you'd like."

"Thanks." She finished replacing the spark plug, straightened up and noticed her mother's wreck of a car. "I'm sorry about Patrick Holden."

"Yeah, thanks. I can't believe it. I guess I'm still in shock."

"How's his dad doing?"

"I haven't talked to him yet. He's pretty busy making arrangements." He replaced the last of the spark plugs and then wiped his hands on the dirty rag. "How's your mom doing?"

"Good. Which reminds me, I gotta go. I told her I'd be at the hospital around ten."

Josh offered her a clean spot on his rag to wipe off her grimy fingers. "Stop by anytime. I can always use the help of a good mechanic." He flashed her a dimpled grin.

Tali nodded. She would definitely be back.

As she rode her bike the last couple of miles to the hospital, Tali passed crowded sidewalks. With less than a week to go before the Fall Festival, the townspeople were busy. They painted fall scenes on storefront windows and attached colorful banners under the flower baskets hanging from the lampposts. A few times, she rode past people talking in whispers or giving each other hugs, probably upset about Patrick Holden's death.

Still, things were happening. A brass band rehearsed in the gazebo and a group of mini ballerinas skipped into Miss Simms' Dance Studio followed by an elegant woman. Miss Simms?

Coasting down Main Street past Joan and Dan's, Tali spotted a teenager in the diner, probably Brendan, serving coffee to three old guys. Her father would say the kid lacked ambition or that his parents homeschooled him so they would have cheap labor. But he didn't know what Quinn had told her: Brendan was leaving soon to study economics at Oxford.

Seeing Brendan laugh at one of the old man's jokes, she wondered what life as a homeschooler would be like. The idea of sitting by herself at the kitchen table while her mom assigned schoolwork made her cringe.

Then Quinn, Will and Josh came to mind and she remembered that homeschooling didn't have to mean school-at-home. They unschooled. With the freedom to do as she pleased, what would she do all day?

She turned the handlebars of her bike and noticed some grime under her fingernails. She could work on cars, especially if Josh helped her. She sighed.

Seeing the sign for Sapori D'Italia, Tali realized she could learn French or even Italian and not be forced to take Spanish. She looked forward to joining Quinn at the restaurant later to learn some Italian phrases to try out on her mom.

But what about prom and cheering for her school at football games? What about finally getting to play for the soccer team or any team? There'd be no yearbook to write for, though she wasn't doing that now. Only juniors and seniors got to be published. And how would she ever get into college? She'd have to ask Quinn.

If she unschooled, she would definitely ride her bike more. The cold air in her face was refreshing. She couldn't remember the last time she felt so alive.


"Hey Mom, how are you?" Tali asked as she entered the hospital room carrying the small pot of daisies she had bought at the gift shop.

"I'm hideous."

"What are you talking about?"

"I demanded that they give me a mirror."

Tali busied herself setting the flowers on the tray table and putting her jacket in the closet.

"You think I'm hideous, too."

She walked over to the bed and took her mother's hand being careful not to jar the IV. "No. You're beautiful."

Alexandra yanked her hand away. "I'm a monster. How can you stand to look at me? Your father can't. It's why he's not here, isn't it?"

"Mom, don't be silly. He had to work. And you don't look that bad." She'd never tell her mom about passing out the first time she saw her. "You're not as puffy and you're mummy look is gone. Just one bandage on your forehead."

"My face looks like a punching bag."

"The bruises will go away." She touched her mother's rich brown hair. "Did you brush your hair?"

"The nurse brushed it after I insisted she give me a sponge bath."

"Good."

"It did make me feel better." Alexandra sighed then looked at the daisies. "Thank you for the flowers."

"Sure." Tali gave her mom a kiss on the cheek then sat down, putting her neglected backpack on the floor. "Has Dr. Anderson been in yet?"

"Yes. He wants me out of bed." Alexandra pointed to the folded wheelchair in the corner.

"Great! How about lunch in the coffee shop today?"

"I don't want anyone to see me like this."

"I could cut holes in a paper bag."

"Natalia."

"Tali." She had asked her mother thousands of times to call her 'Tali' but decided that now wasn't the time to argue. "Really, Mom, it's not so bad. And besides, you don't even know anyone here."

"True." Alexandra smiled, slightly. "I noticed you pulled your hair back."

Tali felt herself blush. She had forgotten about the ponytail.

"I like it," Alexandra said.

"Thanks." She twirled the ponytail with her fingers. "Have you heard from Dad?"

"Yes. He was excited about one of his bills passing through committee."

"The homeschool bill?" Tali hoped not.

"He didn't say. He started to tell me something about Carpe Diem, but was called away."

"Oh, I bet I know what that's about." She shifted to the edge of her chair. "You won't believe what's been going on in this town!" She filled her mother in, starting first with the sabotaged motorcycle. She didn't mention her father's yellow fingers.

"How awful," Alexandra said. "Though I'm relieved he didn't drive into me on purpose."

Tali hesitated. "He died."

"Oh. I'm so sorry. Though it seems impossible a motorcyclist could survive such an accident."

Tali agreed then changed the subject to Leo Townsend and the horrible article. She finished by describing Quinn's life.

"You're sold on this unschooling thing?"

"Nah, it's just interesting."

"Would you want to unschool?"

"No way. There's lots I'd miss by not going to school."

"Such as?"

"Hanging out with friends. Football games. Homecoming." She wove her ponytail through her fingers.

"The social aspects."

"Yeah. I was thinking of asking Quinn how she feels about missing those things."

"Good idea."

Tali nodded. "Hey, you hungry?"

"Starving."

Tali grabbed the wheelchair and set it up next to bed. "The coffee shop?"

"No, I'd rather not."

Tali pulled back the bed sheets and reached for her mother's hand. "Come on, it'll be good to get a change of scenery."

Alexandra shook her head.

"The coffee shop has awesome food."

"Do they also have dark corners?"

"We'll sit in the darkest one."

Her mother smiled. "Okay."

They both liked the coffee shop's spinach quiche, though Alexandra left most of it on her plate. While Tali polished off a brownie, Alexandra told her about the writer's workshop in Chicago and how she couldn't wait to get home to write her book. She talked excitedly about her idea for a new plot twist.

"Mom, why didn't you write before? You love it."

"I did in high school and I was fairly good at it. At least my classmates thought so. My English teacher said my stories were ridiculous. She told me I'd be better off writing recipes."

"No way!"

"And you know how I hate to cook."

They laughed.

"Once I even mentioned to your grandparents that I wanted to be a writer."

"What did they say?"

"They told me I was insane. They said I was too pretty to work and with all their money, I didn't need to. They refused to discuss it after that."

"Wow, they weren't the greatest parents, were they?"

Alexandra shook her head and looked at Tali with teary eyes. "And I haven't been the best mother to you."

"I just wanted you to notice me," she said in a small voice.

Alexandra choked back a sob. "Natalia, I'm sorry. I was raised by nannies. I assumed they'd do a better job raising you than I would. Your father and grandmother agreed. Firing Rosalinda forced me to be a mother. But I didn't even know how to talk to you." Alexandra reached for Tali's hand. "I never guessed my stories would bring us together."

"I'm so glad they did." She looked at her mom's teary, bruised face. "I thought I might lose you." She started to cry.

"It's okay now." Alexandra touched Tali's damp cheek. "We're okay. I love you, Natalia. Tali."

Tali got up from her chair to hug her mother. "I love you too, Mom." She wiped away her tears. "Hey, I have an idea. Why don't we start writing your book here, in the hospital?"

Alexandra held up her right hand with the IV tube and pointed to the cast on her left arm.

"You dictate while I do the typing. I've got my computer," Tali encouraged. "Let's go back to your room and start."

"It's a wonderful idea. Could we do it later though? I'm a bit tired."

Back in the hospital room, Alexandra fell asleep almost immediately.

Tali was exhausted, too. Yet at the same time, she'd never felt better. She took her computer out of her backpack and tried to start her research paper. Typing in "white-tailed deer," she spotted the bit of grease under her fingernail. She pictured Josh reaching for a spark plug, handing her the o-ring, telling her she was pretty. After that, she had a hard time concentrating on what deer eat and how long they live.

When Alexandra woke up they tried to work on her story, but she struggled to recall the details. Tali suggested they put it off a day.

As she packed up her computer, she told her mother about Tom ditching her and mentioned Josh. They discussed boys, cars, and the upcoming American Idol season. The afternoon passed quickly and before she knew it, she had to meet Quinn at Sapori D'Italia.

"Mom, I made plans with Quinn. I could ditch her and stay."

"No, you go."

"I'll be back around six thirty. In time for dinner."

"You've been with me all day. Have dinner with Quinn and stay at the Inn. I'll see you tomorrow."

"Are you sure?"

"Yes."

"Okay. But I'll call you tonight." She kissed her. "I love you."

"I love you, too."

Outside the hospital, Tali zipped up her jacket and pulled on her fingerless gloves. She hopped on her bike, not easy to do with Uggs, and took off for Sapori D'Italia, thinking about how she could definitely get used to hanging with her mom. Unfortunately, they only saw each other at dinnertime. School and soccer practice took up most of her day and this year the teachers were really piling on the homework.

As Tali drove onto Main Street, she forgot all about the terrific afternoon. Television and radio vans with giant antennas clogged the street. Everywhere she looked, cameramen were setting up equipment or videotaping. Shouting reporters confronted shoppers and townspeople.

Tali got off her bike and walked it through the crowd. She heard bits of live newscasts: "homeschooling run rampant," "undisciplined children," and "how can this be legal?"

Chief Billiot and Officer Dennison waved their arms and barked commands, attempting to bring order. Miss Simms, Brendan and another woman yelled at reporters to stay out of the flower beds. A small boy with his arm in a cast, *Jimmy?*, dodged through the crowd calling "Puck!"

"Excuse me."

Tali turned to see a woman in a crisp navy suit approaching, microphone in her outstretched hand. A cameraman trailed close behind. Tali tried to shrink back into the crowd. The bicycle made it impossible.

"Do you feel deprived by not going to school?"

"I go to school in Alanton. I'm visiting."

The woman lost interest and looked around for someone else to interview.

"I think it's cool not to have to go to school though." Why did she say that? Maybe it was Quinn's endless curiosity or Josh's beautiful grimy face, but for some reason she wanted to defend homeschooling.

The newscaster turned back. "Truancy is illegal in this country, young lady."

Tali looked down at her boots wishing her ponytail would come undone so her hair would hide her face. She managed to mutter, "Carpe Diem kids are learning. Why does it matter where they learn it?"

The lady flicked her microphone back on and signaled the cameraman to roll. "What things are they learning?"

"Italian, photography, auto mechanics."

"How do they go about learning these things, Miss—?"

"Shaw. Tali Shaw. By doing them."

The woman laughed. "If only life were so easy. Someone has to be trained to teach these things."

"The teachers in Carpe Diem are trained."

"What teachers?"

Tali took her eyes off her boots and looked into the camera. "My friend is learning Italian from a native speaker and photography from the man who owns the photography studio."

"And your friend, does she take any tests to determine what she's learned? Does she get a report card?"

Tali shook her head.

The woman looked into the camera. "There you have it, from the mouths of babes—"

"Hey!"

"Carpe Diem children do what they want, when they want and neither they nor their parents are held accountable."

"That's not what I said!" Tali tried to get the woman's attention, but she and the cameraman had quickly disappeared into the crowd. Tali considered abandoning her bike and chasing after them then decided she might make things worse. She convinced herself that because she wasn't from Carpe Diem, they wouldn't show that clip on the news. She got on her bike and managed to weave around the groups of people. She didn't want to be late meeting Quinn.

As she left the commotion behind, Tali looked back at all the people and spotted Jimmy sitting on the curb holding tightly on to Puck. Surrounding him were crushed pieces of red and gold mums.

# 18

"Where the hell is Leo?" Ted Nelson yelled through the doorway.

"I've told you," Carmen shouted back, "I have no idea." The layout editor got up from her desk and entered Ted's cluttered office. "His phone goes straight to voicemail." She pushed aside a box of files and sat on the couch. "No one seems to know where he is."

"Guess who I just got off the phone with?" Ted challenged, leaning against the front of his desk and narrowly missing a coffee mug crammed with half-chewed pencils. He crossed his muscular arms over his black t-shirt, blocking out the words: *Journalists do not live by words alone, although sometimes they have to eat them. ~ Adlai E. Stevenson.*

"No clue."

"Raegan Colyer."

"From the governor's office?"

"Yep. She wanted to congratulate Leo on the excellent article. Wanted to talk to him directly. I lied and told her he's on another assignment."

"The governor's office isn't the only one looking for him," Carmen said. "*Time Magazine*, ABC News, *The New York Times*. I've been on the phone so much my ear is numb." Carmen took off her hooped earring to massage the offended ear.

Ted glanced at his watch. "It's almost four o'clock. Where could he be?"

Carmen shook her head.

"Dammit." He slammed his hand on the desk. "I need him here." He looked out the door of his office for the hundredth time. "Oh. My. God."

Carmen stood up from the couch and turned to look into the newsroom. She gasped.

A tattered and bruised Leo Townsend stumbled around the sea of desks toward Ted's office. As he passed by his coworkers sitting at their computers, the clicking of keys ceased. Reporters standing in groups stopped their conversations to watch Leo limp past. One copy editor dropped her cell phone and didn't realize it until a loud "HELLO?" resonated from the floor. The room grew quiet except for the hum of endless commentary from the television monitors.

Leo stopped to look at the closest television. Ted and Carmen stepped into the newsroom to see what had caught his eye.

A picture of a middle-aged man with a pony tail flashed on the screen with the caption, "Dead motorcyclist identified as Patrick Holden, son of John Holden, founder of the town of Carpe Diem, Illinois." Then the camera focused on a sober CNN reporter with a mask of make-up and a helmet of blond hair. She perked up as she described Carpe Diem as an odd town. Leo turned the volume up.

"... there are no laws in place to make sure these children get any kind of education," said the reporter. The camera moved past her and zoomed in on several eleven or twelve year olds sitting by themselves in a booth near the window of a diner. They ignored the intrusive media as they played games on their cell phones. "How can this be legal?" the reporter asked as the camera panned back to her. She shook her head in disgust.

Leo shouted a torrent of swear words, the last of which were drowned out by a loud, insipid commercial for tutoring services. Shaking his head, he continued his awkward shuffle to Ted, dragging his computer bag behind. At the doorway, Leo collapsed. Ted grabbed him. With Carmen's help, he pulled Leo into his office and lowered the crumpled man and his computer onto the couch.

"What the hell happened to you?" Ted demanded as he covered his nose and mouth. "Jesus, you stink."

"Do you need a doctor?" Carmen asked shooting Ted a reproving look. Leo shook his head.

"Can I get you something?" Carmen offered.

"Coffee," Leo croaked.

"Be right back."

Noticing the curious crowd hovering near his office, Ted closed the door behind Carmen. "What happened?"

Leo's head rolled onto the back of the couch. His hair lay in greasy clumps about his grizzled face. Ted rubbed his bald head, for once glad he didn't have hair. Leo's blue jeans were streaked with mud. A nasty rip in the left leg exposed a scraped and bloodied knee. Grime covered the cherished bomber jacket. It hung off Leo's shoulders, exposing his shirt smeared with dirt, sweat, and a bit of blood. The shirt was half-tucked into his beltless pants which were splattered with what appeared to be vomit. Dark circles accentuated his bloodshot eyes.

Leo sighed then told Ted about his visit to Carpe Diem, the sabotaged motorcycle, Patrick Holden's death, and being driven off the road.

"Do you think the driver of the SUV did that on purpose?" Ted asked, alarmed.

"No, it was probably another drunk from one of those godforsaken towns. Anyway, why would someone want to drive me off the road?"

"You mention sabotaged motorcycles and now this. It's fishy."

"Maybe," Leo said, and then continued with his story. When he got to the part about sharing a cell with Vomiting Victor in the Jonesboro town jail, Carmen reappeared with three coffees and a large sandwich.

"Oh sorry, my timing is bad," she said handing him the sandwich.

"Not at all. I'm starving. Thanks." Leo flashed a disarming smile.

Carmen took the last coffee and sat in her boss' desk chair. Ted was too captivated by Leo's story to object.

"They kept me locked up in the holding cell until this afternoon." After swallowing a couple of bites of ham and cheese, Leo continued, "The sergeant claimed he thought I was Leonard Townsends. Apparently, Leonard has a taste for red sports cars and beating up cops. When the officer read the name on my driver's license, he jumped to conclusions."

"That's no excuse. You should sue."

"I don't give a crap about that. I'm just glad to be outta there."

The food and coffee were starting to energize Leo, he looked almost human, but Ted waited until he finished eating before mentioning the Carpe Diem column. "That's one hell of a story you wrote."

"*I didn't write it!*" Leo's face reddened. "Someone hacked into my computer."

"Whoa, hang on buddy." Ted riffled through the newspapers on his desk until he found a rumpled page. "I have the article right here. Before you start accusing someone, take a look." He handed it to Leo who read it three times, each time with increasing amounts of frowns, groans, and swear words.

"I never wrote this." Leo collapsed back onto the sofa. "Sure, there are a few passages of my work, but so much of this isn't backed up with facts. I never even talked to the mayor of Elon. And what's this—'It could be argued that every child is truant.' You know it's not my style."

Ted looked down at his feet, unable to meet Leo's eyes. "To be honest, I thought so too. But it's a solid piece and you made the deadline. It fit in nicely with Barnes' story about the California homeschool case."

"It's caused quite a stir," Carmen chimed in. "All the major networks and papers have called."

"See what ya miss when ya spend the night in jail?"

Leo shrugged.

"Ted even talked to the governor's office."

"Raegan Colyer called to congratulate you personally on an exceptional article."

"It's not an exceptional article. It's total bullshit." Leo pushed himself up from the couch.

"Well Colyer doesn't agree. She insisted on talking to you. I didn't know where you were. I told her you were on another assignment." Ted crumpled his coffee cup and tossed it at the wastebasket. It bounced off the desk and landed a foot from its target. He didn't bother to pick it up.

"I *am* on another assignment. But before I go, I want *The Examiner* to issue a retraction. I have to set the record straight." Leo opened his soiled computer bag. "Do you think Vince in the tech department could fix my computer? I'm hoping it's just a bad battery."

"I'll take it to him," Carmen said, grabbing the computer and leaving.

"A retraction? I don't know. Wait, what assignment are you talking about?" Ted asked. His telephone rang before Leo could answer. "Hello?" He put his hand on the phone. "It's Raegan Colyer." Uncovering the telephone, he said, "Yes, he's right here."

Leo took the phone. "Raegan. How are you? It's been awhile."

'Raegan?' Ted mouthed. "Don't tell me you've slept with her?" he whispered.

Leo shrugged and then continued his phone conversation, "I'm glad you liked it. You want to what?" He sat up straighter. "Well, that's an amazing offer. I'll have to think it over and get back to you. Sure, sure I can let you know on Monday, Tuesday at the latest. Yes, thank you. I'll talk to you then."

"So?" Ted asked.

"She wants to hire me as speech writer for Governor Thomas."

"You're kidding."

"Thanks for the vote of confidence." Leo shot back. "The current speech writer, John Talbot, took a position with the White House press corps. So they have an opening."

"Hang on. You're *not* thinking of taking the job." Ted was pissed. He'd put his neck out for Leo and now Leo was going to quit?

"No, no, of course not." Leo avoided eye contact and quickly changed the subject. "You've got to print my retraction."

"I don't know. It's a good solid piece."

"It's a fabrication."

"Is the whole thing a lie or are there just some parts that are slightly inaccurate?"

"It's full of lies but what does that matter, Ted? I didn't write it."

"I'll have to think about it."

Leo drew to within inches of Ted. Ted jerked his head back from the stench of sweat and vomit.

"Look," Leo said, "I've been through hell to get here to figure out what's going on. You're going to print the retraction. You owe me for printing the damned thing in the first place."

"And if I don't? You gonna punch me?" Ted challenged. He wasn't worried, even though Leo was taller, younger, and in good shape, Ted had black belts in karate and taekwondo.

"No, I'll quit. That wouldn't have been much of a threat a few days ago, but I'm on to a huge story. You need me to write it."

"What story?"

"Sabotage, educational freedom and Carpe Diem."

Ted glared at Leo for a few tense moments before breaking eye contact. He knew he shouldn't have printed the article without consulting the reporter. "All right, I'll print your retraction. Then what?"

Leo turned to look through Ted's office window into the newsroom. The blond CNN reporter was still on the air, pointing to a little boy sitting on the curb, his arm in a cast, holding a cat. "I'm heading back to Carpe Diem to fix this mess."

# 19

"Brendan, do you know where Mayor Evans is?" Leo asked, weaving around the diner's empty tables. "Shit!" he cursed as he whacked his thigh on one of them. Pain pulsed through his leg. "It's after seven. She's not in her office. I drove to the Inn. Her car wasn't there. The concierge wouldn't let me in the front door." He limped up to the counter. "Brendan?"

The teenager opened a bag of decaf coffee and poured it methodically into the coffee maker.

Leo gritted his teeth as the teen picked up a mug and began wiping it out with a nearby cloth. "*Brendan!*"

The teen slammed the mug down, shoved the cloth into it and then looked at Leo. His eyes were small slits, his mouth an angry gash. "Why the hell should I tell you?"

Leo slumped onto the nearest stool, not surprised by the young man's retort. He had seen the trampled flowerbeds and the sidewalks littered with cigarette butts, crumpled Styrofoam coffee cups, plastic lids and chewing gum. He knew a press rampage when he saw it.

Leo rubbed his leg, debating what to say. Before leaving for Carpe Diem, he had stopped by his apartment for a quick shower. It refreshed him, but glancing at the mirror he saw blood shot eyes underlined with dark circles that only a long, deep sleep would cure. He threw on a clean, severely wrinkled cotton shirt and dusted off what grime he could from his jacket. He neglected to dry his mop of hair. He knew he looked like hell, but he didn't care.

As if on cue, *Apologize* by OneRepublic piped through the restaurant's sound system.

"I didn't write the article," Leo said.

"*Right.*"

"Dammit it's true!" He hoped this declaration would be enough. Brendan glared at him. "Someone hacked into my computer." He hesitated. "I think I know who."

"Who?"

"I can't say—"

The teenager scoffed.

"—until I'm certain. Which is why I need to talk to the mayor."

Brendan's scowl deepened.

"I told people I was doing a story about small towns and the Carpe Diem Fall Festival. That wasn't entirely accurate."

The clerk moved as if to go.

"Wait, let me finish, please."

Brendan stopped, though he continued to glare.

"I came to Carpe Diem to investigate how your town operated without schools. At first, I was skeptical, then after spending time with Quinn and seeing what this community is capable of, I started to change my mind. But I still had a lot of questions. I would never submit an article until I'd answered those questions. That's not my style."

Brendan turned toward the back doorway.

"Ask my editor if you don't believe me!" Leo shouted, desperate. "He'll tell you I'd rather miss a deadline than sign my name to a half-assed story."

The teen hesitated then turned around. "The mayor's at the Community Center. She's called an emergency town meeting."

"Thanks Brendan. I really appreciate it." He got up off the stool. "Wait, did you say 'town meeting'?" His pulse quickened.

"Yes. Go in the back entrance," Brendan said, "To avoid the press."

Great, press. Leo limped out of the diner.

When he arrived within a block of the Community Center, he thought Brendan shouldn't have bothered with his warning. The press was anything but subtle. The Dr. Seussish building looked like it belonged in a Tim Burton movie as giant spotlights made it glow while simultaneously casting bizarre shadows. The lights were mounted next to satellite dishes on top of vans in the road, on the lawn, even in the park across the street.

Leo sat in his idling Mustang trying to contain his rising panic. Cameramen loitered near cars and reporters lounged on the concrete front stairs. Apparently the town meeting was closed to the press.

One step at a time, he told himself.

He parked on a quiet residential street a block away from the Community Center. Taking several steadying breaths, he left the safety of his car and made his way through dark backyards to the center's playground. He waited a few moments while a journalist talking on his cell phone hovered nearby. When the man walked around to the front of the building, Leo ran to the rear entrance, opened the door and ducked into the deserted back hall. He leaned against the wall and gave himself a few minutes before going on.

At the auditorium door, he heard a rumble of muffled voices. He rubbed the scar on his chin and considered leaving. Instead, he willed himself to open the door.

"I've talked to the media." Mary's amplified voice echoed around the room.

Leo stayed at the back of the crowd and watched the mayor up on the stage. Her raised arms exposed sweat stains on her blue blazer. Behind her, a burly teenager wrote in a notepad while a second equally large boy took pictures. Leo recognized the one with the notepad as Quinn's editor friend, Billy.

"They've agreed to leave right after my press conference tomorrow morning." Mary's face was shiny red, her voice quivering. She didn't look as bad as he did, but almost.

"Who will pay for the damage? Buy new flowers?" a woman shouted.

"I've talked to the responsible networks. They've agreed to divide the costs between them."

"If they don't?" someone else hollered.

"If they don't cut me a check first thing in the morning, they'll hear about it during the press conference." The quiver in Mary's voice disappeared. "My daughter will provide pictures."

Applause erupted.

Mary smiled at the crowd then spotted Leo. Even from halfway across the room, he saw the color drain from her cheeks.

"It's getting late," she said. "I think we've covered everything—"

"Wait!" Leo shouted. He forced his shaking body to move through the mass of people. He concentrated on taking one step at a time. "Excuse me. Pardon me."

Men and women shifted out of his way, staring at him. Some gasped. Others shouted "Liar!" He blocked the voices out and fixed all his attention on the mayor. He had to get to her before she disappeared. Before his panic took over.

"Mr. Townsend, I think it best if you leave," she whispered into the microphone. Murmurs of agreement and barks of "Get out" rose from the townspeople.

"Wait, let me explain!" Leo pleaded. He stumbled and bumped into Charlotte Jansen. "Charlotte, I'm—" he began until the shop owner's beautiful face contorted with rage. He attempted to maneuver past her, but tripped over her outstretched foot.

He managed to regain his footing and make some progress until Kate Dobbs blocked his way. "Kate, let me pass. I have to explain." She didn't move. He gently shouldered past her. Someone, possibly Kate, grabbed his jacket. He twisted free and clambered up onto the stage.

"Billy, Steve, please escort Mr. Townsend out of the building," Mary said. The young men approached him.

Leo waved them off. "Wait. Please. What I have to say is important."

The boys hesitated.

He maneuvered around them to Mary. She put a shaky hand over the microphone.

"You sent that article," he hissed. "I want to know why."

"I don't know what you're talking about." Mary spoke in a low, even voice.

Leo grabbed the microphone. "Your honorable mayor wrote the article, put my byline on it and e-mailed it to my editor."

Shouts of "No!" and "You're lying!" punctuated gasps and murmurs of disbelief.

Mary hissed, "Why on earth would I do that?"

"That's what I'd like to know," Leo said through gritted teeth. He spoke again to the crowd, "Mayor Evans told me unschooling didn't work. She said this town was a nightmare to govern." Someone shouted "she did no such thing," in an attempt to drown him out, but he continued, "Why she doesn't just quit her position is beyond me. By sending out that article she betrayed you and me both."

Mary raised her arms again to quiet the angry crowd. "May I?" She indicated she wanted the microphone. "Mr. Townsend came to Carpe Diem to interview me about the Fall Festival. We discussed the schedule of events and the artisans who will be here. Unschooling, never came up. I don't know what Mr. Townsend is playing at when he says I sent that article. I can assure you I would never, ever do such a thing." She turned to Billy and Steve. "Please show Mr. Townsend the door so we can finish our meeting."

"Come on, let's go," Billy said, gently taking Leo's arm.

He shook off the teenager's hand and stood his ground for one final moment. He searched the crowd for Quinn, Tali, or even Brendan, anyone who might vouch for him. He was out of luck. He decided his best course was to leave.

As he followed Billy and Steve to the rear door, he heard Charlotte Jansen say, "And to think I considered him good looking."

The teenagers shoved him out into the night.

"Leave town," Billy said.

Leo regained his footing and turned around. Steve was heading back to the auditorium but the assistant editor of the Carpe Diem Daily News stood staring at him. "Billy—"

The teen started to close the door. Leo blocked it with his shoulder.

"Hey man, don't," the kid began.

"You're a journalist, Billy, does this make sense?" Leo pushed on the door. "Think about it. If I wrote the article, why would I come back to town?"

The big kid pushed back. "I don't know shit about you, man. Maybe you came back to find something else you could distort," he grunted, then stopped pushing but held the door in place blocking Leo. "I looked you up. You've written some good stories. I even like your writing style, but word is you're about to reveal your sources to the Smithson grand jury to save your skin. You're desperate. You'll do anything for a story."

"I admit I've screwed up before" Leo conceded. "But not this time. Think about it, if I was desperate for a story, would I come to the auditorium and announce myself to the town?"

"Yeah, I wondered about that."

"It only makes sense if I didn't write the article. And if I wanted to make a name for myself, why would I retract a story that has gotten all this press?"

"You're retracting it?"

"The retraction will be printed in *The Examiner* tomorrow."

The kid opened the door. Leo stayed outside.

"Look Billy, I didn't send the story to my editor. I was with Quinn and Tali Shaw all evening, not to mention Chief Billiot, police officers Ellery and Dennison, Josh Brody, and Francesca Scallini. Lots of people saw me eating dinner at Sapori D'Italia."

"You could have excused yourself and sent it from the bathroom at the restaurant," Billy suggested.

"My computer was locked in my room at the Bradbury Inn."

Shouting came from the one side of the building. Leo thought he heard someone running toward them. "I need a place to stay in town until I can sort this out," he said, "I can't stay at the Inn."

"You can't come to my place. My old man hates you. He wrapped a dead fish in your article and is planning on sending it to you in a week or two."

"You can stay with me," a gruff voice said.

# 20

"It's dead around here," Tali said to Will as she followed him into the Inn's dining room with her dinner plate. She worried that Will and Quinn might see her television interview, but was relieved when she realized the dining room didn't have a TV.

In fact, she couldn't remember seeing a television anywhere at the Inn, even in her room.

"I guess everyone's at the town meeting," Will answered.

"Where are your out-of-town guests?"

"They're leafing it."

"What?"

"Mom knew it'd be a zoo with the press in town so she threw together a day trip. She borrowed the community college's two deluxe vans. I packed them and the Inn's van with local wines, cheeses, and breads. Quinn loaded up the guests. Then our concierge, David, and two of his friends drove everyone to see the fall foliage. They'll go all the way to Galena for dinner. It'll be pretty late when they get back."

"Good plan." Tali said, setting her plate across from Will's on the table nearest the fireplace. "I couldn't believe it when I biked through town. Reporters everywhere. They didn't care about people's privacy or property. It was disgusting."

Will shuddered. "Glad I didn't see it." He glanced over at one of the chairs by the windows and then stared.

Tali followed his gaze. A figure dressed all in black except for a glint of a silver bracelet sat hidden in the shadows. Tali pushed away from the table and followed Will over to the chair.

"Where have you been?" Tali demanded. "I've been looking for you all afternoon."

Quinn, her jacket still on, rocked back and forth, hugging her knees. "I believed Mom. I did. I really did."

"Of course you believe her," Will said. "That article was full of lies. She didn't say those things about Carpe Diem. Why would she? Leo made the whole thing up."

Quinn shook her head, hugging her legs tighter.

This worried Tali. Quinn was always put together, confident, and passionate about everything. Now she looked defeated.

"Join us," Will suggested. "Eat something. I made chicken parmigiana."

Quinn didn't move.

Tali leaned down and whispered in her ear, "Per Favore?"

Quinn shrugged then trudged behind Tali to the table. Will darted into the kitchen for an extra plate and silverware. Tali put half of her untouched chicken onto Quinn's plate while Will slid over half of his salad. Quinn didn't look at the food and didn't raise her eyes to look at either one of them. She ran her fingers through her choppy black hair, exposing blond roots.

"Please tell us what's happened," Will's voice cracked.

Quinn sighed. "After you left the Inn this morning, Tali, Mom asked me to help her arrange the leafing trip. Will and I ended up doing most of the work because she kept getting phone calls from reporters and the town residents. The guests were excited about the trip, and about Will's food, so it was a fun job. After they drove away, I went back into the lobby where I ran into Mr. Wilkinson. You know him, Will, from Indianapolis."

"Sure. I saw him before you did and hid in the kitchen."

"You were lucky he didn't see you. He and his wife decided to spend the day in Carpe Diem because they were tired of driving." Quinn raised her head, her tight lips widened into a hint of a smile. Most of her black lipstick had smeared off. "His exact words were, 'we're not getting our asses back into any stinkin' minivan.' He wanted to talk to Mom about Carpe Diem's restaurants. I told him I could help. He said he'd rather talk to an adult, someone who knew what they were talking about."

"Yep, that's Mr. Wilkinson for you."

Quinn continued, "I was glad I wouldn't have to deal with him anymore. I looked for Mom. When I didn't find her in the lobby or in her office, I got worried that she had left for the Town Hall and forgot to tell me. Remember Will, I came into the kitchen to ask you if you'd seen Mom?"

"I told you I hadn't seen her all morning."

"Right. So I went upstairs to her bedroom expecting her to be gone. Her door was slightly open. I walked in and heard her talking to someone on the phone in the bathroom. The bathroom door was closed most of the way, so I couldn't see her, but I heard her say, 'I'm done doing your shit.'"

"Wow!" Will exclaimed.

"What?" Tali asked, confused.

"Mom never swears," Will answered. "What happened next?"

"I didn't mean to eavesdrop." Quinn picked at the black polish on her thumb nail. "But I couldn't help myself. The swearing really bothered me. Plus, I wanted to know how best to handle the Wilkinsons. I sat on the edge of the bed to wait. 'It worked,' I heard Mom say. 'What more do you want? You've got to be kidding. No, no I won't. NO! Screw you!'" Quinn flinched as she repeated this. "Then she slammed the phone down."

"You're making this up," Will said.

"I wish I was."

"Did you ask her about it when she came out?" Tali asked.

"No, she didn't come out right away. She started to cry. I walked to the bathroom when something on her desk caught my eye."

"What?" Tali asked.

"*The Chicago Examiner.* It was opened to Leo's article. Someone had taken a black pen and scribbled all over the article. In places the scribbling had been so intense that it ripped holes in the paper. Everything was blackened out except his name."

"Freaky," Tali said.

Quinn continued, "Mom came up behind me. I jumped, feeling guilty even though I wasn't doing anything wrong. After all, her door was unlocked and I needed to talk to her. I asked her about the ruined article."

"What did she say?" Tali asked.

"'Therapy.' She said she was so angry with Leo she took it out on his article. It made sense. Then I told her I heard her swearing on the phone. She apologized. She said it'd been an awful day and it was not even noon yet. *That* didn't make sense. We've had horrible days before. Will, remember when the tornado touched down in Elon?"

"'Course." Will turned to Tali. "We had fifty newly homeless people living here for three weeks. And we had to clean up debris, repair siding, mop up the flooded basement. I never heard Mom swear or yell."

"Me neither," Quinn said. "So I couldn't let it go. I asked her why she was crying. I guessed she'd say she was stressed out. But she yelled at me. She told me to mind my own business."

Will gasped.

"What's the big deal? My dad says that to me all the time," Tali said remembering when he finally came home after the Rosalinda incident and she asked him where he'd been. *"Mind your own damn business. I'm home now, aren't I?"* he had said.

"Mom never talks to us like that," Will explained. "What d'ya do, Quinn?"

"I tore out of the Inn, took off for the studio. John was there."

"How is he?" Will asked.

"He looks ten years older but he's going to be okay. He needed a distraction from the funeral arrangements so we put together the Fall Festival pamphlets. He knew something was wrong when he realized I didn't have my camera with me. He asked if the reporters had upset me. I told him they pissed me off, but that wasn't it. I said I didn't want to talk about it. Instead we worked on the pamphlets, raided the studio's fridge for sandwich makings around lunchtime, and talked about visiting Italy."

"So that's where you were," Tali said, a little annoyed. "We were supposed to meet at Sapori D'Italia at four o'clock for Italian lessons, remember?"

"Oh, I totally forgot." Quinn put her hand on Tali's arm. "I'm really sorry. We'll do it another time. I promise."

Tali smiled and nodded.

"Tali helped me in Sapori D'Italia's kitchen," Will said. "She now knows that 'nessun gran cosa' means 'no big deal' in Italian."

Tali felt herself blushing, "It's what Francesca said when I spilled the olive oil."

Quinn managed a smile.

"Did you and John finish the pamphlets?" Will asked.

"Yes. While we waited for them to print, I decided to tell John about my fight with Mom. I mentioned her bathroom conversation, the newspaper, everything. He couldn't believe it. He suggested that I talk to her about it. By then, it was close to five and he had to leave for the town meeting."

"So you haven't talked to her?"

Quinn shook her head. "No. When I came back here, she was gone. I decided I'd go to the Community Center, too, but the Wilkinsons caught me in the lobby before I left. I had totally forgotten about them. I thought they'd be mad. But they were both smiling. Mrs. Wilkinson said that when I didn't return, they sat around for awhile in the dining room."

"And had a huge breakfast," Will added. "I kept bringing out more pastries."

"After breakfast, they walked into town and spent a lot of time at Charlotte's store. Mr. Wilkinson has it for her."

"Who doesn't?" Will asked.

Quinn ignored him. "When they left the store a television reporter asked them if they'd like to answer a few questions. They were thrilled to be on TV. They told me every detail. When I finally got away from them, I went to the Community Center. The meeting had already started. It was really crowded. I looked for you, but didn't see you."

"I was stuck cleaning the kitchen and holding down the fort," Will said.

"Hey," Tali said.

"Tali helped," Will added. "And she shared her grandma's terrific corn and potato chowder recipe."

"Anyway," Quinn continued testily. "Leo Townsend showed up at the meeting."

"What?" exclaimed Tali.

"He looked like hell. He walked, or rather stumbled, up onto the stage. Took the microphone from Mom. He told the town he didn't write the article. He said Mom did."

"What did she say?" Tali asked.

"She denied it. Asked Billy and Steve to kick Leo out. Leo hesitated, then he left with them. Mom continued with the meeting as if the whole thing hadn't happened. I was so upset. I snuck out and came home."

"Wow, that's messed up," Will said.

"I don't think so," Tali began.

"Are you saying my mom wrote that horrible article?" Will's voice quivered.

"No, I don't think she did, it just doesn't make sense," she said, flipping her ponytail around her finger. "I've never heard of a reporter accusing someone else of writing *his* article. And this article is all over the news now. You'd think he'd want all the credit." She stopped twirling her ponytail to pick up her fork and take a bite of the lukewarm, but still amazing chicken. All this drama had made her hungry.

"I wondered about that, too," Quinn began, as she pushed lettuce around her plate. "I also wondered why he'd make such an accusation at a crowded town meeting if it wasn't true."

Will didn't eat. "It's not true. How can you believe that guy? He's crazy!"

"Leo's a nice guy," Tali said as she chewed. "He took me to dinner when Tom ditched me."

"He figured out someone sabotaged Patrick's bike," Quinn added.

"You just think he's hot," Will snorted.

"He wasn't tonight," Quinn said.

They finished the meal in silence. Tali thought about Leo catching her when she almost fainted, how great he smelled. She tried to picture an unattractive Leo. Impossible. She wished she had been at the town meeting. "Do you think Leo's still in Carpe Diem?" she asked.

"Maybe," Quinn said.

"God, I hope not," Will said.

"Where would he be?" Tali asked.

"I bet Billy knows. I'll give him a call." Quinn took out her cell phone. "He's not answering. He's notorious for not having his phone on. Let's drop by his house." Quinn pushed her chair back from the table.

"You're really going to try to find him?" Will asked.

"Yes. Are you coming with us?" Quinn asked.

"No, I might punch him if I see him." He gathered up the plates. "I'll talk to Mom when she gets back. I want her to tell me what's going on."

Quinn started for the lobby. "Grab your coat, Tali. Meet me out front. Mom has the compact car. We'll take our black SUV."

# 21

Leo turned to see the town drunk coming up the back stairs of the Carpe Diem Community Center, crazy white hair, torn ski vest over a baggy sweater, Birkenstock sandals. *Great, that's all I need, a night in a stinking dilapidated shack watching this guy get blitzed.*

"John! I'm sorry about Patrick. How are you?" Billy asked.

"Thank you, Billy. I'm hanging in there."

"*You're* John Holden?" Leo asked. He had seen old photos of John Holden accepting various awards. But this wild old man hardly resembled the eager young teacher in those pictures. That teacher had an army regulation crew cut and wore neat suits and ties.

"Hey guys, look who's here!" a reporter shouted.

"Let's go," Leo said, grabbing the old man by the arm. Together they ran into a neighboring backyard toward the side street where he had parked the Mustang.

Leo heard more shouting but this came from the front of the Community Center. It sounded like the townspeople were leaving the building through the main doors. A news frenzy had started. In the excitement, the press forgot about him.

"I don't mean to sound ungrateful, but why would you take me in?" Leo asked John after giving the grieving father his condolences.

They were seated at John's kitchen table in the stately house on the Carpe Diem farm. The kitchen smelled of pine smoke and baked bread. A wall of curtain less windows reflected the flickering glow from the fireplace on the opposite wall. Edison, an old golden retriever named after homeschooler Thomas Edison, lounged on a braided rug in front of the fire.

"I'm curious about you," the old man replied. "When I first heard you were in town, I wondered why on earth *The Chicago Examiner* was interested in Carpe Diem. We've been under the radar for forty years. Now, out of the blue, a reporter shows up and causes trouble. I want to know why."

"If the town likes being under the radar, why did its mayor agree to be interviewed for a national newspaper?"

John took a swig from his Dos Equis bottle. "Didn't you tell her you were doing a story on small town festivals?"

"No, when I set up the interview, I didn't give a reason. She didn't ask. I didn't know about the festival until Brendan told me."

"So what was your reason for interviewing her?"

Leo picked at the damp label on his beer bottle and thought about wanting to write the story of the century. Instead he had to redeem himself yet again. This time it wasn't just about him, a whole town was in trouble. For that he was partly to blame. If he wanted to fix things, he'd have to come clean. "My boss asked me to do a story about your school-less town. It became an even better story after the ruling against homeschoolers in California."

"How did your boss hear about Carpe Diem?"

"Raegan Colyer, the governor's chief of staff, called him—"

"Christ, we're in more trouble than I thought."

"Why do you say that?"

"Ms. Colyer and I aren't the best of friends. You might even call us enemies."

"Why?"

John waved his hand as if shooing away a fly. "It's a long story."

"I'd like to hear it."

John drank from his beer bottle, emptying it. He went to the fridge, took out two more bottles of Dos Equis, handed one to Leo, and resumed his seat at the table. "Raegan Colyer was the youngest school superintendent in Cook County the year I walked away from teaching. She represented everything I felt was wrong with America's educational system, a system I tried to change with mild success until she took over."

"What happened?"

"I won teacher of the year in Chicago and nationally for three years running," John continued, no trace of bravado in his voice. "I achieved that by circumventing the system.

"At the high school where I taught, the curriculum called for reading *Macbeth*. Predictably the kids grumbled. One girl quoted her dad as saying 'Shakespeare should be seen and not read.' I agreed. Shakespeare can be pretty dull to read. Instead, we decided to perform *Macbeth*.

"In public schools, nothing's that easy. Our high school produced only musicals and the director picked his favorite leads, many of whom were not in my honors English class. Undaunted, we approached the local community theatre. The owner agreed to let the kids run a show in exchange for filling in as ushers throughout the year.

"About the same time," John said, getting up to rummage around in the cupboard, "the district had major financial challenges. The school board, in its infinite wisdom, eliminated the shop classes."

He walked back to the table with a can of peanuts. Leo took a handful.

"One of the worst programs they could cut," John said, resuming his seat. "Most of those kids taking shop weren't going on to college. They needed a vocation. Shop gave them valuable experience which now they wouldn't have. I contacted a local contractor and made a deal. He agreed to show them the ropes in exchange for their helping him dry wall his new condominium complex."

"What did your principal think?" Leo asked.

"She liked the idea. She arranged it so they could leave the high school campus once a week. At the same time, she agreed to let my English students leave campus to rehearse at the theater."

"And the parents?"

"They didn't care as long as the kids did their homework and got decent grades. Giving decent grades was easy; the kids knew the subjects cold. The homework piece was a little harder. I don't believe in busywork. So I convinced the parents extra nights at the theatre or at the building site met the homework requirements." He took a pull on his beer.

"So, Colyer found out?"

"One day the new superintendent of schools shows up, Ms. Raegan Colyer. She questioned why half of my English class was in the Home Ec room sewing Scottish tunics and the other half was in the art room making a bloody head. She wanted to know why I wasn't doing my job, keeping the kids busy at their desks with assignments and textbooks. She demanded to know what the hell was going on.

"Principal Brown stepped in. Good thing. I was struggling to control my temper. She introduced me as the 'Teacher of the Year'.

"Ignoring the principal, Colyer cited the high school English curriculum word-for-word. She said the English curriculum didn't mention papier mâché. Principal Brown told her we were putting on a production of *Macbeth* in lieu of reading the book.

"Colyer cut her off. She didn't want to hear 'excuses.' She said the school's field trip guidelines didn't mention shop kids spackling walls.

"'And do you know why?'" she asked. "Then, right away, she answered her own question. 'Because it's too dangerous.'

"That's when I started laughing," John chuckled. "Which was my big mistake."

"What did Colyer do?"

"Have you met the woman?"

"I've met her," Leo admitted.

"I don't know what she looks like today. Back then she was gorgeous and intimidating. Long black hair flowing down her back, skirts short enough to expose her shapely legs, though long enough to be professional. Perfectly manicured blood-red nails and all her words and actions calculated."

"That's her, although her hair is shorter and the nail polish tends to be pink."

"So you can understand that when her face reddened, I knew I was in trouble." Edison lumbered over from the fireplace. John paused to pet him. "After fifteen years of implementing my own brand of teaching, I was used to school administrators trying to reel me in. This time it was different.

"Colyer insisted on a big inquiry. The final report determined my students were in all kinds of danger. Worse, they weren't learning a thing. We pressed forward with *Macbeth*, which received a standing ovation and a terrific write up in *The Chicago Examiner*."

"The theatre critic's name didn't happen to be Kate Dodds, did it?"

"Oh, you've met Kate, have you?"

"I have."

"Yes, Kate and I've been friends ever since." John stopped petting the dog to scratch the stubble on his chin.

"Parents supported me," John continued. "That outpouring, the great review, not just on the performance but also on my methodology, those weren't enough. By then, Colyer told the parents I'd hit a kid."

"Did you?"

"I've never hit a child in my life. No, Jamal sucker punched me in my right temple. The school secretary saw me block Jamal's second punch, misinterpreted it and told her cousin, who just happened to be Raegan Colyer. I kept quiet. Jamal would have been kicked out of school only a few months shy of graduation. He needed to graduate, to get away from the hell his step-father put him through."

"But he hit you."

"Yep, he sure did. Got a good welt to prove it. But Jamal was a good kid. He wasn't in a gang. I'd heard that he had never hit anyone before. That morning, he told me later, his mom had swallowed a fistful of sleeping pills. She would survive but as the ambulance took her away, Jamal's stepfather laughed and said, 'don't bother bringing the ugly black bitch back.' When I happened upon Jamal at his locker and asked him why he wasn't in class, he snapped. Took it out on his favorite teacher."

John went over to the fireplace. Edison followed and lay down on the rug. The fireplace's metal mesh screen squealed as John pulled it back. He tossed a log on the fire. Sparks danced.

"After Colyer told them I'd hit a kid," he said, dusting bits of wood off his hands, "parents wanted me fired. Principal Brown suggested an unpaid leave of absence. She assumed the pressure I'd been under made me snap." He sat back down at the table.

"I quit. For days I stayed in my apartment. I'd been a teacher in Chicago for fifteen years, fought the system all the way. I thought I'd made a difference. I should have realized it couldn't last.

"A week or two later, I ventured out to the corner diner. A beautiful young woman asked if I was John Holden. When I told her I was, she introduced herself as Suzanne Jacobsen. She said she had read about me and my career. She recognized my face from *The Examiner's* photograph of the president giving me the national award. She applauded me for trying unschooling in a public school. I had no idea what she was talking about. I'd never heard of unschooling.

"A year later I married her. Together we founded Carpe Diem."

"You left Chicago and went into hiding for an ideology?" Leo couldn't believe it.

"Unschooling isn't an ideology. It's a way of life."

"You gave up your career to live a certain way?"

"To offer an alternative to compulsory public schooling. Educational freedom—"

The phone rang. John excused himself. "Yes, he's here." He hung up. "Mary's on her way over. She'd like to talk to you."

"You can bet I'd like to talk to her," Leo replied. He heard footsteps in the hall.

"Who's on the phone, Dad?" Patrick Holden asked, limping into the kitchen.

# 22

Leo gaped at the tall hippie. He had a nasty shiner coloring his puffy left eye, a bandage on half of his deeply creased forehead, and silver streaks through his dark brown ponytail and goatee. At first glance, he appeared to be in his fifties with a worn crusty look women find appealing, a younger version of Clint Eastwood. Yet something mischievous in his grey eyes suggested he was a much younger man.

"I didn't realize we had company," the lanky man said.

"Leo, this is my son, Patrick," John said. "Patrick, this is the reporter I told you about."

"You brought him here, Dad? What were you thinking?"

"I have a feeling we can trust him."

"I, I thought you were... ," Leo stammered. "Chief Billiot said you died."

"I would have," Patrick said matter-of-factly as he grabbed a beer from the fridge. "If I hadn't flown over the top of the car and landed in a rather large haystack."

"Your thick skull helped," John added. "Now I'll never talk you into buying a helmet. Why bother when you're so boneheaded."

"That I am," Patrick chuckled, limping to the table. "Although you won't have to lecture me about headgear anymore. Soon as I can scrape

KRISTIN A. OAKLEY

up enough money for a new bike, I'll throw in a helmet. I was damned lucky to miss the car and have a soft landing. It's remarkable I'm alive, or at least not confined to a hospital bed like Mrs. Shaw. I have a feeling my luck may be running out, though. Someone's trying pretty hard to change it."

The banter frustrated Leo. He wanted an explanation. "Why did the chief say you died?"

"Because that's what Dr. Anderson told him," Patrick said as he eased into a kitchen chair. "Jesus, I ache. I feel like the walking dead."

Leo stood up. "*What the hell's going on?*" His chair crashed to the floor, scaring Edison. The dog ran from the room.

Patrick glared at him. "Lots, but I'm not going to say anything to a reporter, particularly one who will do anything to save his own skin."

Leo put his hands on the smooth wooden table and glared back. "You don't know anything about me."

"You're wrong. The minute you made the appointment with Mary, Dad did some checking."

Leo looked at the old man.

John got up from his seat and repositioned the chair. "Sit down," he said gently.

Leo sat, crossed his arms and waited.

"I told you I was curious," John said. "The internet's an amazing thing and I still have friends in Chicago. For instance, Principal Brown's daughter, Keisha, is a reporter at the *Sentinel*. She told me the two of you dated for awhile until you were too busy training for last year's Chicago Triathlon."

"Principal Brown's *daughter*?" Did Keisha know what happened at the triathlon? Leo hoped not. "Yeah, we went out a few times. So?"

"Did you know she went to the triathlon?" Patrick asked. "She was near the finish line."

Leo dropped his hands into his lap and slowly shook his head.

"All the other spectators focused on the mob, not Keisha. She kept her eyes on you," John said.

"Is it true?" Patrick asked. "Did you stand there and watch?"

"*What?!* God no! I didn't just stand there, I couldn't..."

"What happened?" John asked.

Leo drank the last of his beer and set the empty bottle on the table, wanting a much, much stronger drink. He leaned his elbows on his knees and kept his eyes on the hardwood floor. "Eddie, my younger brother, competed with me in the triathlon. It was his first race. We matched each other in the bicycle portion but he outshone me during the swim. My strength is running and I was in top form that day. I caught up and passed Eddie though I didn't want to leave him behind. If it weren't for him, I doubt I would have been near the lead. Eddie urged me on, told me not to slow down, to finish with my best time."

Leo ran his fingers through his hair. "I was a half-block ahead of him on Columbus Drive, not far from the finish line, when the shot rang out."

"I remember the news reports," Patrick said. "Some kid thought it'd be fun to stop the race by shaking up the crowd."

"Yes," Leo said. "He fired a gun in the air. The crowd panicked and ran into the racers' lanes. I turned around when I heard the gun shot. I saw the mob engulf Eddie." He trembled, remembering Eddie's confused and panicked expression. The crowd barreled into him, pushing him to the ground. Others stepped on him. "He called out for me. I fought my way through the crowd. But I couldn't get to him.

"One very large woman punched me. Jesus, she had a huge diamond ring. Her left clip dazed me for a moment. I didn't realize how bad my chin was bleeding until much later."

"Keisha Brown said you froze," John said quietly.

Leo glared at the older man. "Froze? No. I struggled with the crowd and have the scars to prove it." Both physical and emotional, he thought, touching his chin. "I finally got to Eddie. But he was in bad shape by then, trampled by the crowd."

"He died?" Patrick asked.

"It was touch and go for weeks, but he survived." Leo hesitated then added, "He's paralyzed from the waist down."

"I'm sorry," John said.

"Rationally, I know I couldn't have done anything, but I tell myself I should have tried harder. Not left him behind. For months after it happened, I drank everything I could get my hands on, slept with any woman who would have me. I almost lost my job."

"Why didn't the paper fire you?" Patrick asked.

"When I became a finalist for the Pulitzer Prize for my Carl Smithson piece, they decided to give me another chance. I'm still on probation."

Leo leaned back in his chair and recrossed his arms, mad at himself for saying too much. Now it was their turn. "I've answered your questions. I'd appreciate it if you answered mine. What the hell's going on?"

Patrick shook his head, then winced. He massaged his left temple. "Someone has tried to kill me, twice."

"Twice? Someone sabotaged your bike…"

"One of the nurses at the hospital spotted a man dressed as a doctor leaving my room. She didn't recognize him so she checked on me. She found me struggling to breathe. He'd shot me full of morphine. They didn't catch the guy, but they did increase hospital security."

Leo remembered passing three uniformed policemen at the hospital.

"That wasn't good enough for Dad," Patrick continued. "He and Dr. Anderson smuggled me home. They told people I had died to protect me."

"Do you know who tried to kill you?" he asked.

"Possibly. But I'm still not sure I can trust you."

"Christ!" Leo got up from his chair. It wobbled, but stayed put. "Look, I could've stayed in Chicago and forgotten about this town. I didn't."

"It's too great a story," Patrick hissed.

"Yes, it is a great story," he replied through gritted teeth. He had warmed to John Holden. Patrick was harder to like. "But the story that's being told will ruin this town."

"Patrick," John intervened, "Leo confronted Mary at the town meeting tonight."

"Seriously?" Patrick looked at Leo with a bit of respect. "That was ballsy."

"The lady screwed the town over," he said. "The town blames me for this current mess when, in fact, she's to blame. I wanted to set the record straight."

"I would have done the same," Patrick admitted. "Though Mary's not to blame, I am."

"*You* sent the article?"

"No, I sent the article," Mary Evans said as she entered the room making Leo jump. She leaned against the door frame, black jacket in her hand. The circles under her eyes were almost as dark as Patrick's shiner and couldn't be hidden by her glasses.

"I knew it," Leo said feeling vindicated.

"*How could you?*" John said, standing, his deep voice shaking. "Do you have any idea what you've done? How you've exposed Carpe Diem?"

Mary bowed her head.

"Dad, she didn't have a choice. It's my fault," Patrick said.

"You're wrong, Patrick," Mary said. "Raegan Colyer's behind all this."

John walked over to Mary then put his hand on her arm. "Quinn came to me. She was very upset. She told me you had mutilated Leo's article. She overheard you swearing on the phone. Were you talking to Colyer?"

"Yes."

"Does this have to do with Raegan sending Leo to Carpe Diem?"

"She didn't send me," Leo said. "She told my editor about your town and suggested I investigate."

"The governor's office is in the habit of assigning stories to *Examiner* reporters?" Patrick asked. "I knew the current administration had the press in its back pocket, but this is too much."

"We're not in any government pocket," Leo said with more anger than he intended.

"And yet, here you are."

"Patrick," John intervened. "Let's give him the benefit of the doubt."

The younger man pushed up the sleeves of his grey shirt revealing nasty cuts and bruises. He sat back and studied Leo for a moment. "What's your connection to Colyer?"

"We met when I was doing background work on Governor Thomas for a different story. We, ah, went out a few times," he admitted.

Mary raised an eyebrow. "Isn't she at least twenty years older than you?"

Leo gave her a sheepish grin. "She's hard to resist. Anyway, that was years ago. Now, all of a sudden, in addition to suggesting the story on Carpe Diem, she's offered me a position on the governor's staff."

"Why?" Patrick asked.

"She didn't say. My guess is she's gotten what she wants from the Carpe Diem story. She doesn't want me investigating any further." He looked at Mary. "What's your connection to Raegan?"

"She told me she sent you to Carpe Diem. She wanted me to feed you lies about unschooling."

"Which explains the 'unschooling isn't successful' and 'it's a nightmare to govern' comments."

"Yes, and why I scheduled my appointment with you at the same time as the town meeting. I asked Will to run the meeting knowing you'd probably see it as chaotic and attribute it to a teenage boy behind the podium."

"Why go to all the trouble when you knew you were going to write the article anyway?" Leo asked.

"That wasn't the original plan. Raegan assumed you'd talk to me, attend the meeting, write up your story and head back to Chicago. She told me you'd do the minimum amount of work because you were lazy." Mary shrugged apologetically and studied her hands. "When I told her you pressed me on unschooling over dinner and you planned on staying in town for a couple of days, she panicked and made me write the article." She looked at Leo. "Raegan told me to watch you, to call her when you left town. I did."

"On the way out of town, someone almost drove me off the road," Leo said. "And a cop threw me in jail. My editor wondered if someone was out to get me. It was Raegan all along."

"Oh Leo, I'm sorry," Mary said.

"Mary, why on earth would you do any of that?" John demanded.

"She was blackmailing me," she answered. "I had no choice."

"Blackmail? What are you talking about?" John asked.

"Christopher Shaw."

"She knows about Shaw?" John gasped.

"Yes."

"Knows what about Shaw?" Leo asked.

Mary shook her head. Brown strands of hair fell loose from behind her right ear. "I can't tell you now, but I will, soon."

Leo looked at her pleading eyes and decided to let it go. "Okay, so tell me this much. Is Raegan against this town just because you unschool?"

"There's more to it than that," John said. "First, Mary, why don't you sit down? Can I get you a beer?"

"Yes, please. I'm overdue for one."

Once everyone was seated, John said, "Raegan Colyer is incredibly intelligent and considers herself superior to other people. She thinks she knows what's best for everyone, particularly children. As a young superintendent, and even now as the governor's chief of staff, she believes children need to be molded into good citizens. She doesn't give a damn about their individuality."

"And to you their individuality is paramount?" Leo asked. "Raegan sees you as a threat?"

"Exactly."

"You left the system. How much more of a threat could you be?"

"Soon after I left, parents of my former students began looking me up. Their kids had thrived in my classes. Now they were despondent. The parents were desperate. They begged me to teach again. I knew with Raegan as superintendent that would be impossible. But I wanted to help. I cared about the kids. I couldn't abandon them."

"So you suggested homeschooling. Wrote a few books on the subject, if I remember," Leo said.

"Ah, you've done your homework, too," John said approvingly.

"Then you disappeared."

"While writing my first book on homeschooling, Suzanne and I bought some land. By the third book, we owned several hundred acres. We decided to establish an unschooling community with ten other families.

"Raegan was now the state superintendent of education based in part upon her continued criticism of me, my books, and what she called my 'homeschooling following'. She described homeschooling as 'educational abuse'. She claimed all homeschooling parents were potential closet child abusers. Can you imagine what she'd think about a community of unschoolers? I thought it best to keep a low profile."

"Now that she's found you, do you think Raegan's out to destroy you and this town?" Leo asked.

"Yes. I and Carpe Diem threaten everything she believes in and everything she's worked for."

"It's more than that, Uncle John," Mary interjected.

"*Uncle* John?" Leo asked.

"Years ago," Mary continued, ignoring him, "Mom told me you dated Ms. Colyer, then dumped her."

It was John's turn to give her a sheepish grin. "Yes. We dated for many months. I think it was during my sixth year of teaching. Anyway, Raegan was possessive, controlling. I didn't handle it well. She saw me with another woman. She confronted me. I told her I didn't love her. She's never forgiven me for rejecting her."

"And she took it out on you by getting you fired years later," Mary said.

"That's right," John agreed.

"So this isn't just ideological. It's personal," Leo said.

"Yes," John said.

Patrick sat up quickly. The sudden movement made him groan.

"Patrick, take it easy," Mary said. "I still can't believe Dr. Anderson agreed to release you from the hospital."

"I'm fine," he said rubbing his temple. "I saw Raegan at Senator Shaw's office."

"During your meeting?" Leo asked.

Patrick gave him a quizzical look.

"Tali Shaw was at the police station when we discovered that someone had sabotaged your bike," Leo explained. "She mentioned your meeting, said it didn't go well. She was worried he was involved in the sabotage."

"Oh, he's involved all right," Patrick said, his face flushing. "And the meeting *was* a disaster. We had started to talk when he walked out. I think he took great satisfaction in slamming the door."

"Did your meeting have to do with Shaw's anti-homeschooling legislation?"

"You have done your homework, haven't you?" Patrick asked.

"It's my job."

"And Patrick's job is protecting the rights of Carpe Diem citizens and ensuring educational freedom for all," Mary teased.

"Definitely," Patrick replied with a wink. "Like Dad, I've written a few books on unschooling, though I spend most of my time lecturing at universities, school board and PTA meetings, and homeschool conventions. Most of the time people listen politely, although they rarely hear me. Once in awhile parents will thank me for the advantages unschooling has given their family."

"Don't be modest, Patrick," Mary said. "You do more than lecture. The term 'radical infiltration' comes to mind."

"Wait a minute," Leo said straightening up. "Radical infiltration? Wasn't that an *Examiner* headline a few years back?"

"Yes," Mary said, finally using her beautiful smile.

"I vaguely remember the article," Leo said. "The vice president of the American Federation of Teachers demanded the dismantling of the union on the grounds that government-run education was unconstitutional and so was the union. Was that you?"

"The very same."

"That was ballsy," Leo said repeating Patrick's words.

Patrick laughed.

"It was stupid," John said.

"Hey, you were subversive in your day. I was following in your footsteps."

"I did it quietly, on the local level."

"I know, and no offense Dad, but it didn't work. You needed to be flashier."

"Patrick, the only thing your flashy stunt accomplished was solidifying the teachers' union and accumulating death threats."

"Not true, it helped to start many grassroots homeschool groups throughout the nation."

"Those groups were necessary only because you drew the government's attention to homeschooling in the first place."

Leo suspected the men had argued about this for years. He was more interested in Raegan Colyer's involvement. "Patrick, you mentioned seeing Raegan at Senator Shaw's office right before the accident."

"Yes. I went back to his office to try to persuade him to table his anti-homeschooling legislation."

"Back?"

"I had met with him the week before. He called me a few days later to set up a second appointment, telling me he had considered what I'd said. He even offered to meet me at nine o'clock at night to accommodate my schedule. I took it as a good sign. Boy, was I wrong.

"Anyway, I bumped into Raegan leaving Shaw's office. We exchanged 'hellos.' She didn't seem surprised to see me although I wondered why she was there so late."

Patrick picked at the label on his beer bottle. "As I've said, my meeting with Shaw didn't go well. After he stormed out, I wondered why he wanted to meet with me in the first place and why he set up this second meeting. I left pretty dispirited, thinking that instead of getting him to scrap his legislation, I'd actually encouraged him to push harder to get the damned thing passed. "I was driving my motorcycle home," Patrick continued, "forming a different strategy, when I lost control. The next thing I knew, I was in the Carpe Diem hospital looking up at Dad and Dr. Anderson."

"You think Senator Shaw set up the second meeting so he could sabotage your bike? Is he capable of that?"

"More than capable," Mary said. She stood up and put her jacket on. "I'm sorry. I should go. I've got to find Quinn, talk to her before the press conference tomorrow. She needs to know."

"Know what?" Leo asked.

"Do you want me to come with you?" Patrick asked.

"No, thanks. It'll be okay. I want to talk to you later. Have you explain how Raegan found me." She glared at Patrick then walked to the hallway, pausing to look at Leo. "I'm so sorry you got sucked into this."

# 23

Tali stood next to Quinn on Billy Turner's front porch. They hoped he could tell them where Leo was. Tali couldn't believe that Leo had written that crappy article. She wanted to hear his side of the story.

The porch light was on but no one answered the doorbell. Billy hadn't returned Quinn's calls. Discouraged, they were walking back to the car when Quinn's phone beeped. "It's a text from Billy," she said. "He says Leo is at John's."

They climbed into the SUV then pulled out of the driveway just as Tali's phone rang. She didn't recognize the number. "Hello?"

"Is this Tali Shaw?"

"Yes."

"Miss Shaw, I'm Margaret Simpson, a surgical nurse at Carpe Diem Hospital. Your mother, well, there's been a setback. We've tried to contact your father, but haven't been able to reach him."

"Setback?"

"We've discovered a brain hemorrhage. Dr. Anderson is performing emergency surgery. I think it would be best—"

"I'll be right there." She hung up and turned to Quinn. "We need to get to the hospital." Quinn whipped a U-turn as Tali filled her in.

"Is your dad coming?" Quinn asked, tires squealing as she turned onto

Main Street.

"They can't reach him." Tali tried his number and got his voicemail.

"I'll stay with you if you'd like," Quinn offered.

"You wanted to talk to Leo…"

"It can wait."

She nodded, then called Tom. He picked up on the fifth ring.

"What?" Tom said.

"Mom's back in surgery. It's bad. I can't reach Dad," Tali tried not to cry. "I know it's late, but can you come—"

"Tonight? You're shitting me right? It's Friday night. There's a big game against East."

"I thought that was tomorrow night."

"It is. But the boys and I have a lot of preparation to do — you know, to the visitors' locker room. Make sure those East bitches are properly welcomed."

"Hazing football players? *You're shitting me, right?*" She never talked to Tom like that.

"*Hey—*"

"Mom might not make it," she hesitated, "I'm scared. Please come."

"Not tonight. Besides, by the time I get there your mom will be fine. You won't need me."

She couldn't believe him. She glanced at Quinn who kept her eyes on the road. "Screw you. We're through."

"What the f—"

She clicked the phone off and shuddered.

"For what it's worth," Quinn said, "I think you did the right thing."

Tali's phone played "I'd catch a grenade for ya" from the Bruno Mars' song *Grenade*. Tom's ringtone. She ignored it. When it stopped, she took him off her contacts list. She waited for the singing to begin again. It didn't. She actually felt relieved.

Quinn pulled the SUV into the hospital parking lot. "I'll drop you at the front door then meet up with you in a few minutes."

Tali got out even before the SUV came to a complete stop. Her cell phone played the opening notes to *Jaws*. Her father. "Dad, Mom's gotten worse—" she began as she scrambled up the concrete steps.

"I'm in the office," Christopher said, interrupting her, "when someone tells me my daughter is on the news advocating homeschooling. What the hell is that about?"

"It's not important."

"Not important? Do you realize what I've been working for all these years and here's my daughter—"

"*Dad!* It's Mom—"

"Don't you dare yell at me! You have a lot of explaining to do. I'll be at the hospital within the hour." He hung up.

Tali shoved her phone into her pocket. He and Tom were prime candidates for assholes of the year. She wasn't looking forward to facing her father, but she couldn't worry about that now. She hurried through the hospital's open doors and bumped into Josh.

"Oops, sorry," he said. His smile faded. "What is it? Is it your mom?"

She nodded, walking past him, and tripped on her own feet. He grabbed her elbow to stop her fall. "I'll come with you." Together they ran up the stairs to the fourth floor nurses' station.

"I haven't heard anything yet," Denise said. "As soon as she's out of surgery, you'll be the first to know."

Tali must have looked lost. Denise touched her arm and said, "The surgery may take a few hours. The surgical waiting room is downstairs, but you don't have to stay there. I'll give you a local distance pager. We'll be able to reach you anywhere in the hospital."

Tali took the pager and pictured sitting in a waiting room crowded with anxious families. "Can I hang out in my mom's room?"

"Yes."

"Would you tell my friend Quinn where I am? She'll be here soon."

"Sure."

Tali turned to Josh. "You don't have to stay."

"It's not a problem."

"Is it okay if my friends wait with me until Mom's out of surgery?" she asked Denise.

"Of course."

She walked with Josh into her mother's hospital room. Seeing the empty bed, the sheets in a crumpled mess, a pillow on the floor, she started to cry. Josh hugged her. He smelled wonderful, like musky soap.

She pulled away, embarrassed. "Sorry." She wiped her moist cheeks.

"It's okay. How 'bout we sit down."

She nodded and took off her coat, dropping the pager on the floor.

"I'll get it," Josh said. H grabbed it then handed it back to her in exchange for her jacket.

Tali sat in the recliner and fingered the pager as Josh hung up her coat. Somehow holding the device made her feel like she was doing something.

She watched Josh take off his North Face jacket and add it to hers. He wore faded jeans and a black hoodie, slightly unzipped to reveal a white t-shirt. She had been wrong, he wasn't skinny. His mechanic's uniform hid a pretty decent body. Then she noticed the bandage on his left hand.

"What happened to your hand?"

He looked down as if he had forgotten all about it and blushed. "I was leaving tonight's town meeting," he said, picking up the pillow and placing it back on the bed, "when one of the reporters from Channel Six shoved his microphone in my face and asked me if I knew how to read."

"What?"

"I ignored him and started down the steps. His cameraman blocked me and said, 'Come on son, tell us what it's like to have never been in the real world.'

"I lost it. I knew they were yanking my chain, but I didn't care. In all the excitement, I wasn't the only one throwing punches. I cut my hand, probably on the guy's camera. By the time I got to my car, it was bleeding like crazy. I thought I'd better get it checked it out. Here I am, five stitches later."

"That's awful." But that was all she could say. She stared at the empty bed and turned the lifeless pager over and over in her hands.

Josh sat in the vacant recliner. "Look, I'm sure she's going to be okay. Dr. Anderson is one of the best surgeons in Illinois. Probably one of the best in the country."

The door opened. It was Quinn.

"What did the nurse say?" Quinn asked.

"My mom's in surgery," Tali answered. "I'm really worried."

"It's going to be okay. I totally believe that," Quinn said. "How about your dad? Did you get ahold of him?"

"Yeah, he's coming." She sighed.

"Good." Quinn peeled her black jacket off, exposing more layers of black. She sat on the edge of the bed. "Hey, what happened to your hand?" She asked Josh.

"A cameraman got in the way."

"Excellent. I hope he's in worse shape than you."

"He's fine. I can't say the same for his camera."

Quinn and Josh laughed. Tali managed a smile.

"A hell of a night, isn't it?" Quinn asked her. "Your mom and then Tom."

"Tom?" Josh asked.

"Tali's boyfriend. Or rather, he was Tali's boyfriend. She broke up with him."

"Oh," Josh hesitated slightly. "I'm sorry to hear that."

Was he really? Tali hoped not. "Actually, I'm relieved," she admitted. "We weren't good for each other."

"I didn't think so either," Quinn agreed.

"Do you have a boyfriend?" she asked Quinn.

"Not at the moment. I dated this guy a few times," Quinn pointed to Josh. "He took me to the Masquerade Ball." She noticed Tali's quizzical look. "It's similar to a high school prom."

"Homeschoolers have proms?"

"Sure. Homeschoolers get together for all sorts of things. Dances, sports, orchestras even."

"You'll have to come to a Carpe Diem rugby game," Josh added.

"You should, they're awesome. You're in the presence of the team's legendary captain," Quinn said, giving Josh a playful nudge.

Tali felt a twinge of jealousy. "Why did you stop dating?"

"Because it was too weird."

"Definitely," Josh agreed.

"Weird? Why?"

"We've been best friends since we were, what? Six?"

"That's about right."

"Our friends talked us into going out. It made sense at the time until the first kiss—"

Josh laughed.

"What?" Tali asked, wondering what could possibly be wrong with kissing Josh.

"I'm not sure how to put it." Quinn looked at Josh. "I felt like I was kissing Will."

"Your brother?"

"Yeah."

"And I felt like I'd just kissed my sister," Josh added.

"I don't think either one of us was surprised," Quinn said. "We've always treated each other like siblings."

"Still do," Josh said, winking at Quinn. He looked at Tali, his eyes sparkling. "So I've got some news about that car we fixed."

For the next half hour or so, Josh did his best to keep Tali's mind off of her mother's operation, but Tali couldn't concentrate on his words. She played constantly with the pager willing it to light up, vibrate, do something. When Denise opened the door, Tali jumped, sending the pager clattering to the floor.

"I'm sorry," Denise said, carrying in a bundle of linen. "I don't have any news. I just need to change the sheets."

Quinn slid off the bed, picked up the pager, and handed it back to Tali. Tali sunk back into her chair.

"It shouldn't be much longer," the nurse said. She pulled off the old sheets and quickly replaced them with fresh ones. As she finished changing the pillow case, she said, "The next time I drop in, I'm sure I'll have good news."

Tali tried her best to believe Denise. She started tapping the pager on her thigh, barely aware she was doing it.

"How about I tell you about the latest Fall Festival plans?" Quinn asked, leaning against the bed.

"Sure." She really didn't care, but she knew Quinn wanted to help pass the time. It worked. Discussing festival plans led to talking about Quinn and Josh's lives in Carpe Diem. Tali, in turn, told them about life as a public high school student.

"I'd like to do more, but homework gets in the way," she said.

"What would you like to do?" Josh asked.

"I wanted to go to with Mom to Chicago on Tuesday. Though I guess it was lucky I didn't." She shivered. "Dad thinks she went on one of her shopping trips. She actually went to a writing workshop. She's writing a book. I've been helping her with it. She wanted me to come along but Mrs. Schaefer, my social studies teacher, wouldn't give me an excused absence. Plus, my paper on entrepreneurship was due that day and she wouldn't extend the deadline. She said there were no exceptions, especially when she 'didn't see the relevance.'"

Josh laughed.

"What?" she asked.

"As an author, your mother is an entrepreneur," Quinn said. "I'm sure her workshop included stuff about marketing and selling her book. You'd think your teacher would want you to take advantage of that."

"I never thought of it like that. You're right. I would've learned more about it by being there instead of just reading about it on the internet."

"She's coming around to our way of thinking," Josh said.

"But in school it only counts if I do the assigned work."

"If you're learning things, why does that matter?" Quinn asked.

"It matters because I wouldn't be able to prove I learned it."

"Prove it? Why?"

"To get my diploma, go to college. Don't you want to go to college?"

"I'd like to go to a fine arts school," Quinn admitted, crossing her legs, "after I do some traveling."

"But if you don't have a high school diploma, how will you get into college?"

"The same way you will. Send a transcript, take the ACT, and submit a portfolio of my photography."

"Without homework, tests or grades, how will you have a transcript?"

"My mom and I will create it by describing my accomplishments in a transcript format. For example, a year learning Italian with Francesca equals a credit of a high school foreign language. As for grades, we'll talk about what I've done and assign our own grades."

"In my case," Josh said, "I'm already a college student. My courses at the Carpe Diem Community College will transfer so I won't need a high school transcript and I won't have to take any entrance exams." He checked his bandage and tucked a loose piece of gauze back into place. "A lot of unschoolers don't even go to college."

"Like Billy Turner," Quinn said.

"Right. He's been assistant editor of the Carpe Diem Daily News for two years and will take over when Old Man Hauser retires. He's also working on publishing an unschooling magazine."

"That's amazing, but doesn't he want to get a journalism degree?" Tali asked.

"He says it's a waste of time and money. Says he's already doing what he loves and is successful…"

His voice trailed off as the hospital room door swung open.

# 24

Leo excused himself from John and Patrick and hurried down the hall to catch Mary. He was halfway across the front lawn before he caught up with her.

"I retracted the article," he told her, slightly out of breath. "The retraction will be in *The Examiner* tomorrow morning, before your press conference."

"What does it say?"

"It says the article was intentionally full of inaccuracies." He ran his hand through his hair. "It also says the person who wrote the article, someone with access to my computer, had a bone to pick with Carpe Diem."

"Does it say I wrote it?"

"No. I thought you were responsible though I wasn't sure, so I didn't name you. It wasn't until I saw you at the town meeting that I knew you wrote the article and then I thought you were the major threat to this town. I wanted to warn the townspeople. I'm sorry."

"It doesn't matter," Mary said, walking the rest of the way to her car. "I planned on admitting I wrote the article anyway. I'll become the story, not the town." She started to open the car door.

Leo realized he admired her convictions. She was planning on sacrificing herself for the town. He wouldn't let her.

"You can't. Don't you see," he said. "If you admit it, the scandal will bring more negative attention to Carpe Diem. People will assume that if the mayor of the town thinks unschooling is a disaster, then maybe it is, maybe it should be outlawed."

She closed the car door. "If I say I made it all up—"

"No one would believe you. They'll think the town council forced you to hold the press conference and made you say how great unschooling is."

"If that's the case; it will be the perfect justification for getting Chris' anti-homeschooling legislation passed." Mary's eyes filled with tears. She lifted her glasses and angrily wiped them away. "But that's not my main problem. If I even appear at the press conference, Chris will know—" She stopped.

"Know what? What does Shaw have to do with this?"

"I can't tell you. Not yet." She reached for the door handle, her hand quivering. "What am I going to do?" she wondered out loud.

And then Leo realized something. Mary was willing to sacrifice herself for her community, John had left everything behind and Patrick had risked his life; all for what they believed in.

The only thing Leo had ever believed in was winning a Pulitzer Prize. Sure he cared about uncovering the truth, but that was for a story. The Pulitzer, the one great story, his career, suddenly it didn't seem like enough.

He put his hand on Mary's. "Wait here," he told her. He ran back inside the house then quickly returned with his cell phone.

She looked at him, her eyebrow raised.

He clicked on the phone, noticed it was nine thirty, and called Ted.

"Hey Leo. How are things in Carpe Diem?"

"Heating up, Ted. Are you still at the office?"

"Yeah, why?"

"I need you to pull my retraction."

Mary put her hand on his arm, shook her head and mouthed "No."

"First you want me to pull the article," Ted said. "Now you want me to pull the retraction. What the hell's going on?"

"I'll explain later."

"You told me you didn't write the Carpe Diem piece."

"I didn't."

"Then let's print the retraction. Christ Leo, you threatened to quit if I didn't."

"I can't clear the record, not yet. I'll explain later," he repeated. "Please Ted, pull the retraction."

Silence. He wondered if Ted's next words would be "You're fired."

"All right." The words were clipped. "You'd better know what the hell you're doing." The editor cleared his voice. "I'm sending Barnes to cover Carpe Diem."

"*What?*"

"You were there all day yesterday and this evening and what do I get? A retraction I can't print. Carpe Diem has been all over the news. This is front page stuff. Where's your article?"

"Look, if you send Barnes, he'll get the same story as everyone else. I've made connections here. I have the inside scoop. I promise you, this will be one hell of a story."

"I'm sending Barnes," Ted said.

"No!"

"Hear me out. Barnes will do the reporting. When you give me your 'inside scoop' as you call it, I'll print it, but only if it's as good a story as you claim. This is nonnegotiable."

Leo sighed. "All right. I suppose it makes sense."

Mary looked bewildered.

"I hope you know what you're doing."

"I do." He clicked off his phone.

"Why are you pulling the retraction? People will believe you wrote those things about Carpe Diem. They'll believe those horrible things are true."

"I've got it all figured out," Leo reassured her. "John and I will go to the press conference. You won't even have to be there. We'll say you've come down with the flu. Better yet, we'll say you couldn't attend due to an illness in the family. I'll explain I was overzealous. That I screwed up and didn't get my facts straight. Made up your quote and a few other things.

With my track record, people will believe it. I'll become the story. Take some of the heat away from Carpe Diem."

"You'd do that? What about your reputation? Won't you be jeopardizing your job at the paper?"

"I'll explain it all to my editor. It'll work out. It always does." He hoped he sounded more convincing than he felt.

"Do you think saying you screwed up will work?"

"It's better than having the mayor of Carpe Diem admit that she wrote the article. Can you imagine the press feeding frenzy?"

Mary shuddered. "Thank you so much for doing this." She put her hand on his chest. He leaned closer.

"I thought you had to find Quinn," Patrick called from the front door.

Mary stepped back. "I do. I have to talk to her."

"Once you do, will you tell me what all this is about?" Leo asked her.

"Yes. I owe you that." Mary got in her car and drove off.

Patrick and Leo walked back into the house. As they rejoined John at the kitchen table, Leo said, "Mary and I were discussing tomorrow's press conference. Mary won't be there, but you and I will be, John."

"Why?" Patrick asked.

John looked at Leo, nodded once and smiled.

# 25

When the hospital room door swung open, Tali expected Denise. It wasn't the nurse.

"I can't tell you how disappointed I am in you—" Christopher said, barging in. He stopped when he saw Quinn and Josh.

"Kids, could you give us some privacy?"

"*Dad!*"

"No, it's okay," Quinn said as her phone beeped. Glancing at it, she cringed. "My mom's looking for me."

"I have to get going too," Josh added.

"Thanks for staying with me."

"Anytime," Quinn said, grabbing her coat and then giving Tali a hug. "Be sure to call when you have some news."

She nodded.

Josh put on his coat, then touched her arm. "Can I see your phone?" He pressed a few buttons and handed it back. "There, now you've got my number. Call me too, okay?"

She nodded, smiling.

"See you back at the Inn," Quinn called over her shoulder.

"That was rude," she said to her father.

"Don't you lecture me, young lady. Do you realize the embarrassment you've caused me? I'm pushing through legislation to eradicate home-schooling while my daughter is telling reporters it's cool not to go to school."

She studied the toes of her boots. "Sorry, I didn't think—"

"No, you most certainly did not. I've handled the situation. I've told the press you're distraught over your mother's accident and that you don't want to deal with school right now. You're not to speak to any reporters ever again, do you understand me?"

She noticed a blue smudge on the toe of her left boot. She wondered what it was and how it got there.

"Do you understand me?"

She nodded.

"Good."

"Mom's in surgery," she mumbled.

"I know. Her nurse called me." He set his briefcase on the floor and took off his overcoat, revealing a charcoal grey suit, white shirt, and maroon tie. His work attire.

"Weren't you in Springfield? How did you get here so fast?"

Christopher put his coat and the briefcase in the closet. "I was already on my way when the hospital called." He checked his gold watch. "Almost ten. No wonder I'm hungry. I didn't stop for dinner. Let's go to the coffee shop. Hopefully it'll be open this late."

"I kinda wanted to stay here in case something happens."

"We'll tell them where we are. This hospital isn't very big."

Tali remembered the pager. She held it up. "They can page me," she said.

"Then let's go," Christopher said turning toward the door.

Tali followed him into the hallway. His dress shoes clicked on the tiled floor. Her Uggs shuffled. "I thought you were going to stay in Springfield. I'm glad you changed your mind to be with us."

"Uh huh," he said, pushing the down button next to the elevators. "Who was that girl?"

"Quinn Evans."

"She's from Carpe Diem?"

Tali nodded. "You've met her mom. She owns the Bradbury Inn."

"No, I didn't meet her. The concierge checked us in, remember?" They stepped into the elevator.

"And the boy, he's from here, too?"

She nodded. She didn't want to discuss Josh with her father.

"He's what, a junior?"

The elevator doors opened and they stepped into the quiet lobby.

"I guess he'd be a junior if he went to school. He doesn't." She snatched a glance to see her dad's reaction.

"Oh, yes, one of those aimless Carpe Diem teens roaming the streets."

"Josh isn't, he doesn't—"

"According to a terrific *Chicago Examiner* article, Carpe Diem teens run wild. That article is helping me pass my legislation."

"I've read the article, too." Tali dodged a nurse hurrying by. "It's full of lies."

"I don't think *The Examiner* would print—"

"Well, they did. The article says Quinn's mom doesn't believe unschooling works. She'd never say that."

"Quinn's mom? Oh yes, the mayor of Carpe Diem and the owner of the Bradbury Inn," he said, mockingly, pushing the café door open to the smell of fresh coffee. At this time of night, only a few doctors occupied the restaurant.

"The article quoted you, too. When did you talk to Leo?"

"Who?" Christopher asked, sitting at a table.

"Leo Townsend, the reporter," she answered, sitting opposite him.

"Townsend. Yes, he called me when I was driving back to Alanton. I told him about my anti-homeschooling legislation."

She placed the pager on the table and fingered her car charm. "I think the legislation is wrong."

"You know nothing about it."

"I haven't read your bill, but I think unschooling is pretty cool, especially in Carpe Diem."

"That's why I'm here," her father said, accepting a menu from the waitress.

"*What?*"

The waitress set Tali's menu down on the table and quickly departed.

Christopher glanced up. "I'm here to see you and your mother, of course, but I'm also curious about this town."

"Wait a minute. You said you were already on your way when you got the hospital's call. You weren't coming to see us. You came because of your job!"

"That's not entirely true—"

A muffled ring interrupted him. He dropped the menu on the table and fished in his pocket for his phone. "Yes, Adam. I've made it to Carpe Diem. There's been a development with Alexandra. I'll have to call you later." He hung up.

"There's been a development with Alexandra?" Tali shouted. "Is her emergency surgery getting in the way of your job?"

The doctors sitting nearby stared. She could feel her face reddening from embarrassment or anger or both.

"Don't be dramatic. If you'll calm down, I'll explain." He let her fume for a moment then went on, "Yes, I came back to find out more about Carpe Diem. As I said, finding such an excellent example of the ills of homeschooling will help move along my legislation. But I also came to see how you and your mother are doing."

She looked at the dark eyes she'd inherited, framed by smile lines. She always thought he was the best looking dad in the world. But now, with his perfectly trimmed blond hair and clean shaven face even at this time of night, he looked plastic to her, like a Ken doll.

Something vibrated on her leg. The shaking, glowing hospital pager.

They hurried out the coffee shop, down the hall to the elevators and then decided to take the stairs. They were out of breath by the time they got to the nurses' station.

"Oh good, you're here." Denise looked relieved. "The surgery went well."

Tali felt shaky with relief.

Denise continued, "Mrs. Shaw is in recovery. Dr. Anderson should be here any minute. Oh, here he is."

"We were able to stop the bleeding quickly," Dr. Anderson said. "And, as a result, there was very little cerebral edema. Swelling. Mrs. Shaw will be fine."

"That's great news, doctor," Christopher said.

"Can we see her?" Tali asked.

"She's in the post-operative recovery room. When the anesthesia wears off, we'll bring her back here." The doctor's pager beeped. "I need to go. I'll check back later when Mrs. Shaw is in her room."

"Thank you," Christopher said as the doctor left the room.

*Things are going to be okay*, Tali thought.

Later that night, Alexandra was moved back into her room.

"Hi Mom, how're you feeling?" Tali asked.

"A little nauseous." Alexandra looked past her. "Chris."

"I came as soon as I could. The operation was a success. You're going to be fine."

Alexandra managed a smile before falling asleep.

Tali thought about doing her homework, but knew nothing would sink in. Instead, she played games on her phone and lounged in her favorite recliner. Her father sat in the other one with his laptop open. She debated talking to him about homeschooling then decided she wasn't up to it. Bored with the games, she felt herself dozing off.

"I'm going to take you to the Inn," Christopher said, waking her up.

"No, I—" Tali began.

"I don't feel good," Alexandra said. "I think I'm going to be sick." She leaned over the side of the bed and threw up.

Tali hurried to her mother and touched her forehead. "You're hot." She stepped around the vomit, found the nurse's call button and pushed it so hard she was afraid she had broken it.

"I'm sorry, I didn't mean to," Alexandra's voice trailed off. "I'm having," she gasped, "trouble breathing."

A nurse peeked into the room. "Did you—"

Then she saw Alexandra struggling to breathe. "Page Dr. Anderson," she called over her shoulder to the nurses' station. She yanked an oxygen mask from the wall. "Would you two mind stepping into the hall?"

Christopher left. Tali couldn't move. Other nurses came into the room.

She watched her mother struggle. One of the nurses put her arm around Tali's shoulders and gently eased her out.

Tali trudged down the hall and joined her father in the waiting room. After what seemed like a lifetime, Dr. Anderson and the nurse appeared.

"There's been a complication," the doctor said, stating the obvious. "Mrs. Shaw has developed an OPSI, an overwhelming post-splenectomy infection. It's rare, but it does happen. We're treating her with antibiotics. Since we caught the infection immediately, her chances are very good, ninety percent."

His pager buzzed. "We'll keep a close eye on her to make sure the antibiotics are working." More buzzing. Looking at the pager he said, "I have to go. It will be best if you stayed in the waiting room. I'll be sure to apprise you of any changes in Mrs. Shaw's condition." He hurried away.

Tali turned to her dad. "Ninety percent?" Her voice shook. "Which means she has a ten percent chance of dying." She could feel the tears coming again.

Christopher didn't reply. Instead he turned to the nurse. "Can you get me my computer? I've left it in Alexandra's room."

Tali felt cold all over, realizing she hated him. She wandered over to the opposite end of the waiting room, as far away from her father as possible, sat on a small sofa, and pulled herself into a ball. Throughout the night, she stared at her tattered jeans or the TV until she couldn't keep her eyes open. The last thing she saw before dozing off was her father silently cursing his computer.

# 26

Quinn sat on the corner of her bed picking at the black polish on her thumbnail without taking her eyes off her mother.

"I shouldn't have told you to mind your own business," Mary said. "I'm sorry, sweetie." She started pacing in front of the bedroom window. "There's something I have to tell you, that I should have told you years ago." Her steps made the oaken floor boards creak.

"When I was twenty-one, I worked as a paralegal at a law office in Alanton. I wanted to make enough money to go on to law school, to follow in Grandpa's footsteps." She hesitated, sighed and continued, "I fell in love with one of the firm's junior partners. A married man."

Quinn's hand flew to her mouth.

"I know. It's horrible," Mary admitted, her voice quivering. "He was twenty-seven and had been married for five years. He and his wife were having problems. When he told me he planned on divorcing, I believed him." She stopped pacing. "But he never actually intended to leave her. I guess I knew that all along."

She sat down near the head of the bed.

"I definitely knew that what I was doing was wrong. I couldn't help it. Tall, handsome, and incredibly smart; I couldn't resist him. We spent hours debating the finer points of law. On Sunday afternoons, he'd make

KRISTIN A. OAKLEY

up tunes on his guitar while I painted. Every minute we were together, he made me feel beautiful. I loved him. Our affair lasted over a year."

She took one of Quinn's fidgeting hands in her own, cold hands. "I got pregnant."

Quinn pulled her hand away. She did the quick math in her head. "Me," she said in a small voice. "You were pregnant with me."

"Yes."

Quinn's stomach lurched. For a moment she thought she'd be sick. She pictured her dad, Troy Evans, giving her piggyback rides and whittling dolls out of sweet smelling pine wood. "Who is he?"

"I'll tell you in a minute."

*It's someone I know.* "Does Will know?"

"No, not yet. I'll tell him… later… after we've talked."

"What did the guy say when you told him you were pregnant?"

"He insisted I get an abortion."

Quinn rubbed her nauseous stomach, wishing she hadn't eaten Will's chicken parmigiana.

"I refused. I begged him to leave his wife. Things were bad between them and, at the time, they didn't have any children. He told me he couldn't leave his wife because it would ruin his political aspirations. Back then, infidelity killed a political career. We argued, yelled at each other." Mary paused. "He hit me."

"Oh God," Quinn mumbled, then clasped her hands over her mouth as she ran to the bathroom. She lifted the toilet seat lid just in time.

"Honey?" Mary asked, rushing into the bathroom. "I know it's a lot to take." She began to stroke Quinn's hair.

"Don't touch me," Quinn hissed.

Mary jerked her hand away as if it had been burned.

Quinn wiped her mouth with the back of her hand, flushed the toilet then washed up in the sink. Her head pounded. She tried to ignore it. Pushing past her mother, she sank down on the bed.

Mary sat on the edge of the chaise. She quietly continued, "I didn't know anything about abusive men, how they operated. It was only after I'd moved in with Grandma and Grandpa in Springfield that I realized his efforts to control me were signs of abuse."

"Control you?" Quinn asked.

"Yes. For instance, we had stopped going out to dinner. He insisted that we eat in my apartment. At first I thought he was worried his wife would catch us. But lawyers' hours are such that you grab dinner whenever you can and more often than not it's with your staff. No, he was jealous. You may not believe it, but I could turn heads."

Quinn looked at her mom's mousey brown hair, pale skin, thick brown glasses, sweatshirt, and holey jeans. She snorted. No one ever checked out her mother. People noticed her height but once they saw her boring features, they stopped looking.

"I'm not much to look at now," Mary said pushing her glasses up the bridge of her nose. "But back then…" Her voice trailed off.

"Soon he asked me what I did when we weren't together. I thought it was sweet. I thought he missed me, until he demanded specific details of where I'd been, who I'd been with. I tried to ignore his questions, to make light of them." She hesitated. "Then the managing partner of the firm hired a young male paralegal."

"Did you have sex with him too?" Quinn asked viciously.

"No," her mother answered in a small voice. "One morning while the paralegal and I discussed a case in the coffee room, my attorney walked by. The next day, the managing partner fired the paralegal for lying on his job application. But I had worked with him. I knew he wouldn't lie.

"I realized," Mary went on, "that the attorney's behavior explained his marital problems. I had met his wife, talked to her at a firm picnic. She was a nice lady, not at all like the nagging witch he described."

"How do you do it?" Quinn asked, resting her chin on her knee.

"Do what?"

"How do you meet someone, shake her hand and make polite small talk, knowing all along you'll fuck her husband that night?"

"*Quinn!*" Mary's face flushed. Her features hardened.

"How is that possible? What type of a person are you that you could do that?"

"I convinced myself they were on the verge of divorce," Mary answered, hugging herself. "I began to believe they weren't truly married. I know it's self-serving. It's the only way I can explain it. Now, having been married, I realize how horrible my actions were. But," her voice softened, "I have you."

Not to be appeased, Quinn said, "So you're pregnant and living with Grandma and Grandpa in Springfield. That must've been a kick. I can't imagine Grandpa would've been too keen on the idea."

"It was tough for both of them, but they loved me," Mary whispered.

Quinn felt no sympathy. "When did you marry the man who until a few minutes ago I thought was my dad?"

Her mother started to say something, stopped, then started again. "Your father," she emphasized these words, "built Grandma and Grand-pa's screened-in porch when I moved back in. We were high school sweethearts, we've told you that story a million times. We realized we still loved each other. When I told him I was pregnant, he didn't care. He wanted to marry me anyway. The Alanton lawyer—"

"You still haven't told me his name," she pointed out.

"I will. Anyway, he called me constantly. Apologized. He wanted me back. He claimed he had left his wife. I knew better. Jan, his secretary and my friend, kept me filled in.

"I insisted he stop harassing me. When he didn't, I threatened him. I told him if he didn't stop contacting me, I'd tell his wife about our affair. It did the trick, or so I thought. Not long after the calls stopped your dad—"

"*Which dad?*" Quinn asked, tears welling up in her eyes.

Mary came over and put her arm around her. "I'm sorry I didn't tell you sooner. I should have."

"Why didn't you?" she asked, tearing up.

"Oh honey, I didn't want you to know what kind of man fathered you."

"Why tell me now?"

"Because he's about to find us."

"What do you mean, find us?"

"We came to Carpe Diem to hide from him."

"What?"

"Let me tell the rest of the story. Then you'll understand."

Quinn rested her head on her mom's shoulder. She felt very tired.

"Troy and I got married. Soon after that, I had you. For the next few years, things were great. I worked at the state capitol in Springfield while I went to law school at night. Your dad founded his own construction business. I had Will. Then came your dad's accident…," Mary's voice trailed off.

"His death devastated me. I don't know what I would have done without Grandma and Grandpa." Her voice shook. "They insisted I finish my law degree. I did. After I graduated, I landed a job in the governor's office. I immersed myself in state politics and rediscovered unschooling which I knew about from Great Uncle John. When I mentioned it to your grandparents, Grandma confessed she had always wanted to homeschool me. But Grandpa wouldn't hear of it. He didn't want me raised like that hippy cousin of mine, Patrick."

"Grandpa never liked Patrick, did he?" Quinn said.

"Patrick can be hard to take," Mary admitted. "Eventually, Grandpa warmed up to the idea of homeschooling you.

"Homeschooling came up at work, too," Mary continued. "When I met our newly-elected governor, he made small talk, asked about you and Will and where you went to school. I told him I thought I might homeschool you. I was excited about it at the time, so I'm afraid he heard more about homeschooling than he wanted to.

"About a week later, I was called to the governor's office. When I walked in, the Alanton lawyer was sitting in a chair talking to the governor.

"He had been elected to the state Senate a few months before. I had always dreaded running into him. Still, I didn't expect to see him there. The governor introduced us and said the new senator had an interest in homeschooling and thought we should meet."

"Wait, wait, hold on a minute." Quinn felt dizzy. She was afraid she'd be sick again. "An Alanton lawyer who became a state senator? Is my biological father Christopher Shaw?"

"Yes."

"Whoa. This is too much. I don't think I can take any more."

Mary hugged her. "You should hear all of this."

"O-kay."

"After the meeting, Chris told me things were going well with his wife.

They had a child."

"*Oh my God! Tali's my sister?*"

"Yes, she is." After a minute, Mary continued. "Chris wanted to apologize for the way he treated me. He wanted to talk to me in private. I didn't want to be alone with him, but he seemed sincere. I suggested we go to my office. I thought I'd be safe enough there.

"He apologized for his behavior, for hitting me. He said he didn't know what had made him do that. He said he had never hit anyone before or since. I accepted his apology. I thought that would be the end of it."

Mary rubbed her hands together before setting them in her lap. "He asked me about my work on various bills. It was like old times. He steered the conversation to homeschooling, so we debated that, too. Then I made the mistake of mentioning I intended to unschool you."

"What happened?"

"He yelled that his child wouldn't be a socially deficient moron. I demanded he leave. He came around my desk, grabbed me around the throat and shoved me up against the wall."

Quinn gasped.

"I couldn't breathe. He hissed in my ear, 'if you insist on unschooling Quinn, I'll sue for custody. You'll never see your daughter again.' He threw me aside and left.

"I didn't know what to do. As a successful attorney and a well-liked senator, I was afraid he'd win a custody case. And I knew he'd hurt me. I left the office early and raced over to Grandma and Grandpa's."

"What did they say?"

"I'd never seen Grandpa so angry. He wanted to press battery charges. Then he said he'd fight the custody case all the way to the state Supreme Court if necessary. Grandma made him look at it practically. She made us both realize Chris would always be a threat, whether I homeschooled or not. She's the one who suggested we move to Carpe Diem."

"It doesn't make sense," Quinn said. "He'd just follow us here."

"That's what I thought. Plus, I didn't want to leave my job and Grandma and Grandpa. But the night I decided to stay and fight, they were killed in the car accident. After the funeral, Uncle John talked me into moving to Carpe Diem."

"Why didn't Senator Shaw look us up."

Mary gave her another hug. "I changed our last name."

"Dad's name wasn't Troy Evans?"

"No. Troy Conrad."

Quinn shook her head.

Her mother tweaked her blond roots. "I'm not a brunette either. I'm naturally blond, like you."

Quinn studied her mother. Blond hair would suit her pale skin. Now the comment about turning heads made sense. Her mom was a tall, leggy blond. "And the clunky glasses?"

"Don't need them." She took them off, set them aside and massaged the bridge of her nose. "Moving here did the trick. Knowing Uncle John wanted privacy, I never mentioned him or Carpe Diem to anyone. To Chris, I basically disappeared."

"Then why run for mayor?"

"I love this town, the people, and I love politics. Plus, Carpe Diem has stayed under the radar for thirty years. I thought we'd be safe. We were safe, until a few days ago. Governor Thomas' chief of staff, Raegan Colyer, discovered Carpe Diem. And me."

"You mean that woman who's got it in for homeschoolers?"

"Yes. She called, wanted me to tell a *Chicago Examiner* reporter Carpe Diem's a cesspool of ignorance. She demanded that a negative article be printed. She said if I couldn't convince the reporter, I'd better write it myself."

"Leo told the truth. You did write the article. Why? Just because Raegan Colyer asked?"

"She blackmailed me. She knew Chris. They worked together on the governor's commission to revise the school code. She said if I didn't write the article, she would tell Chris our whereabouts."

"But I'm seventeen. Don't I have a say when it comes to custody?"

"I'm not worried about that. I'm worried about our safety."

"Well, guess what. He's in town. I met him."

"*You met him?* When? Where?"

"At the hospital. Tali's mom isn't doing well so I stayed with Tali until he showed up."

"Did he know who you were?"

"No. He barely acknowledged me."

Her mom paced the room. "He's here for tomorrow's press conference."

"No, Mom, he's here because his wife's in emergency surgery."

"I don't think so. My guess is he was already on his way."

"How can you say that?"

"I know him. I know what he's capable of."

# 27

Someone was shaking Tali's shoulder.

"Wake up."

Tali rubbed her eyes. Where am I? She looked at the sunlight streaming in through a wall of windows. The hospital waiting room. It must be Saturday morning.

"Is Mom—"

"You mother's fever has dropped," the nurse hovering over her replied. "The antibiotics did the trick."

"That's great! Dad, did you hear?" She looked around the empty room.

"He isn't here. Left about a half hour ago. He said he had to go to a press conference."

Leo hid in the darkened anteroom with the door ajar, giving him a good view into the Town Hall's large conference room. His pulse quickened as the room filled with people. Cameramen set up their equipment, illuminating the podium. Chicago television stations jockeyed for position. CNN, MSNBC and FOX had muscled into the key places. The CNN cameraman filmed the perky blond reporter as she gave a pre-

KRISTIN A. OAKLEY

liminary report. Behind Blondie, other reporters filed in leaving room for only few citizens in the back. Leo spotted his co-worker, Barnes. Large, bald-headed and black as coal, he was an easy man to pick out from the crowd.

John Holden's back came into view as he approached the podium carrying a water bottle in his hand. He had dressed up for the occasion. His tan, cable-knit sweater wasn't patched or holey, and his dark brown dress pants were clean and pressed. Brown loafers replaced his Birkenstock sandals. Clean shaven and his wild Albert Einstein hair tamed, he looked like a kindly old professor.

John smiled in the direction of Leo's hiding place. Leo wiped beads of sweat from his forehead. He'd have to face the crowd soon and admit to something he didn't do.

John addressed the crowd, "Ladies and gentlemen of the press, citizens of Carpe Diem, thank you for attending this morning's press conference." His bearlike voice echoed around the room.

Conversations stopped and chairs scraped the wooden floor boards. One last person slid into the room; a tall, blond man Leo couldn't quite make out.

John began, "I'd like to apologize on behalf of Mayor Mary Evans who is unable to be here today due to an illness in the family. She asked me to take her place."

There were a few murmurs.

John continued, "I'll make a few short statements and then open it up to questions."

He moved to the side of the podium and leaned against it giving the scene a more relaxed, conversational air. "For those of you who don't know me, I'm John Holden. I founded this town thirty years ago."

"After teaching for fifteen years in the Chicago public school system, I became frustrated and disillusioned. My wife, God bless her, introduced me to homeschooling.

"Back in those days, homeschooling focused on the need, interest and ability of the child. It was pure child-led education. Today that philosophy is called 'unschooling' to differentiate it from other homeschooling techniques which copy public school methods in varying degrees." He took a gulp of water.

"My wife and I embraced the unschooling lifestyle for ourselves and for our son. We bought a few acres and built the farm you might have seen on your way into town. Several like-minded friends joined us. Together we built up Carpe Diem to what it is today.

"I'll admit Carpe Diem is unusual because it lacks a public school system, but it's not very unusual if you simply think of us as a community of homeschoolers." He took another drink of water, and then set the bottle on the podium. "Are there any questions?"

Shouts erupted.

John raised his hands, hushing the crowd. "One at a time, please."

"Your mayor said this town is a nightmare to govern," a reporter in the third row said. "She said, and I quote from an article in *The Chicago Examiner*, 'unschooling isn't successful'."

Before John could answer, another reporter added, "Rumor has it, your mayor actually wrote the article."

Leo took that as his cue. As he emerged from hiding, he shouted, "The rumor is false." He was relieved that the words came out as a strong declaration and not a frightened croak. "My name is on the article. I wrote it."

Camera flashes blinded him. Several people shouted from the back of the room. He fought the urge to bolt but managed to make his way over to John.

To look professional, Leo had borrowed a dark brown jacket and matching pants from Patrick, what Patrick called his "courtroom suit". Under that, he wore a crisp white shirt, unbuttoned at the collar. The suit was an inch too short in the sleeves and snug through the shoulders. Mary hadn't thought anyone would notice. In fact, she had predicted that once the female journalists spotted him they'd forget why they were there.

"Mr. Holden," he managed as he approached John. "I'm Leo Townsend, a reporter for *The Chicago Examiner*." He held out his hand.

John didn't shake it according to their plan, but he couldn't resist giving Leo a slight wink only Leo could see. "I know who the hell you are," John growled. "No one wants to hear what you've got to say."

Several of the reporters balked in protest. "I'd like to hear him," Billy Turner shouted from the back of the room, waving his notepad in the air.

John hesitated, giving Leo the opportunity to ease into his place at the podium. He cleared his throat and then started, "Good morning. I'm Leo Townsend, a reporter for *The Chicago Examiner*." He avoided looking at Barnes then spotted the blond man standing near the rear door. Senator Shaw.

Earlier that morning, Mary had called to warn him that the senator might make an appearance. Leo had thought this unlikely with Shaw's wife in critical condition. Yet, here he was. Unbelievable.

Leo pressed on, "At the risk of losing my job, I admit the article was a sloppy piece of work." He was surprised at how easy the words flowed.

John crossed his arms, taking an angry stance for the audience's benefit.

Leo sighed for full effect. "To be honest, being assigned to write about this town seemed like a demotion, a fluff piece. In fact, most journalists in this room are probably thinking the same thing."

Several chuckled.

"I hate to say it, but because of that I was lazy. I wrote most of the article off the top of my head. I threw in my own prejudices against homeschooling. I didn't bother with investigative reporting.

"In fact, for a majority of journalists, myself included, investigative reporting is becoming a thing of the past. Particularly in Carpe Diem."

This elicited outbursts of protest from almost every reporter in the room.

Leo wanted to back away, retreat into the anteroom, but didn't. "I've seen the trampled flowers and media litter," he shouted over their outbursts. "I've also watched the television reports and read the newspapers. Every story regurgitates what I wrote. I can't tell you how many times I heard the talking points 'hedonistic society' and 'Carpe Diem children run wild.' There haven't been any attempts to dig up new facts or to get the existing facts straight."

This quieted the crowd.

"Like many of you, I wanted to get the article written and then head back to Chicago, where the real news is. What I didn't anticipate was how the article would be received. The damage it could do to this town."

"But," a reporter Leo recognized as Jake Cannon from *The Chicagoan* called, "based on my *exhaustive investigation*," several people around him chuckled, "the kids do roam the streets."

"Kids in Carpe Diem use the streets like other human beings — to get from one place to the other."

"Leo, how can this be legal, just letting the kids do whatever they damn well please?" Barnes asked.

"The citizens of Carpe Diem follow the law. Their children attend school from the ages of seven to seventeen."

"You said there aren't any schools in this town," Barnes countered.

"Yes, but the townspeople believe 'school' is everywhere. They believe that you can learn from every situation, from everyone. So when a Carpe Diem child is counting pennies to pay for a pack of gum, he's learning mathematics. When children rehearse their parts for the town play, they're learning reading, public speaking, and literature."

"But the law also says they have to be taught the same basic subjects taught in public schools," Blondie threw out.

John tapped Leo on the shoulder. "May I?"

Leo stepped aside, thankful to be out of the spotlight.

"Our children are taught those subjects," John began. "I'll admit Carpe Diem children don't sit in desks filling out worksheets and learning testing skills for the next Illinois State Achievement Test. Instead, we provide a rich educational environment where learning language arts, social studies, math, fine arts, physical science, physical education, and health simply can't be avoided. I assure you we operate under the full extent of the law."

"The law is about to change," a voice bellowed from the back of the room. Everyone turned their heads to see Senator Shaw making his way to the front. Anticipating this, Leo had called Billy and his equally large friend Steve to ask for assistance. As the senator tried to maneuver around the teens, they seemed unable to move out of the way.

"The point," John bellowed, regaining the crowd's attention, "is that the people of this town haven't broken any laws. We lead full, productive lives. Our children are being educated. We ask you leave us alone to go about our business. Thank you," John started for the door but turned back to the crowd.

Leo had hoped to hurry the old man into the anteroom before Shaw made any kind of statement or a townsperson asked why Leo had accused the mayor of writing the article. But John had more to say. "Please come back next weekend for our annual Fall Festival. It's quite a crowd pleaser."

Several reporters laughed. One began to shout out a question, but the chatter and shuffling of chairs as people got to their feet drowned out his words.

"Close one," Leo said to John back in the anteroom. "I'll have to be sure to thank Billy and Steve for their help."

"I don't know if the press conference will be enough," John said in a worried tone. "I'm afraid those reporters will get ahold of Senator Shaw."

"Not if I can help it," a female voice said.

"Christ, Mary, you scared me. When did you get here?" Leo closed the door.

"I snuck in about the time you lied to the press," she answered touching him lightly on the arm.

"What are you going to do?" John asked her.

"I'm meeting Chris in my office," Mary answered. "I'll tell him if he doesn't leave Carpe Diem alone, I'll go straight to his wife. Tell her everything."

"No. I won't allow it," John said.

"Really, Uncle John, you won't *allow* it?"

"I have to agree with John," Leo said. "It's too dangerous. You don't know what Shaw might do." Before he had left for the press conference, Mary told him her history with Shaw. He knew the senator could become violent.

"It's too late. Right about the time Billy and Steve blocked Chris, I texted him. I told him I was the mayor and I wanted to meet with him immediately."

"Which explains the clothes," Leo said looking at Mary's black suit and matching pumps.

"My mayoral look," she admitted. "Anyway, I asked him to hold off talking to the press until he talked to me first. He agreed. He's probably in my office right this minute."

"Okay," Leo said, "But I have a better plan."

# 28

Mary stopped at the doorway of her office. Christopher Shaw occupied the same chair that Leo had sat in just a few days before. With Christopher's back to her, she could see his blond hair was thinning though his shoulders were still broad under his suit coat. She took a deep breath, straightened her jacket, and walked in.

"Senator Shaw," she said as she passed him. She didn't stop to shake his hand. Instead, she hurried to her swivel chair, putting the desk between them. She wished she had bought the massive oak desk Will had liked instead of this delicate Shaker.

"Mary," Chris said, rising from the chair.

"Please sit," she said, placing her black clutch purse on the desk. She snapped it open and pulled out a cloth to wipe her glasses.

Chris continued to stand, taking his time to look her over fully, then settled back into the chair. "So here you are," he said. "You've changed quite a bit since I last saw you." He smirked.

Mary put her thick glasses back on, fingered her mousy brown hair and debated telling him he was right, she no longer fell for creeps. She stared into his dark eyes which had once seduced her, but now mocked her. "You haven't changed a bit."

"I'm sure that's not true, but thanks anyway." He patted his already perfect hair in place.

It wasn't meant as a compliment, but she let it go. "I wanted to meet with you to ask you to reconsider the homeschool legislation. What it would do to this town, to homeschoolers all over the state—"

"You mean," he interrupted, "what it would do to you and my daughter. I want to see her."

"Chris, she's seventeen. She doesn't even know about you," she lied.

"It's time she found out. And you can forget about dropping the legislation. It will never happen."

"Why? Why do you care if people homeschool their children?"

"People, no, you homeschooling my daughter, yes. That, I care about. I told you years ago no child of mine was going to be homeschooled. She's probably an illiterate misfit moron."

Earlier that week, Quinn had sat in the Inn's dining room writing notes in the margins of Plato's *The Republic*.

"I'm going to ignore the moron comment," Mary replied and then added under her breath, "If she were a misfit moron it would be because of your malfunctioning genes, you arrogant jerk."

"What did you say?" he demanded.

"I said she's seventeen. It's over. She's been homeschooled. No law will ever change that."

"The new law will." He grinned, his perfectly white teeth gleaming. "It states that children have to attend school until the age of eighteen. I'll see to it that Quinn's sent to a nearby high school until Carpe Diem builds its own. And it's up to the school to decide which grade level to put her in. With her total lack of education, I'm sure they'll start her as a freshman. Sophomore, if she's lucky."

"Don't do this."

He stood up and leaned across the desk. Mary wanted to push her chair away, but didn't.

"I don't give a shit about homeschooling," he said. "In fact, I don't give a shit about education at all. For years I tried to track you down. Tell you how much I love you. How much I wanted us to be a family."

Her stomach flipped. This guy was delusional.

"But I couldn't leave my wife and her money. And I had Natalia to think about. So I gave up trying to find you. Yet I knew if I worked on anti-homeschooling legislation, and if you were still in Illinois, that someday I'd flush you out. You were that passionate about it. It worked."

"Okay, then drop the legislation."

"Too late. It's a done deal. Besides, getting the legislation passed will be icing on the cake. It'll do wonders for my career."

"You'd ruin the lives of tens of thousands, maybe hundreds of thousands of homeschoolers, YOUR constituents, for your career? You're sick."

He grabbed her wrist. His touch had once electrified her. Now it disgusted her. "I didn't realize how much I loved you until you left me. Now that I see you, I realize we can make this work."

She tried to yank free. His hand tightened. "What about your wife and her money? Tali?"

"Natalia's a child. She'll come around. And Alexandra won't be with us for much longer."

"What do you mean?"

"Her medical prognosis doesn't look good." His fingers dug into her skin. Her wrist throbbed, her hand tingled.

"Did you sabotage Patrick's motorcycle?" Mary managed through the pain.

He abruptly let go of her wrist. She shook out her hand while he paced the little room. "Did you know the son of a bitch blackmailed me?"

She laughed, but knew it was true. Patrick had confessed it.

Chris stopped. "I'm not making it up. He came to my office. Demanded I withdraw my 'Education for All Bill'. When I refused, he told me he knew I'd fathered Quinn. Said he would go directly to my wife with that juicy bit of news if I didn't do what he asked."

"You're lying."

He shook his head. "I told Patrick I'd think about it. A few days later, he called me, said he'd come to his senses and wanted to discuss the legislation."

Mary knew this was a lie. Patrick said Chris set up this second meeting.

"I thought it might be a good opportunity to end this once and for all," he said.

"And?"

"Patrick ranted about educational freedom. He threatened me. I couldn't get through to the guy."

"You don't have to worry about Patrick anymore, do you? He's dead."

"That's right."

"*You bastard!*"

Chris reached across the desk, grabbed the back of her neck and pulled her so close that she feared he would kiss her. "Seems to me the only bastard around here is your daughter," he hissed, bits of spittle hit her face. His other hand enclosed her throat.

She clawed at his hands and felt her nails cut into his skin. Chris didn't flinch. He pulled her up by her neck, lifting her out of the desk chair. She couldn't breathe. She couldn't scream. The room darkened. *She was going to pass out. Die. He was going to win. What would he do to Quinn? Quinn.*

Mary kicked back as hard as she could. The chair toppled against the wall.

Leo charged into the room and threw himself at Chris, forcing Chris to drop Mary. Coughing, she dove out of the way as the men struggled against the desk. Chris roared and swung his fists wildly. Leo's accurate punches hit Chris' temple, then his jaw and finally his stomach. Chris crumpled to the floor, moaning.

Leo grabbed Mary's purse off the desk, knelt next to Chris and waved a tiny digital recorder in front of his eyes. "Mary recorded your entire conversation. This will make one hell of a nice article," Leo said.

Chris moaned again and then passed out.

Leo hugged Mary. "Are you okay?"

She rubbed her neck. "Yes," she croaked.

"When I saw his hands around your beautiful throat—"

She grabbed his face and kissed him.


Leo shut off the recorder and looked across the police station's conference room table at Chief Billiot. "There you go, he confessed. The district attorney has grounds to charge him with attempted murder."

The Chief took the recorder, replayed it and shook his head. "His involvement is only implied. He doesn't actually say he sabotaged Patrick's bike."

Leo and Mary protested, but Chief Billiot raised his hand. "However, this definitely helps the case. It shows motive and opportunity." He sat back in the swivel chair. "When we discovered Patrick Holden's bike had been sabotaged, our investigation led us to the last person Patrick saw before the accident, Senator Shaw. Shaw managed to be conveniently unavailable when the state troopers stopped by. Luckily, his secretary was helpful. She gave them full access to his office."

"And?" Leo asked.

"They found traces of nitric acid on his desk." The chief smiled. "I went to his cell and glanced at his fingers. Several were yellow and peeling. With that evidence and your tape, Senator Shaw might be spending the next thirty years behind bars."

# 29

"I'm sorry. Not even her daughter can see her. Please stop calling."
Denise slammed down the hospital phone.

"What was that about?" Tali asked as she approached the nurses' station.

"The press wants to talk to your mother. They won't take 'no' for an answer. It's the fourth time they've called in ten minutes."

"Why?"

"They mentioned something about your father before I cut them off. I guess they've discovered she's a state senator's wife. Whatever it is, they're not getting in to see her."

"Are you sure I can't see her?" Tali asked, catching a whiff of Denise's soap and shampoo. Tightening her greasy ponytail, she knew she didn't smell half as good.

"Yes. I'm sorry. The doctor thinks it's best to hold off on visitors for a few hours."

Tali sighed.

"I know it's hard not seeing her, but she's been through a lot. She needs to rest."

Tali nodded and yawned.

"Speaking of which," Denise said, "You look like you could use some sleep. You're staying at the Bradbury Inn, right?"

She nodded again.

"Go to the Inn, get some rest, and grab a bite to eat. When you come back, I'm sure you'll be able to see her."

Tali's stomach growled in response. It had been three hours since the nurse said her mom was going to be okay and there was still no word from her dad. She didn't want to spend one more minute in the waiting room. But she couldn't leave the hospital until she heard from her father.

"I can't leave. I'm waiting for my dad," she said to Denise. She checked her phone for the hundredth time. 11:52 a.m. The press conference must be over. "He's not returning my calls."

"Maybe he's on his way," the nurse suggested.

Tali nodded and trudged back to the waiting room. Sticking her hand in her back pocket, she discovered a crumpled ten dollar bill. Lunch money. She texted Quinn to see if she'd join her.

"Tali!"

She turned around.

"Who the hell do you think you are breaking up with me?" Tom yelled as he stepped off the elevator. Seconds later, he was in her face.

She backed against the waiting room wall. "Tom, calm down."

"Fuck that shit."

"What are you doing here? Isn't there a football game tonight?"

"Coach suspended me for trashing the visiting team's locker room. It's bullshit." He slapped the wall above her head making her jump. Then he pointed a beefy finger at her.

"Nobody dumps Tom Olson. Not even trash like you."

"It wasn't working out," Tali shot back, surprised at the strength in her voice. "You only went out with me so you could cheat off my test papers."

"You got that right," he said, picking a zit on his chin. "But I decide when it's over," he pointed to his chest, "not you." He stepped closer. His breath stank of stale peppermint gum and, she was pretty sure, alcohol. "What's with the ponytail?" Before she could answer him, he yanked Josh's o-ring out of her hair. Blond strands came with it.

"*Ow!*" She rubbed the back of her stinging head. "Give it back."

"What the hell is this?" He laughed as he stretched it until it broke. "Oops." He grabbed the front of her sweatshirt and crammed the rubber pieces in then pulled her to within inches of his face, lifting her so that she stood on her toes.

"I'm gonna make you sorry. No one dumps Tom Olson, you sorry excuse for a girl."

"Hey! Neanderthal!" Quinn shouted from behind Tom.

Tom tossed Tali against the wall then whirled around with his right hand in a fist.

"You're kidding, right?" Josh hissed as he came to within inches of Tom.

The two glared at each other. Tom puffed up to full size. His Alanton Tigers football jersey stretched tightly across his broad back. Josh, his open jacket exposing a Carpe Diem rugby shirt underneath, remained calm and looked slightly amused.

"This is a private conversation between me and my girl," Tom hissed.

"I'm not your girl. Not anymore." Tali moved next to Quinn, who put her arm around her.

"You heard her. It's time you left." Josh moved to one side, opening a path for Tom.

Tom clenched and unclenched his fists without taking his eyes off Josh. Although the two were the same height, the linebacker outweighed the mechanic by a good forty pounds. Still, there must have been something about Josh that made Tom back down or, Tali guessed, Tom really was a coward.

"You're not worth my time," Tom spat. He gave her a hate-filled glare then shouldered Josh on his way to the elevator. Before the elevator doors closed he shouted, "Bitch!"

"Thank God you guys showed up," Tali said, giving Quinn a hug, the older girl's spiky black hair tickling her cheek. The broken o-ring fell to the floor. Josh picked it up and shoved the pieces into his jeans pocket.

"We were on our way over to see if you wanted to grab lunch when I got your text," Quinn said.

"You came just in time." Tali shivered.

"Forget about Tom. It's over. Let's concentrate on more important things. Like your mom, is she going to be all right?" Quinn asked.

Tali nodded. "The antibiotics worked."

"Have you been in to see her?" Josh asked.

"No. She needs to rest. Denise, the nurse, suggested I get some sleep, too." Embarrassed to be so skuzzy, she tucked a limp strand of hair behind her ear. "I could use a shower."

"We'll take you to the Inn," Josh suggested.

"I have to wait here for Dad. I haven't been able to get ahold of him."

"There's something we need to tell you about your dad," Quinn said.

"What? Where he is? Is he okay?"

"He's fine."

A young family walked past them into the waiting room. Their four small children squealed and took off for the playhouse. The parents took a seat nearby.

"It would be better if we told you about it in private. Back at the Inn."

"Tali, you look exhausted. Let's go," Josh suggested.

Too tired to argue, she agreed.


After a hot shower, change of clothes and a heaping portion of Will's pasta, Tali felt better. "So," she said to Quinn and Josh, who had joined her for lunch in her room, "Where's Dad? What's going on?"

"Hang on," Quinn said. "Mom!"

Mary and Leo entered the room.

"Why are you here?" Tali asked Leo and then said to the mayor, "I'm surprised you'd want him around after he wrote that horrible article."

"Actually, I wrote it," Mary admitted.

"*What? Why?*"

"We have a lot to tell you," Mary began, sitting in the rocker. Her hands fidgeted with the brightly colored scarf around her neck. "I'm afraid you're not going to like me very much once you hear what I have to say."

"Why wouldn't I like you?" Tali asked as she sat on the bed. And then, for some reason, that faded slip of paper with the words, *Chris and Mary*

*Tomlinson* came to mind. Something clicked. "Wait. Is your maiden name Tomlinson?"

"Yes it is. How did you know?"

"You and my dad…you're… you're having an affair," she said through gritted teeth.

"*Had* an affair, a long time ago," Mary said. "Before you were born."

"But my parents were married?"

"Yes."

She wanted to slap Mary. No punch her, beat her.

Mary continued, "I won't make any excuses. It was wrong. I'm sorry about what I did." She paused. "Though something good did come out of it."

"*Really*. Enlighten me," Tali spat.

"I had Quinn."

"You—" she turned to Quinn. "You're my half sister?"

"Yes."

Staring into Quinn's dark eyes, she was surprised she hadn't noticed the resemblance before. She supposed the dyed black hair had thrown her off.

"Your father," Mary went on, "looked for me, for us, for years. I eluded him until now. When he came to the press conference, I decided to meet with him. I wanted to convince him to drop his anti-homeschooling legislation. We argued and I discovered that your father—" the mayor's voice trailed off.

"That my father what?" she asked.

"He sabotaged Patrick Holden's bike," Leo said.

Tali recalled her father's yellowed fingers. She didn't want to believe it, but a part of her suspected all along that he was involved.

"He confessed on tape," Leo said.

"Why would he do that?"

"He agreed to meet me in my office after the press conference," Mary said. "When he did, I recorded our conversation."

Tali shook her head. "This doesn't make sense. Why would he want to hurt Mr. Holden?"

"Patrick wanted your dad to drop his anti-homeschooling legislation,"

Leo said. "Christopher refused. Patrick threatened to tell your mother about Christopher's affair with Mary. I suppose Christopher thought a motorcycle accident was a good way to eliminate the problem."

"But Mom already knew about the affair," Tali said in a small voice.

"She did?" Mary asked.

She nodded. "A couple of days ago, I found a faded slip of paper with the names *Chris and Mary Tomlinson* and a question mark in her purse. I assumed they were people Mom met at her writer's workshop." At that moment, Tali wanted more than anything to be with her mom.

"There's more," Leo said. "Your father's been arrested. He's in the Carpe Diem jail. He's facing one count of attempted murder for sabotaging Patrick's bike. And he's facing a charge of causing great bodily harm to your mother."

Before Tali could process this, Mary pressed on, "He's already been charged with battery. He attacked me, in my office," she said, taking off her cotton scarf. Her neck was covered in nasty red marks.

Tali pictured her mother's favorite crimson and gold scarf. The room spun. She slid to the floor.

Quinn helped her back onto the bed, whispering, "It'll be okay."


"I've given Barnes most of the details he needs for a front page story," Leo said, speaking into his Bluetooth headset to Ted.

Lounging in one of the Inn's high back chairs, he held a much needed beer in one hand and Mary's hand in the other. Mary rested in the companion seat with her head back and her eyes closed. The fake eyeglasses were gone. Her half-empty glass of red wine sat on the table between them.

"Most?" Ted asked.

"There are some details I'm working out. It'll take a few days." He hesitated, took a sip of beer. "I'd like to stay through the Carpe Diem Fall Festival next weekend. Thoroughly research this town. Make sure I get my facts straight."

"Did you or did you not write the original article?" Ted sounded exasperated.

"I did not write it."

"You lied during the press conference?'

"Yes. I can't explain my reasons right now. It'll all come out in the piece I'll write after the festival. Please bear with me. I promise I'll have one hell of a story for you when this whole thing is over."

"Well, you did nail the senator. I'll give you that. I can't believe you'd let Barnes run with the story."

"Barnes is a great reporter. He can cover the preliminaries."

"Preliminaries? You're being mysterious," Ted said. Leo pictured the editor in some profound t-shirt, crossing his scarred arms.

"Sorry, I don't mean to be." Leo had convinced Chief Billiot to withhold the information about Mary's involvement from the press and he certainly wasn't about to leak that information. "I don't want to say too much in case my assumptions are wrong."

"All right," the editor said. "I'll go with your instincts on this one, but if you wait too long, it'll be old news. No one will care."

"They'll care all right. I'll be in touch." He switched off the phone. No protestations, no threats to fire him? He smiled and swallowed the last of his beer.

Quinn entered the room, greeted an elderly couple enjoying mid-afternoon cookies and tea, and then walked over to Leo and Mary.

"How's Tali doing?" Leo asked her.

"She's okay. Josh brought her a checkered flag scrunchie which made her smile. It looked really cute in her hair."

"Where on earth did he find something like that?" Mary asked.

"Charlotte's Fair Trade Store."

"Really?" Leo asked.

"Apparently it was made in some remote village in Ethiopia." Quinn leaned against the side of her mother's chair. "Anyway, after Josh left, Tali and I talked for a long time. She had a lot of questions. Knowing that I just found out made her feel better. We sat together for a long time until she dozed off."

"Hopefully she'll sleep for awhile," Mary said.

Quinn pulled up a chair from the nearest dining room table. "She mentioned that she had noticed that her father's fingers were yellowed. She didn't mean to, it just slipped out. I think she felt she had betrayed him."

"You can reassure her she hasn't. Chief Billiot already knows about Shaw's yellowed fingers. He saw the stains," Leo said. "It was the last bit of evidence the police needed."

"Okay, I'll tell her." Quinn turned to her mother. "This changes everything for Tali, doesn't it Mom?"

"I'd say. Do you think she'd want to stay with us, at least until her mother's released from the hospital?"

"I think she'd like that. She's upset with you though most of her anger is directed at her father. She's also afraid to tell her mom about her dad being arrested."

"Her mother's going to find out sooner or later. It's all over the news. Reporters will want to talk to her. Maybe it would help Tali if you were with her when she told her mother."

"If she wants me to be there, sure."

"You're a good kid," Leo said.

"Thanks." Quinn turned to leave.

"Quinn, honey," Mary called out. "I love you."

"I know, Mom," Quinn hesitated. "I love you, too."

"It's going to be okay, isn't it?" Mary asked Leo.

He studied her face. "Yes, everything's going to be fine." He hoped he sounded convincing. But he couldn't get Raegan Colyer off his mind.

# 30

Early Sunday morning, Leo felt restless. He wanted to go for a run, something he hadn't done in almost a year. But he had only a pair of jeans and loafers with him in his room at the Inn. Then he remembered the beat up duffle bag in the trunk of his Mustang.

Sure enough, it contained an old sweatshirt, sweatpants, and pair of running shoes. He took the bag back to his room and changed.

As he ran down the driveway, fallen leaves crunched under his feet. He couldn't believe how stiff he was. Still, it was great to be moving again. He exhaled steamy puffs of air into the cold October morning and felt invigorated. He'd have to dust off his good running shoes when he got back to Chicago.

Turning the corner onto Main Street, he thought about Raegan Colyer. Something gnawed at him. He pictured her, several years ago, uncharacteristically talkative after a night of champagne and a toss in bed. He remembered her bragging to him about a scheme to make millions. He'd chalked it up to too much alcohol. Now he wondered.

Slowing to a walk, he pulled out his phone and called Al Kennedy, an educational lobbyist and his former University of Chicago roommate. "Hey Al, it's Leo," he huffed. "I'm curious about something. You got a moment?"

"Sure, what's up? You sound out of breath."

"I've been running," he held on to the stitch in his side. "And it's got me thinking."

"Running always did."

"What I'm wondering about is how could a well-connected political insider with an interest in education make millions of dollars?"

"There are a number of ways — illegal and legal. Like your friend Smithson, embezzling teacher union dues. But there's lots of legit money in textbooks."

"What about homeschooling?"

"There are homeschooling curricula, educational supplies, teaching support, tutoring, legal advice—"

"Legal advice?"

"In some parts of the country, parents of homeschooled kids who aren't meeting strict state educational standards can be hauled into court. There are cases of children being taken from parents who refused to meet those standards and refused to send their children to public school."

"Seriously?"

"Oh yeah. There are at least two national legal organizations that represent homeschoolers," Al said. "These organizations aren't very active in Illinois because the law is favorable to homeschooling. Illinois homeschoolers typically don't need legal advice."

"If the Illinois law were to change?"

"Those organizations would make a shit load of money."

Leo stopped walking. "Can you do me a favor?"

"Anything."

"Pull a few strings and find out who's on the board of those organizations and see if there are any ties to the governor's office."

"I'll make a few calls."

"And Al, I need this as soon as possible."

"Right."

Leo ran back to the Inn. He showered, threw on a white button-down shirt and jeans and padded barefoot across the hardwood floor to the small desk by the bedroom window. He pulled his computer out of its case, his fingers itching to use it. He couldn't remember the last time he'd gone a few hours, let alone days, without touching his laptop. He plugged the cord in, set the machine on the desk, and flipped the switch. Nothing. Damn. So much for that technician at *The Examiner*.

He slipped on his socks and loafers, packed up the computer, grabbed his bomber jacket from the hook on the door, and headed downstairs. After breakfast, he'd try to find a repair shop.

Stepping into the lobby, he looked for Mary. The registration desk was vacant and so was her office. He went into the dining room and grabbed a table by the fire.

"Good morning, Leo," Will said, pouring him a glass of fresh squeezed orange juice.

"Hey, Will. How are you holding up?"

Mary had mentioned Will took the news about Shaw remarkably well. He didn't seem surprised to find out his sister had a different father. Instead, standing next to Quinn, whose black leggings accentuated her long skinny legs while his baggy blue jeans couldn't hide his short, bulky ones, he had said, "I always wondered if we came from different stock," then had hugged his sister.

"I'm fine considering my reality has shifted a bit," Will answered. "Going to do some writing today?" He pointed to the black case leaning against Leo's chair.

"Not with this thing," Leo said. "It's shot."

"Oh?"

"The damned thing won't turn on. Completely blank."

Will put down the pitcher of orange juice. "Can I take a look?"

Leo pulled the case up onto the table, pushed his juice glass aside, and took the machine out. "Have at it."

Quinn entered from the kitchen carrying a bowl of fresh fruit. "No, don't let him on your computer. We'll never get him back in the kitchen."

"A computer whiz, is he?" Leo asked.

"An obsessive geek is more like it," Quinn answered. "Have you seen his room? He's got parts everywhere. He's rebuilt three or four computers. He's even designed and built one from scratch."

Leo laughed. "And I thought you were just a lowly cook."

"Very funny," Will said, although his attention was on the blank screen.

He grabbed a pocket knife from his back pocket, flipped up the screwdriver, and started to open the computer.

"Are you sure you know what you're doing?"

Will didn't answer.

"Don't worry, he knows," Quinn said over her shoulder as she took the fruit to the buffet table. "Even though he's never read a manual."

"She's kidding, right?"

"Nope," Will answered. "I'm not the best reader in the world."

"Then how did you learn to build computers?"

"By working on them." Will popped out a circuit.

Leo was fascinated. He knew a bit about software but never paid much attention to the hardware. Several questions came to mind but Will was intent on fixing the machine so he kept quiet. Instead he helped himself to a hearty bacon and egg breakfast from the buffet table. As Leo chewed on the last piece of bacon, Will showed him the screen. A sparkling night photo of Michigan Avenue winked back at him.

"That's amazing! You got it to work."

"Really not that amazing."

"You shouldn't be so humble. Our technician at *The Examiner* couldn't figure it out."

Will closed his knife and shoved it in his pocket. "I should know what's wrong with it considering I broke it in the first place."

"*What?*"

"Well, yeah." Will avoided Leo's gaze. "A few days ago, Mom brought me your laptop and told me you were going to send a nasty e-mail to your editor about Carpe Diem. It made me mad. When she asked me to disable it temporarily, I didn't hesitate."

"You sabotaged my computer?"

"I did. I'm really sorry. It works now." Will attempted a grin.

Leo knew he should be upset, but the kid had thought he was helping out his mom and the town. He might have to have a few words with Mary, though. He gazed at the picture of the Magnificent Mile. The image faded.

"Looks like it still needs some work." He showed the screen to Will.

Will made some adjustments. "This isn't something I did. This computer has other issues. It's kind of old. You should probably get a new one."

"So I've been told. But it means a lot to me."

A burst of laughter rang out from the lobby as a large group of women in purple hats entered the dining room.

"I can mess with it if you'd like," Will suggested. "After the breakfast crowd."

"Great," Leo said. "If there's anything you can do to fix it, I'd really appreciate it."

"No problem. It'll be fun. A challenge. It might take me a while though."

"That's fine. I've got my chisel and stone tablet." Leo touched his coat pocket. "I'll still be able to get some work done." He packed up the computer then handed it to Will. "I'll fill up with your most excellent coffee, write in my favorite chair over there by the window and then check out the town. I'll stop back later this afternoon to see how you're doing."

"Sounds good," Will said.

"And Will, no funny stuff this time."

"I promise." Will smiled then took the case with him into the kitchen.

Leo filled his coffee mug and walked over to the window where he settled into a wide armchair. For a few moments he watched the purple-hatted ladies helping themselves to large quantities of eggs and cinnamon rolls. Then he jotted notes about the past few days' events.

Three cups of coffee later, he had recorded all the necessary information and made a list of unschooling questions. He decided to start the day with Peyton Blaney, Carpe Diem's librarian, to gather historical information about homeschooling. Then he would head over to John's photography studio.

He also wanted more evidence of unschooling in action. He was wondering how to go about getting it when Quinn walked by.

"Quinn?" he asked. "Do you have a minute?"

"Sure."

"If I want evidence of unschooling as it's actually happening, how do I go about finding it?"

"Unschooling is life. Any activities kids are doing can be considered unschooling."

"I get that, but I'm looking for educational things."

Quinn smiled. "No, you don't get it. Why label activities as educational or non-educational? It's like some activities are more important than others."

"Don't you think those activities that lead to learning and growth are more important?"

"Importance is subjective. Will just fooled around with your laptop. Waste of time or unschooling? Maybe it's a matter of semantics.

"Anyway, if you're looking for unschooling in action, your best bet is the town square. People are setting up the festival booths." Her mouth curled into a sly grin. "You'll probably find lots of evidence of learning and growth there. I could come with you and take some pictures."

"Good idea. I might need you as a bodyguard. I don't think I'm very popular after yesterday's press conference."

"Wrong again. People know you came to Mom's rescue and helped her stop Senator Shaw."

"They also think I wrote that damned article."

"We're used to people making wrong assumptions about us. And you admitted it was a sloppy piece of work which couldn't have been great for your career. I think you'll find we can be pretty forgiving. Also, you're curious about Carpe Diem and unschooling — our favorite topics." She glanced around the deserted dining room. "I could go with you now since breakfast is over."

"Sounds good."


"I didn't see your mom this morning," Leo mentioned to Quinn as he drove his Mustang down the Inn's driveway.

"I haven't seen her either, but that's not unusual. On Sundays she drives out to the farm to buy produce for the week and to the Farmers Market in Hadley for anything else the kitchen might need. Will and I serve breakfast while she's away."

A few moments later, Leo parked the Mustang in front of Dan and

Joan's Diner. Across the street, the town square was bustling. The journalists, reporters, and cameramen were gone. Small groups of townspeople were gathered in what looked like assigned locations throughout the park. Laughter, hammering, and distant music mingled with the gentle October breeze.

"I'm surprised there are so many people here," he said to Quinn as she grabbed her camera from the back seat.

"Why?"

"Well, it's Sunday morning. I assumed most of the townspeople would be in church. Aren't most homeschoolers Christian fundamentalists?"

"You can't really lump homeschoolers into one group or category," Quinn said. "We come from all faiths, though the Christians hold a slight majority. But unschoolers tend not to be Christian."

"Why not?"

"Most fundamental Christian homeschoolers argue that the Bible gives parents the authority to control their children's education. Unschoolers leave the control up to the kids, so Christian unschoolers are rare. We only have a few of them in Carpe Diem."

Together they crossed Main Street to where a pick-up truck with a trailer was parked alongside the curb. Three men opened the back of the trailer, letting out the smell of freshly cut lumber. Quinn introduced them as Colin and Dale McCarthy and Dean Smith. They were polite but restrained. That was better than Leo had expected.

"Can I give you a hand?" Leo asked.

They exchanged glances. Colin shrugged.

As they pulled out large wooden panels, Dean explained, "These are for a few festival booths that are structured more like permanent buildings. The concession stands and Quinn's photography booth are among those. We'll haul the panels to the individual sites and put them together. Colin has the map. The rest of the booths, most of those at the festival, are constructed of PVC pipes draped with canvas. We're putting those up today, too."

Colin pulled a map out of his back pocket. "Let's start with the kids' food booth which we'll set up under that red maple." He pointed at a nearby tree.

KRISTIN A. OAKLEY

As they unloaded, other people came to their assistance. Before long the trailer was empty.

"Thanks for your help," Dean said to Leo as he shook his hand.

"Not a problem."

"Why don't we go over to the photography booth and help put that together?" Quinn suggested to Leo. "John should be coming soon. You can pick his brain about unschooling."

While they walked, Quinn photographed a mother showing her daughter how to use a handsaw and three young children mixing paint to get the right shade of green.

When Quinn took several pictures of a father demonstrating the use of a carpenter's triangle to his son, Leo said, "Okay, so you're getting some great evidence of learning, but what we're seeing isn't very different from what school kids learn on the weekends."

"True," she admitted. "But this happens all the time, not just on the weekends."

As they approached the photography booth, Quinn introduced Leo to Jimmy Edwards' parents and uncle. They had been busy; the darkroom was already taking shape. Jimmy sat cross-legged in a director's chair with Puck in his lap and his head in a paperback book. He scowled.

"Whacha readin'?" Leo asked the boy and winked at Stan Edwards. Jimmy was only six. He couldn't really be reading the book.

Jimmy showed him the cover. "Cuz of Winn-Dixie," he said. "It's my favorite book. I'm reading it again."

This surprised Leo. "If it's your favorite book why are you frowning?"

The boy patted his cast. "Doctor says I can't use the saw to shave off the boards this year cuz of my arm."

"I'm sorry to hear that," he replied.

Leo walked over to Stan. "How did you teach Jimmy to read at such a young age?"

Stan finished pounding in a nail before answering. "We didn't. We surround him with good reading materials and we're avid readers. My wife calls us bookaholics. We have a pretty decent library at home, books everywhere. And we read to Jimmy at bedtime and throughout the day, whenever he asks for a story. He picked it up naturally at a young age."

Leo held up the other end of the board for Stan to nail into place. "He must be unusually bright," he said.

"Being his dad, I'd like to agree with you," Stan chuckled. "But honestly, reading books at his age is not unusual in Carpe Diem. It probably wouldn't be unusual elsewhere if schools simply fostered the love of reading like we did."

"They do."

"Not really. Schools look at reading as a task children have to learn at a certain age. They break the written word into what they consider digestible parts and then force-feed the kids those parts before they're allowed to put them together. By the time the kids figure it out, reading is a boring chore."

"But the schools' methods work. It's how I learned to read."

"People learn to read despite what the schools do, not because of it. Most kids have developed the ability to read by age seven or eight and would do so with or without any school program. And if the schools' methods really work, why are so many high school graduates illiterate?"

They hammered another board in place.

"I heard some unschoolers don't learn to read until they're teenagers," Leo countered, remembering one of the facts that the president of the National Homeschooling Parent Organization gave him during a phone interview yesterday. He'd had the impression the man was not a fan of unschooling.

"True, though that's rare. Still, those kids develop heightened memories and when they do decode the written word, they're reading challenging material. It's like the child who doesn't talk until age three who suddenly spouts out whole sentences."

"We all develop at different ages," Judy Edwards chimed in, grabbing a few nails from a nearby toolbox. "But if school children don't pick reading up at the same age as everyone else, then they're put in a remedial reading group. That's not what it's called though the kids know what it is. It's discouraging, humiliating. Reading is the last thing they want to do."

"In Carpe Diem there's no illiteracy," Stan Edwards added. "Everyone learns to read eventually. *When* doesn't matter. How many people have you asked, 'how old were you when you learned to read?'"

Leo looked at Jimmy ensconced in his book, oblivious to the cat squirming in his lap. Bob Marley sang from Leo's pocket. "Excuse me," he said, pulling out his phone.

"Hey, Ted. Working on a Sunday?"

"The wife's having one of those girlie spa parties. Didn't want me around. I thought I'd get a start on the work week. How's the research coming?"

Leo looked at Jimmy. "Good. I'm getting a totally different take on reading at grade level. In Carpe Diem—"

"Great. You can fill me in later." Ted hesitated. Cleared his throat. "Raegan Colyer called."

"Today?"

"With her workload the weekend probably means nothing to her. Anyway, she called to apologize about suggesting that I send you to Carpe Diem. Said she didn't realize what a disaster you'd be."

"That's rich." Leo stopped short of saying 'considering she effectively wrote the article.' "I find it hard to believe Raegan would apologize about anything."

"So did I until I realized the real reason for her call."

"Which was?"

"She wanted to find out if I'd fired you. She was surprised when I told her I hadn't. Then she tried to talk me into letting you go, 'for the good of the paper and all.'

"When I told her I'd given you a second chance, she pointed out all your screw-ups and said you didn't deserve it. I told her I'd already made my decision and you were on assignment in Carpe Diem. She went ballistic and hung up. She has it in for you. You'd better watch your back."

"I'm not worried. Raegan is always going ballistic about something. Her bark is worse than her bite."

"I'm not sure," Ted said. "Bad things happen to people who cross her. Do you remember Jim Harrison, the city councilman who was killed in a car accident the day after he admitted taking bribes?"

"Sure, the toxicology report said he had a high blood alcohol level."

"Uh huh. That's what it *said*. And Raegan was the one who gave the bribes."

"*Allegedly*. Ted, you're being paranoid."

"All I'm saying is you need to be careful."

"Okay. Anything else?"

"No. I'll call you in a few days to see how you're getting along." Ted hung up.

Stan Edwards looked at him with one eyebrow raised. "Problems?"

"Nothing I can't handle," Leo replied, touching his scar.

# 31

As she sat by her mother's hospital bed the next morning, Tali thought about the last few days. Her father was an adulterer and was now locked in a jail cell waiting to be charged with attempted murder. She couldn't wrap her head around it.

She dreaded going back to Alanton. The mocking, the teasing. And Tom. She pictured walking down a deserted hallway, her footsteps echoing off the metal lockers. She'd turn the corner to Mrs. Wallace's art room and there he'd be, waiting for her. Would he ignore her, taunt her, attack her? She fingered her car charm.

"Good morning," Alexandra said as she woke.

"How ya feeling?"

"Stronger." To prove it, she tried to sit up. Tali rushed to raise the bed and adjust the pillows.

The hospital room door opened. Denise entered, carrying a breakfast tray.

"Good morning, Mrs. Shaw, Tali," Denise chirped. "How's the patient this morning? Hungry?"

Tali moved over to the recliner as Denise placed the food on the tray table. "We'll have to stick with clear liquids and Jell-O for the next day or two. Then, gourmet breakfasts, I promise. Buzz me when you're done."

She gave a slight wave as she left the room.

Tali flipped through a magazine while her mother ate. When Alexandra finished, Tali set down the magazine and asked, "Did you know about Dad's affair with Mary?"

"I suspected it," her mother said, patting her mouth with a napkin. "Then decided I was being paranoid. Women always flirted with him. And even though he spent long hours with Mary, I rationalized that he had to because she was on his staff."

"Did Dad ever, um, ever…" her voice trailed off.

"Attack me?"

She nodded.

"Yes," Alexandra said in a small voice.

"Oh, Mom." Tali's stomach turned. "You wore scarves to hide the marks, didn't you?"

Alexandra's eyes filled with tears.

Tali went to the bed, pushed aside the tray table and hugged her mother. "Why didn't you leave him?"

"I thought if I was a better wife—" Alexandra began, her voice shaking.

"So you *deserved* to be hit?"

"No, no that's not what I mean." Alexandra shut her eyes, sighed and began again. "No one deserves to be hit.

"But he was so persuasive. I guess most abusive men are. He would apologize, ask my forgiveness and tell me he loved me. He would promise to never hurt me again. I believed him.

"I wanted to believe him, for your sake and because of your strict Catholic grandparents. In their eyes, divorce wasn't an option no matter what the circumstances. They would have disowned me."

Tali remembered her potbellied, red-faced grandfather ranting about the sins of divorce after she told him her favorite teacher had left her husband.

"Despite all that, when he ran for the state Senate, I told him I wanted to get a divorce. He begged me not to. He told me he would get counseling, which he did. Things did get better. The campaign kept him busy, and after he was elected he rarely came home, particularly when I stood

KRISTIN A. OAKLEY

my ground and fired Rosalinda."

Tali realized that good old Dad may have had an affair with Rosalinda, too, but she couldn't bring herself to ask. Instead she said, "He has a bad temper, but I never thought he'd hit anyone. Especially you."

"I worked hard at hiding it. If he had ever hit you, we would have left."

"He makes me sick." Tali took her mother's hand. "I talked to the Carpe Diem police chief. When the charges come through, they'll move him to the Alanton jail where he'll await trial. If he's convicted, he could be in prison a long time."

"Yes."

"What about us?"

"We'll go home to Alanton. I'll file for divorce; hopefully write a book, and you'll finish high school."

Tali pulled on the loose threads hanging from the hole in the knee of her jeans. "I don't want to go back to Alanton."

"Why not?"

"It'll suck. People will ask stupid questions about Dad. They'll stare. School will be awful. Britney Crandall and her clique will make my life so hard. She's already sending horrible text messages." Tali covered her mouth. She hadn't meant to say that. She didn't want to worry her mom.

"She did? What does she say?"

"Hi, white trash," she mumbled.

"That's awful."

"It's no big deal. I've blocked her phone number."

"Have you checked your Facebook page?"

"No," Tali admitted. "I'm afraid to."

"She's something else."

"She's not the only one giving me grief. I heard Tom's telling everyone he knew my old man was no good so he broke up with me."

"I never liked that boy. What does his sister Danielle say?"

"She's tried sticking up for me, but her mom believes her brother. She won't let Danielle hang out with me anymore."

Alexandra shook her head. "Unbelievable."

"I don't want to go home. I want to move to Carpe Diem. I want to live here."

"We won't run from our problems."

"I don't see it as running. I see it as starting a new, better life. Really Mom, other than Danielle, there isn't anyone else I'd miss. And now I won't be able to see her. Here, I've become good friends with Quinn even before I knew we were sisters. I want to get to know her."

"But don't you see how difficult it would be for me to live in the same small town as Mary and her daughter — Chris' daughter?"

"Quinn can't help being his daughter any more than I can. She's amazing. You'd like her." Tali fingered her car charm again. "And Mary wants to talk to you. I think she wants to apologize. I don't know her as well as Quinn. She seems nice. She got Dad to say he tried to kill you and Patrick Holden."

"*Tried* to kill Mr. Holden?"

"He's alive."

"How can that be?"

"He survived the motorcycle accident. He's been hiding out at his dad's. They were afraid whoever tried to kill him might come after him again."

"He won't have to worry about that anymore."

Tali nodded. "So…can we stay in Carpe Diem? Try unschooling?"

"You want to drop out of high school?"

"Yes. Think of all the time we'd have to work on your book." And work on cars. She pictured rebuilding engines with Josh.

"I don't know." Alexandra frowned. "I have a lot of questions about this 'anything goes' attitude."

"I could call Mary and Quinn and ask them to come over. They can answer your questions and Mary can apologize."

Alexandra didn't reply.

"Please, Mom."

"I don't want to see her. I don't want to hear what she has to say. Besides, I look like hell."

"No, you don't. And I'll help you with your hair and make-up if you'd like. You're ten times prettier than she is."

Alexandra shook her head.

"It would mean a lot to me." Tali held her breath.

"Fine," her mother sighed. "But have them come today before I change my mind."

Tali twirled her ponytail into a jumbled mass. She was trying to finger-comb the tangles when the hospital door opened and Quinn and Mary entered.

Something about Quinn looked different but Tali couldn't figure out what it was. She was dressed in black from head to toe as usual and had even blackened the white tips of her high top sneakers. But something was missing. When she gave Quinn a welcoming hug, it came to her.

"You're camera-less."

"Mom insisted I leave it in the car. I think she was afraid I'd take pictures of the bed pans."

Tali laughed, easing the tightness in her stomach. She looked at Mary, who actually looked pretty. She had ditched the ugly glasses and replaced her usual boring business suit with a cream-colored sweater and long, flowery skirt. She wore a matching silk scarf which, Tali assumed, hid the marks of Christopher's attack.

Tali made introductions. When Mary told Alexandra it was nice to see her again, Alexandra glared. Tali went back to tangling her ponytail.

"I was young," Mary began. "Selfish, easily manipulated. Chris told me he'd filed for divorce. I believed him. When I met you, and saw the two of you together, I knew he had lied. Who brings the wife he's divorcing to an office party? The next day I found out I was pregnant. When I told Chris he attacked me. I fled." These last words came out in a muffled croak.

Mary cleared her throat and began again in a shaky voice. "My affair with a married man has been eating at me all these years. There's no excuse for what I did. I'm so sorry I hurt you."

There was a long awkward silence until finally Alexandra nodded her head slightly and eased the tension. "I don't excuse what you did, but I know most of the blame falls on Christopher," she said. "He was hard to resist and he knew it."

Tali sat on the edge of the bed. She took her mother's hand and gave her a kiss on the cheek. Then she said to Mary, "How about a mini-seminar on unschooling? Mom was wondering how it works."

"Okay," Mary said, brightening. "Let's see. Where to start?" She and Quinn settled in the chairs by the window.

"Unschoolers explore what interests them at the time. It's similar to when we're babies. As infants, we're in a constant state of trying to make sense of the world. Think about all we achieve in the first few years of our lives. We learn to walk, talk, feed, and clothe ourselves. How do we do that without schools to teach us? We learn through observation and trial and error. We have an instinctive motivation to learn what it means to be human."

"That's fine for babies but what about getting into college?" Alexandra pushed.

"A lot of unschoolers decide not to go to college for the same reasons they've never been to school. Why sit in a classroom for four years to learn business administration when they're already running a business?"

"You're not going to college, Quinn?" Alexandra asked.

"Actually, I plan on going to a fine arts school after I do some traveling."

"How will you get in if you don't have a high school transcript?"

"We'll make our own transcript," Quinn answered.

"It's difficult explaining natural learning to college admissions, but not impossible," Mary added. "We simply translate Quinn's experiences into a high school transcript. You could do the same for Tali."

"Really? How?" Tali asked.

"What would you do if you didn't go to school?" Quinn asked.

"Watch YouTube and check Facebook," Alexandra teased.

"No, well, maybe a little," Tali admitted. "Actually, I've been thinking about this a lot. I'd like to write for a newspaper. I'd also love to learn more about how cars work and I think it'd be great to learn a language from a natural speaker like Francesca."

"You'll need history, geometry, chemistry," her mom said.

"All three of those can be covered simply by studying one subject like auto mechanics," Quinn said. "Josh can tell you more about this than I can, but history plays an important part in how the American car was invented and developed. Also, he talks a lot about things like steering and engine block geometry."

"Josh told me about multi-valve geometry when we were changing spark plugs," Tali said. Hr mom looked shocked.

"I stopped by the police garage and asked if I could help. The car we worked on was rusty, so Josh explained oxidation and how he'll use phosphoric acid to remove the rust."

She turned to Quinn. "Would that count for chemistry?"

"Definitely."

"You worked on a car?" Alexandra asked.

"Yeah. It was great." She fingered her car charm necklace. "I had so much fun I didn't realize until now all the stuff I was learning."

Mary added, "You can see how the study of one thing is actually the study of many things. The trick is translating real life activities into what the college is looking for. Plus, most colleges today are eager to enroll homeschoolers. They've realized homeschoolers make great college students because they want to learn, not just get a degree."

"I think I understand," Alexandra said, "Though it's hard to think so drastically outside the box."

"I'm sure the more you think about it, the more questions you'll have," Mary said. "I've brought along several books about unschooling which might help." She set them on the coffee table. "And I'd be more than happy to come by again to let you pick my brain."

"Thank you," Alexandra said. "And not just for the books. Thank you for all your kindness and generosity to Tali, for catching Chris, and for apologizing." She held her hand out. Mary took it and gave it a gentle squeeze.

# 32

Monday afternoon, Raegan Colyer smoothed her jet black hair into place. Her bangs were longer than she liked, but she'd cancelled her styling appointment that afternoon with Jacques. There was simply too much to do.

She had a vague notion that she should be anxious. Ordinary people whose plans fell through would feel that way. But she always had back-up measures and these, she knew, would be foolproof. A smile crept onto her face as she opened the door to the governor's office.

"Ah, Raegan," Governor Thomas said, straightening in his chair and running his hands through his thinning hair. "How was your weekend?"

"Excellent, Governor." It was pathetic how he tried to look attractive. She slid into the nearest chair and crossed her legs, letting her skirt inch up. "The secretary of state was very friendly."

"That's right. He took you to the Lyric Opera."

"*Carmen* puts him into the right frame of mind."

"Why bother when a cheap bottle of wine will get you the same results?"

She inspected her boss. Flecks of dinner roll and what looked like steak sauce decorated his loosened tie, remnants from lunch. A half-eaten Snickers bar sat on his littered desk next to a coffee cup. It was

KRISTIN A. OAKLEY

filled with whiskey, no doubt. Yes, women would have to be drunk to have sex with him.

"Assuming you got results?" the governor said.

"I never kiss and tell."

The governor laughed, clapping his beefy hands together. He shuffled through an odd assortment of letters and torn envelopes on his desk until he found the Monday edition of *The Chicago Examiner*. "Interesting developments in that little town of yours." He tapped the paper's picture of Senator Shaw.

"Quite. Shaw surprised us all, as did Mr. Townsend."

"I thought you had them both in your back pocket."

"Apparently not. But it doesn't matter anymore." She brought her manicured fingertips together.

"Why not?" The big man asked, resting his hands on his massive stomach.

"I'll get to that in a moment. First, the 'Education for All Bill' may be dead."

"Dead?" He raised his bushy eyebrows high above his beady, bloodshot eyes. "Because of Shaw?"

She looked at the obese idiot and felt a raw desire to grab the man's fat head and beat it on the desk. Unfortunately, she needed this imbecile to help. And she didn't want to break a nail. Instead, she counted to twenty until the murderous feeling passed. "Senator Shaw's arrest brought homeschoolers scurrying out of the woodwork," she explained. "They've been harassing members of the Education Committee, demanding that they drop the bill. Without Shaw's leadership, the senators are caving. It looks like they won't return the bill to the full House."

"But what about the article and the news reports?"

"Townsend's press conference, as they're calling it, seems to have negated the effects of the article."

"What about the teachers' union? Outraged citizens? Aren't they putting on the pressure?"

"They certainly could. But they're not. The word's out that the motorcyclist Shaw allegedly killed was Patrick Holden."

"Who?"

"Someday you'll have to read up on the history of the state you run," she hissed.

"I don't have to take that—" the whale attempted to get out of his seat.

She watched him struggle for a minute, repulsed by the way his bulging belly caught on the chair arms. Then, his government seal tie clip reminded her she needed this man, if only as a tool. "Sorry, sorry, I shouldn't take this out on you."

The governor settled back down, maneuvering his fat into strategic places. He then managed to pull out a whiskey bottle and two glasses from a desk drawer. "Have a drink."

"No. Thank you." She only drank as a prelude to sex. Thankfully, she got her way with the governor without having to sleep with him. The only way she'd have sex with him was if she were dead.

She picked up *The Chicago Examiner*. "Patrick Holden was a homeschooling activist." She opened the first section of the paper to page three and handed it to him.

"This guy Barnes makes it sound like Holden was a hero championing the little guy against the big bad government," the governor said.

"Exactly. You can see why the teachers' union doesn't want to get involved. Holden's been a thorn in their side for decades. If they push now, it might look like they were involved with his death, or at least are being disrespectful. So they're backing off. And those concerned citizens you mentioned aren't getting into the act because they're preoccupied with Shaw's story. It makes for great gossip. They've forgotten about the evils of homeschooling."

"That's it then," the governor said, throwing the paper aside. "Hell, there's always next year."

Raegan slowly stood up. "No, that's not *it*." She paced the room.

"I don't understand," he said. "You said the bill was practically dead in committee and no one is pushing for its passage. Even if it had support, the deadline for bringing it to the floor is Wednesday."

Raegan stopped pacing to look out the windows. "First," she said, more to the city scene below than to the governor, "I've talked Senator Fritz into seeking an extension of the bill's deadline. It took a bit of wrangling and the giving of more than one favor. She's agreed." Raegan examined her French manicure and then walked back to her seat.

"An extension doesn't make sense," the governor countered. "That gives homeschoolers even more time to talk the senators out of the legislation. It's best that this waits until next year. Besides, I've got enough on my plate." He shoved the remainder of the candy bar into his mouth.

"What I have in mind would make passage of this bill the easiest thing on Earth, eliminate homeschoolers from Illinois — ultimately the country — and make you a hero."

"Right, and Julia Roberts is going to give me a blow job."

Her hand itched to slap him. She counted to ten. "Pour us a drink. You'll want to hear this."

# 33

*Pursuing our passions, unschooling, is ultimately what we all would like to do. But because of schooling, we assume we don't have the luxury. Public institutions can't or won't allow children to unschool because of their assembly line structure, constraining rules, and pointless regulations. The years of forced study have taught us that learning is unpleasant and only happens in the classroom. Once we escape from this system, via graduation, job responsibilities and family supersede the pursuit of passions.*

*In Carpe Diem, Illinois, children and adults are pursuing their passions each and every day and profitably so. What are the rest of us doing? In school, our children study arbitrary material and forget it the moment they finish a test. At home, they spend an hour or more on additional arbitrary material, called homework, then watch four hours of television (the current national average). Sure, the Carpe Diem kids enjoy "Glee" and have Facebook pages, but they are too busy selling their photography, learning how to cook Italian dishes, rebuilding cars or reporting for the local paper to be glued to the tube. The irony is that while we watch life, the people of Carpe Diem experience it.*

"*The Examiner* will never publish this," Mary said.

Leo jumped. He had been so intent on his story that he hadn't noticed her or her guests enjoying the Inn's happy hour wine and cheese.

He shrugged. "I think my editor might let me get away with it. He wears t-shirts with quotations. His favorite is by Nietzsche: 'The surest way to corrupt a youth is to instruct him to hold in higher esteem those who think alike than those who think differently.'"

"I'd like to meet your editor," Mary said. "Do I get to read your article before you submit it?"

"Only if you promise not to make any changes to it."

Mary laughed. "I promise. I see your computer is working."

"Will did a great job, though his magic might not last. I'm afraid this computer might be getting too old."

Mary glanced around the dining room and then back at him. "I've prepared a private happy hour out on the veranda for the kids and me. Care to join us?"

"Definitely." He saved his article, packed up his computer and followed Mary and the smell of her soft perfume out onto the porch.

The afternoon sunlight illuminated the red, gold, and yellow leaves of the maples lining the Inn's long drive. Their rustling mingled with the gentle laughter and Vivaldi's *Four Seasons*, which drifted out of the dining room's windows. Missing were the honking cars, screeching tires, and shouted obscenities he heard daily in Chicago. Instead of cigarette smoke and exhaust fumes, he smelled damp earth and falling leaves.

"Hi kids," he said to Tali, Quinn, and Will. The girls sat together on the wicker porch swing while Will occupied a matching chair.

Will raised his glass of what appeared to be champagne. When Leo gave him a quizzical look, Will said, "Sparkling pear juice."

"Hey, Leo." The girls toasted him with their own glasses of the bubbling liquid. Now that they were inseparable, he noticed similarities between them. Even the intonation in their voices harmonized.

Mary had set two goblets, a carafe of red wine and a plate of aged cheeses on the small table between two chairs. Leo set his computer bag next to the table. "Is this the same wine you're serving in the dining room?" he asked as she filled his glass.

"No. This is from Dan and Joan's collection. I save it for special occasions."

He smelled the peppery aroma of the Merlot and then sampled it. "I can see why. What's the special occasion?"

"Mom and I are moving to Carpe Diem," Tali said.

"Excellent news."

"I'm really excited. At first I didn't think Mom would agree. Mary and Quinn helped her see the light."

"Amen, sister." Quinn gave Tali a high five.

"It'll be a big change for you. New town, no school," he pointed out. He noticed an amazing transformation in her already. No more drooping shoulders or curtain of hair covering her face.

"That's what I'm hoping."

"A big change for her?" Will asked with false indignity. "I'll have two big sisters!"

"You'll love it," Quinn said. "You'll have someone else to taste test your concoctions."

"Which reminds me," Will said. "How do you like the cheese, Leo?"

Leo took a slice of the cheese and bit into it. It tasted of fresh herbs and garlic. "It's great," he admitted. "Don't tell me you made this."

"Yep. When I was ten I went through a whole cheese making phase and set several aside to age."

"I'm impressed." He ate another slice then turned to Tali. "When will you move to Carpe Diem?"

"Once the festival is over," she replied. "Quinn and Patrick are going to help me get the house in Alanton organized and ready to put on the market."

"Tali's mom," Quinn interjected, "will be in the hospital for awhile longer, so we offered to help her out."

"When Mom's released," Tali added, "we'll stay at the Inn until our house sells. Then we'll buy a house in Carpe Diem." The swing creaked as she swung her legs. "And the best part is John's helping me with my school withdrawal letter!"

"As soon as she mails it, she'll be an official dropout." Quinn gave her a playful shove.

"No, a drop-in," Tali corrected her half sister.

"Drop in to life?" Quinn asked. Both girls laughed.

"Hey, that's a good line," Leo said. "Can I use it in my article?"

"Definitely."

A distant rumbling overshadowed the squeak of the porch swing. "Sounds like Patrick is on his way," Mary said.

"Did he get another motorcycle?" Tali asked.

"Does a bear shit in the woods?" Quinn replied.

"Quinn!" Mary scolded. She was drowned out by the roaring Harley coming down the driveway.

Patrick pulled around to the front steps, took his helmet off, and limped up the stairs.

"Out in public?" Leo asked. "Weren't people surprised to find you're not dead?"

Patrick set his helmet on the floor and eased into the nearest wicker chair. "No. I made a public appearance at Keagan's last night. Word spreads quickly around this town."

"Yeah, it does," Quinn said. "I heard that when you walked in, Charlotte Jansen threw beer in your face."

"Oh, Patrick, did she really?" Mary asked.

"Yep. She was a tiny bit angry that I'd lied to her and everyone else about being dead. Eventually she came around." Patrick grinned. "Anyway, I came to tell you there's a good possibility that the 'Education for All Bill' is dead."

"Terrific," Mary said.

"That's good news," Leo agreed.

"Apparently, Shaw had persuaded the Educational Committee to sign the bill. But when they got word of his arrest they tabled it."

"You're meeting with Chris did the trick after all," Mary said.

"How so?"

"Without your accident, the bill would have passed," she teased.

"I would have preferred to go about it another way, but you're right. Though I still may have my work cut out for me."

"What do you mean?" Quinn asked.

"Raegan Colyer has pushed for an extension to the deadline for passing the bill. The senators have agreed. So it's still in play."

*Raegan won't go away*, Leo thought. He wondered what information his friend, Al, was digging up. He made a mental note to call him.

Patrick took a slice of cheese. "I have the feeling that even with the deadline extension, the bill isn't going anywhere. The committee members are exhausted. They want the whole issue to go away. They're just humoring Raegan to get her off their backs."

"The bill will be tabled after all?" Leo asked.

"I think it's a done deal," Patrick answered.

"Then how about some wine to celebrate?" Mary asked, starting to rise.

"Maybe a beer. But sit still, I'll get it. It's good for me to exercise my leg," Patrick said. He limped across the veranda and into the Inn's lobby.

"Is that the Moores, Mom?" Quinn asked, pointing to a sleek, black limo pulling into the drive.

"No, they're not coming this year. Their daughter is about to have a baby."

They watched the car come closer.

"I'm not sure who it is," Mary said.

The limo parked beside Patrick's motorcycle. The uniformed driver got out, walked around to the passenger door, and opened it. Two shapely legs ending in spiked black heels appeared. Raegan Colyer exited the limo.

"What the hell does she want?" Leo said as he rose from his chair.

Raegan straightened her tight black skirt and adjusted her blouse to expose ample cleavage. She looked in disdain at the Inn's country façade.

"I thought I might find you here, Mr. Townsend," she said spotting Leo. "And Mayor Evans, how are the Fall Festival preparations coming along?"

"What can we do for you, Ms. Colyer?" Leo asked, descending the front steps in an attempt to stop the woman's approach. He didn't trust her and wanted to keep her as far from Mary and the kids as possible.

"Actually, it's more of what I can do for you, Mr. Townsend. I'm wondering if you would accompany me on a short drive. This is such a pretty part of the state."

Leo glanced at Mary who mouthed "No," but he knew this meeting was unavoidable. "Sure," he said trying to sound nonchalant.

The interior of the limo smelled of crushed leather and expensive perfume. As the car took off, Raegan selected a crystal carafe filled with an amber liquid and offered him a drink. He refused. He didn't want to extend this visit any longer than necessary.

"What's this about? Are you going to take me to jail and have me booked on more trumped-up charges? Or drive me to an abandoned field and have your hired gun get rid of me once and for all?"

"Oh, Leo," she laughed, and touched his arm. "Sometimes I don't understand your sense of humor. No, I was in the neighborhood and thought I'd drop by. See the town for myself." The limo pulled onto Main Street. The sidewalks bustled with shoppers. "It's quite charming, isn't it?"

He didn't answer.

"More importantly, I wanted to issue my job offer in person. You do remember I offered you a job?"

"Certainly."

"You promised to get back to me Monday. Tuesday at the latest. Since it's now Tuesday, I decided to get your answer in person. You see, I like to meet with my staff, talk about the duties and benefits, and get to know my employees better." She rubbed his thigh with a manicured hand.

He gently removed her hand from his leg. "You said I'd be writing speeches for the governor."

"That is correct, however, you will be directly under me." She touched the corner of her red-lipsticked, smirking mouth. "You'll be responsible for writing the governor's State of the Union address in addition to speeches for any educational events since education seems to be your forte. The governor wants you to start work tomorrow."

He'd never work for this woman. "The job sounds intriguing though I certainly won't be able to start tomorrow. I'm putting together a piece for *The Examiner* on Carpe Diem and unschooling." He knew she was well aware of this. "It'll take a few more days, through the weekend at least. And I have my job at *The Examiner* to consider."

"I'm prepared to offer you double your current salary."

*How does she know what my salary is?* "That's very generous, but I can't take your offer. I've invested a lot in this story, and in the paper."

"Your job at the paper is tenuous at best. Ted Nelson needs only the slightest excuse to fire you. I'm offering you job security."

"For only as long as the governor has a job."

"Oh, it's much more than that, Leo. If you accept this position, I'm prepared to take you with me when I become education secretary in the president's cabinet in January. In a few months you'll be writing speeches in Washington."

He stopped breathing. She was offering him the job of a lifetime. He thought of the possibilities, then glanced past her, out the car window. He saw Jimmy sitting on a park bench reading *Because of Winn-Dixie* with Puck curled up in his lap. Leo pictured the boy holed up in a classroom with a mob of other six-year-olds, filling out worksheets designed to teach him to read. They'd probably put him on Ritalin to control his precociousness.

He turned his attention back to Raegan. "It's a terrific opportunity, but I have to decline. I came here to write a story and I intend to do that."

Her face hardened. "This is a one-time offer, Mr. Townsend. Think of your career. You'll regret it if you don't take the job."

"I don't think so."

A vein on her forehead throbbed. "You're throwing your life away for this miserable town." She called to the driver, "Take Mr. Townsend back to the Inn."

"What do you have against Carpe Diem?"

"I am a woman of law and order," she said.

He wondered how a woman of law and order could afford a limousine and driver on a government salary.

"Carpe Diem," she continued, "is a community of anarchists. Children need structure, guidelines. They have no self-control. Left to their own devices they become animals. That's readily apparent in Carpe Diem."

Leo laughed. "What are you basing this on? The kids I've met here are polite, considerate, interesting people. A few years back, I did a story about Chicago public school funding and visited urban high schools as part of my research. I was shocked at the foul language and lack of respect kids showed the teachers. Only a few teachers could handle their students."

"Yes, so imagine a system without restraints."

"What I've discovered these last couple of days is that if children are

KRISTIN A. OAKLEY

interested in what they're doing, if they're trusted and respected, they don't need to be caged."

"Children need to be controlled."

"Who does the controlling? *You?*"

"Yes, me. Because I am the government and I have the people's best interests in mind."

The limo stopped at the end of the Inn's driveway. As Leo exited, Raegan hissed after him, "Carpe Diem should not exist."

The limo sped away, its tires kicking up dried leaves. Leo shook his head as he walked down the long drive back to the Inn.

"What was all that about?" Mary asked as he sat in the wicker chair. The kids were gone. Patrick now sat on the porch swing.

"She offered me a job. I declined. She got pissed." He took Mary's hand. "I don't suppose you'd consider cancelling the Fall Festival?"

Mary laughed until she noticed his expression. "You're serious. Why?"

"Raegan is powerful and angry. She said, 'Carpe Diem should not exist.' I think she meant it. I hate to think what she might do."

"To hell with that!" Patrick slammed his beer down. "We'll be damned if we'll let a politician run our lives."

"That's exactly what she wants to do."

"Well, it ain't happening."

"Patrick's right," Mary said. "The festival will go on as planned."

"I understand, but you have to realize what this woman is capable of. Remember she blackmailed you into writing lies about this town and pinned it on me? She probably hired someone to drive me off the road and bribed a cop to throw me in jail. She has the Senate's Educational Committee in her back pocket and now she's trying to stop me from writing my article. Why?"

"Because she knows you'll write the truth about Carpe Diem," Mary said.

"Do you think that's why she wants me out of town?"

"Sure, so you'll stop researching the town."

"Maybe. Or maybe she's got something planned for Carpe Diem and doesn't want me here when it happens."

# 34

Wednesday afternoon, Leo and Mary walked down the paved path through the town square. They stepped over boxes of gourds, around stacks of plywood, and under half-hung banners. Every few steps, Mary answered a question about the master schedule or Leo helped hold a board in place.

Eventually they passed the spot where, only a week earlier, Mary had tripped and he had caught her. So much had happened since then, including Raegan Colyer's ominous visit yesterday. But Raegan hadn't resurfaced. Leo's concerns about her were fading. Besides, it was hard to be paranoid on such a beautiful fall day surrounded by townspeople excited about tomorrow's Fall Festival kickoff.

*I Gotta Feeling* sang out from Mary's pocket. She pulled out her cell phone.

"I thought the *Mission Impossible* theme was your ringtone," Leo said.

"It was, but with Chris behind bars, I've switched it to the Black Eyed Peas." She gave him a giant grin then answered her phone. "This is Mayor Mary Evans." Her smile faded. She stopped walking. "You can't be serious. There's been no evidence of—" She swayed.

Leo helped her to the nearest park bench.

"Excuse me, Attorney Richmond," Mary said, "you're basing this on false accusations."

He mouthed, "State Attorney General Allison Richmond?"

Mary nodded. "Nine counts of child abuse? Against who?

"No, we don't have an Edward Smith living in this town. We had a Eugene Smits, but he died last year on his hundredth birthday." She stood up, regaining her composure.

"Well, yes, a little boy was recently injured. Not from child abuse or neglect. He ran in front of a car to rescue his cat. The driver couldn't stop in time. Certainly, feel free to look at the police report. Talk to the boy's parents. No, there's never been an incident of child abuse in Carpe Diem, let alone nine of them. People here don't even believe in spanking their children.

"I understand you have to investigate. Visit our town, see for yourself. Yes, you can contact me anytime if you have further concerns. Goodbye." She clicked off her phone and slumped back onto the bench. "The attorney general is investigating charges of child abuse in Carpe Diem."

"You're kidding!"

"No. Someone suggested that physical, sexual, and emotional abuse is common here."

Leo put his arm around her. He kept her close as they continued on the path.

"There's no doubt who tipped her off," he said.

"Raegan Colyer?"

"Who else has so much pull as to get not only the AG's office involved, but the AG herself? I hope the press doesn't get wind of the allegations."

"I don't think they will. Attorney Richmond mentioned these kinds of allegations are kept quiet until an investigation finds actual evidence. A false accusation can ruin people's lives." She shivered. "If Raegan was behind this, she'll probably give up her obsession with Carpe Diem when she sees nothing can be proven. Don't you think?"

"Or she will become more desperate," croaked someone behind them.

"Hey, John," Leo said, shaking the older man's hand.

"You think she'll try something else, Uncle John?" Mary asked in a shaky voice.

"Yes I do." He hugged her. "But I have some good news. The 'Education for All Bill' is officially dead."

"Excellent! The committee members came to their senses?"

"Yes. They withdrew their support for extending the deadline. They've decided to concentrate on redrafting the school code rather than worry about a small minority of kids who are being homeschooled. Apparently Raegan isn't as influential as she thought."

"Except when it comes to the attorney general," Mary said. She told John about the phone call.

"You handled that well. My guess is that the AG will just drop it," John said.

"So you think Raegan will give up?" Mary asked.

"If you believe that, you don't know Ms. Colyer." John brushed his hand against her cheek. "Don't worry, whatever Raegan decides to do, it's nothing we can't handle."

"John's right," Leo said. "This town hasn't done anything wrong. The families are successful and happy. There's nothing Raegan can prove."

"I hope so." Mary sighed.

Nearby, several adults put the final touches on the corn stalk labyrinth. They laughed as two small faces peeked through the stalks.

"Let's forget about Raegan Colyer," Leo said. "It's a beautiful day." His stomach growled. "Come on, I'll treat you to Joan's famous lamb meatballs."

"Sounds good to me. John, will you join us?"

"Certainly."

They wound their way through the park, stopping periodically to help put up a banner or carry supplies. As they left the town square, they waved to the two McCarthy brothers who were relaxing under an elm tree.

Brendan greeted them at the diner's door. "You're in luck. The dinner crowd hasn't started coming in yet so I've got a couple of tables by the window."

Once they were seated, John asked Leo, "How's your piece on unschooling coming?"

"He's sold on the concept," Mary answered for him. "So much so I don't think *The Examiner* will print what he's written," she teased.

"I am sold though not a hundred percent," he replied.

Brendan handed them menus. "Our special tonight is white bean chicken chili," he said. "It's enhanced with homemade tomatillo salsa."

"Wow, does that sound good," Leo said, "though my heart was set on the lamb meatballs."

"Get the meatballs, I'll get the chili and you can have a taste," Mary said.

"Or," Brendan added, "I could get you a cup of the chili."

"Excellent. Thanks."

Brendan finished taking their orders then left for the kitchen.

"What are your misgivings about unschooling?" John asked Leo.

"Well, you wouldn't advocate unschooling for everyone, would you?"

"I would, but, as you can tell by Ms. Colyer and the media, our culture is very resistant to it."

"Because it's so radical?"

"Because they think it's radical when actually, if they understood it, they would slap their foreheads and say, 'oh yeah, it does make sense.' It's hard for adults in our society to let go of control over other peoples' lives, particularly the lives of their children."

Brendan appeared with a cup of the chili. Leo tasted it as Bob Marley shot the sheriff.

"I thought you didn't believe in cell phones during meal times," Mary teased him.

"I don't. Having the phone handy is part of my 'being on our guard' plan." He glanced at it. "I don't recognize the number. Excuse me." He got up from the table then left the diner. "Hello?"

"Mr. Townsend, this is Jane Carlton from the clerk's office at Dirksen Federal Courthouse in Chicago."

"Hello, Ms. Carlton. You're working late. It's past six."

"Oh, that's nothing. I'll probably be here until ten. It's been a crazy week here what with the Smithson trial going on. That's why I'm calling you. The grand jury wants to hear your testimony tomorrow."

"*Tomorrow?*"

"Yes, I'm sorry about the short notice. You know how these things go."

"What time do I need to be there?"

"Nine a.m. They probably won't get to you until after lunch, but they want you here just in case."

"Do I have a choice?" He didn't like the idea of leaving Carpe Diem on the day of the Fall Festival kickoff. He still thought Raegan Colyer would pull another stunt.

"No, Mr. Townsend, not really."

Maybe they'd take him early and he'd be back in plenty of time for whatever mischief Raegan planned. "Okay. I'll be there. But if you have any say in the matter, I'd prefer it if I could testify in the morning."

"It's not up to me, but I'll give them your message."

When he sat back down at the table, now covered with plates full of food, he said, "I've got to head back to Chicago tonight."

"Oh?" Mary asked.

"The grand jury in the Smithson case is ready to hear my testimony and they want me to be there first thing in the morning."

Mary looked down at her food.

"Look, it's going to be okay. I'll do my thing and get back here as soon as possible."

John shook his head.

"What?"

"I didn't know Raegan could manipulate a grand jury investigation."

"Oh, come on. Now you're being paranoid."

"Am I? The timing is perfect, don't you think?"

Leo ran his fingers through his hair. "I'm sure Raegan doesn't control the grand jury. Honestly, there's nothing to worry about. I'll be back in plenty of time and even so, Raegan can't hurt this town. She's run out of legal options."

"'Legal' being the operative word."

Leo said nothing.

# 35

Leo spent three hours Thursday morning avoiding journalists in the halls of The Dirksen Federal Building in downtown Chicago. At noon, he managed to escape to the Elephant & Castle Pub on West Adams for bangers and mash. He washed the food down with coffee though he craved a Guinness.

When he got back to the courthouse, a reporter from *The Chicagoan* accosted him. He asked Leo if he was going to add 'squealer' to 'lack of credibility' on his résumé. It took every ounce of Leo's strength not to punch the jerk. He pushed past the reporter and escaped to the men's room where, for the hundredth time that day, he tried to figure out what he'd say to the Smithson grand jury.

If he named his source, he'd be back in Carpe Diem in a couple of hours but he'd lose his job at *The Examiner* and any possibility of ever working for a paper again. No one would publish his Carpe Diem piece.

If he didn't name his source, he would keep his job and what remained of his dignity but the prosecutor would ask the judge to hold him in contempt of court. He would spend the next few days or months in jail, far away from Carpe Diem. Leo tried to convince himself nothing bad would happen to the little town while he was gone. He didn't succeed.

Bob Marley called from his pocket. "Al?"

"Hey Leo, I'm sorry I haven't gotten back to you sooner. My mom's been sick. Had to fly to California to be with her."

"Not a problem. How's your mom doing?"

"She's much better, thanks."

"Leo Townsend!" a muffled voice called from out in the hall.

His heart raced. "I've gotta go. Can I call you back in a few hours?"

"Sure, but I think you should know there's a connection between a homeschool legal organization and the governor's office. Raegan Colyer, Governor Thomas' chief of staff, is on the board of FLASH."

"FLASH?"

"The Federation of Lawyers Advocating for School at Home. She took over after city councilman Jim Harrison was killed in that car crash."

"Jim Harrison was on the board of FLASH?"

"Heck, he founded it."

"Townsend. Leo Townsend!"

"Thanks Al. Gotta go." Pocketing his phone, Leo adjusted his blue tie and straightened his grey suit jacket. Too busy thinking about what Al had said, he wasn't bothered by the reporters heckling him in the hallway and he didn't acknowledge the grand jurors in the conference room. He passed by the prosecutor without a word and sat at the table where she directed.

For the next hour, he was quick and to the point as he answered the prosecutor's questions. He explained how he had gathered facts for his story which uncovered Carl Smithson's fondness for other people's money. As president of the Illinois State Teachers' Union, Smithson had used union dues to finance his gubernatorial campaign, remodel his Kenilworth mansion, and host a month-long European vacation with fifty of his closest friends. Smithson had hid his embezzlement well. Most assumed he had inherited the millions from his late father, the founder and owner of Chicago Confectionaries. Leo's source discovered that Smithson had sucked his inheritance dry years before.

As the prosecutor listened to Leo's testimony, she paced in front of the grand jury. Her skirt swished against her pantyhose. Her brown suit was a bit rumpled, her curly black hair kept in place with reading glasses pushed high up on her head. In her left hand she carried a yellow legal pad blackened with scribbling which she tapped with a pen. She walked around the conference table and approached Leo.

He knew what was coming. She would ask for his source and this time he wouldn't be able to evade the question. His stomach churned. He shifted in the chair.

"Mr. Townsend, the grand jury must have evidence to substantiate your testimony. These accusations you're making against candidate Carl Smithson are serious. We need more than your word."

He said nothing.

"Unfortunately, if I don't get the name of your source, then I won't have any choice but to request that Judge Connors hold you in contempt of court."

There it was, the threat he'd been waiting for. He wiped his damp palms on his pants. "Be my guest. It would be a waste of your time. My source is protected under both the Illinois Shield Law and the Federal Reporter's Privilege." He crossed his arms.

"Oh, I don't think I'd be wasting my time. We both know there are exceptions to the Shield Law. Additionally, a seventh circuit court case—" she flipped several yellow pages over, squinted then read, "*McKevitt v. Pallasch* questions a reporter's right to claim confidentiality." She glanced at him.

"No, unless you cooperate, it's very likely you'll find yourself living in a cell at the Metropolitan Correctional Center. With looks like yours, you'll be very popular there."

A few jurors chuckled.

He ignored the remark, but knew jail wasn't an option. He couldn't shake the feeling that Raegan Colyer was up to something. He had to get back to Carpe Diem.

"Look, Mr. Townsend," the prosecutor continued, "you obviously want Mr. Smithson brought to justice or you wouldn't have written this story. The best, surest way to achieve that is to give us the name of your source. Make it easy for yourself and this proceeding. Cooperate."

Could he redeem himself by cooperating? By bringing down Smithson? Maybe he'd be viewed as a hero. An unemployed hero. And writing the story of the century and winning the Pulitzer, it wasn't going to happen.

He glanced at the wall clock: 2:15. If he left Chicago within the next half hour he might make it back to Carpe Diem by five just as the festival started. How could he give the prosecutor the evidence she needed without divulging his source?

The prosecutor tapped her pink manicured fingernails on her pad of paper. Suddenly, Leo knew what to do.

"Who is your source?"

He loosened his tie and took a deep breath. "I think," he began, hoping he appeared to struggle with his testimony, "Raegan Colyer."

Several jurors gasped. One even said, "Oh my God," before covering her mouth. Murmured conversations broke out among the jurors.

"Quiet, please," the prosecutor demanded. She turned back to him. "Raegan Colyer, the governor's chief of staff? She's your source?"

"I received three phone calls over the course of several weeks which alluded to Mr. Smithson's activities," he said. "These calls led me to investigate further. I then uncovered concrete evidence which I provided to the police, and about which I've testified today."

"Starting with the first phone call," the prosecutor began, "tell me the date and time and the exact conversation, to the best of your recollection."

An hour later, Leo finished his testimony. As he shouldered through the throng of reporters outside the grand jury room, he came face-to-face with Ted.

"How did it go?" the editor asked, his black linen jacket barely covering the Shakespearean quote, "Truth will out."

"I'm not going to jail."

"You named your source."

"I had to—"

"You son of a bitch!"

"You don't understand," he pushed past Ted, "and I don't have time to explain. I have to get to Carpe Diem."

"Townsend, you're fired! Your reporting days are over!"

Leo had expected this and, for the first time in his life, he didn't care.

Exiting the building, he sprinted two blocks down East Adams, hop-

KRISTIN A. OAKLEY

ing his testimony would be enough to keep Raegan the hell away from Carpe Diem. He tried not to think about how he'd damaged his career. As he entered the parking garage, he pulled out his phone and pushed the number for the Cook County Sheriff's Office.

"Sergeant Zachary Davies."

"Zach, Leo Townsend. Do you have a moment?"

"Just a moment."

"What can you tell me about city councilman Jim Harrison's accident? What caused the crash?"

"Officially, Harrison was drunk."

"And unofficially?" Leo stopped on the garage steps.

"I'll deny anything you print."

"Zach, I'm not going to write about it. I just need to know. I give you my word."

The police officer hesitated. "The two front tires were flat. That's not unusual after an accident of that magnitude. But it was unusual that the steel rims melted away. The car had caught fire so at first we assumed the fire melted them. But the fire didn't reach the left tire rim and that was definitely melted. We never looked into it further though. Hell, Harrison was a known alcoholic. And right after his accident a gang war broke out."

"Okay, Zach, thanks."

"Are you going to tell me what this is about?"

"It's just a hunch. If it pans out, I'll give you a call." He took the remaining steps two at a time, jumped into his car, and then called Mary. He had to warn her about Raegan.

The phone rang a few times, then silence. The battery was dead. He dug into his glove compartment for the charger and plugged the phone in. Now he'd have to wait until the damned thing was charged. Swearing, he tore out of the garage, pulled into traffic, and made some progress until the Adams Street Bridge began to lift. Cars boxed him in on all sides.

*"God Dammit!"*

As *Beautiful Liar* by Beyonce and Shakira came on the Mustang's radio, Leo watched a policeman on horseback saunter by.

He wondered how much jail time he'd get for lying to a grand jury.

# 36

Until now, Tali had never felt that what she did mattered. Sure, she "played" for the Alanton High School soccer team, which meant cheering from the bench. She did raise a lot of money for the team by selling more than four hundred raffle tickets, the second-largest number sold. But Britney Crandall's dad sold a thousand to his company's employees and everyone made a big deal out of that.

Helping with the Carpe Diem Fall Festival was different.

At the journalism booth, Billy couldn't turn the crank on the antique printing press so Tali borrowed tools from the woodworking booth and fixed it. While she worked on the crank, she suggested to Billy that they offer a writing contest. "Kids stopping by the booth would get note pads to write about their festival experiences," Tali explained. "At a set time, they would stop back to drop off their stories. We'd print the best ones in the *Carpe Diem Daily News*."

Billy loved the idea. They finished working out the details just as Josh arrived.

After storing away the last of the newsprint rolls, Tali, Josh and Billy picked Quinn up at the photography booth. There, Tali suggested to John Holden that he post an extra set of developing instructions at the entrance to the portable darkroom. "Good idea, thanks," the old man said.

Then the teens walked to the gazebo to hear the band's rehearsal for that night's show. Brendan and his dad, Dan, dueled on their fiddles to Charlie Daniels' *The Devil Went Down To Georgia*, their loose bow strings flying. When Brendan won the duel, Tali and the others cheered.

They then left the gazebo and walked around the pond filled with squawking geese to Will's vegetarian food booth. Pots and pans and warming trays covered the counter top, the portable stove, even the grass around the booth. Peyton Blaney sat on a stool drawing pumpkins on the blackboard menu, oblivious to the mess. As Will shoved equipment under the counter, he told Tali he had decided to offer her grandmother's corn chowder.

"I've tasted it," Peyton said. "It's amazing."

Tali beamed.

"I'm all set," Will said. "Let's get to the parade."

Leaving Peyton to finish her artwork, they joined the flow of people heading toward Main Street.

"There's our spot," Quinn said as she maneuvered past a large family. As they reached a beautiful blond woman sitting cross-legged on an Indian blanket, Quinn said, "Hey, Charlotte, thanks for saving us a spot."

"It's a good thing I did," Charlotte replied. "I can't get over this crowd. I don't recognize half the faces."

"It's a great turnout," Josh agreed. "Charlotte, this is our friend, Tali."

"Nice to meet you, Tali."

"You, too." Tali glanced down Main Street. Grandparents relaxed in lawn chairs with cameras in their laps, young children squirmed on blankets checking every few minutes to see if the parade had started, and adults chatted about the warmer than usual fall day, perfect for a parade.

At five o'clock, Tali joined the spectators in cheering as a black cat sauntered down the middle of the street, followed by Jimmy Edwards and another little boy carrying the "Carpe Diem Fall Festival" banner. With his arm still in a sling, Jimmy couldn't wave to the crowd like the other boy, so he concentrated on keeping the banner straight, his face stern. Leading the parade was serious business. Then he saw his mother and giggled.

A float carrying the Carpe Diem Jazz Ensemble followed. The musicians sat on hay bales next to carved pumpkins or stood next to corn stalks. Their brass instruments reflected the setting sun.

"Ooo, what's this song?" Tali asked Josh as she nodded her head to the music.

"I think it's called, *Dancing in the Moonlight.*"

"The beat's great."

Josh pulled her up from the curb and into the street and they started to dance. He was a terrific dancer, easy to follow. When he ended the dance in a dip, the crowd cheered. Tali felt herself blushing but didn't care.

Sitting back down on the curb, she watched princesses, a prince, a villain, and a beautiful bird dance around a proud Miss Simms.

"The costumes are gorgeous," Charlotte said. "They'll look terrific performing Stravinsky's ballet *The Firebird.*"

The Firebird and the prince held hands as they skipped by.

"They're so cute!" Tali said.

"The Firebird is Becky Downs and the prince is Ben Stoddard," Will told her. "They're both eight. They've been talking about getting married since they were two." He pointed down the street. "Here comes Mom."

"It'd be worth being mayor to be able to ride in one of those," Josh said.

Mary sat on the back of a midnight blue 1969 Corvette convertible driven by Chief Billiot.

"Whose Stingray is that?" Tali asked.

"The chief's," Josh answered. "He bought it as a kid and rebuilt it himself."

Mary waved to them and the chief beamed. "It's too bad Leo isn't here," Tali said. "He'd love that car."

"I wonder where he is," Josh said.

"Mom said he was called back to court," Quinn said. "He hoped to be back in time for the parade. I guess he's running late."

"*It's the mayor of Freaksville!*" someone shouted.

Quinn grabbed Tali's arm making her jump. "My mom's bleeding!" Quinn cried.

Mary's golden turtleneck sweater was splattered red. It was a horrific sight until Mary wiped off what looked like bits of tomato. Another tomato hit her on the shoulder; a third hit her in the face. She crouched down low in the back seat of the car and urged Chief Billiot to drive on. But with dancers in front of him and fire trucks behind, he couldn't move. He climbed out of the car and got hit in the side of the head with an egg. Yolk dripped from his feather earring.

As Tali watched the chief dodge another flying egg, someone shoved her. People pushed by her, stepping on Charlotte's blanket. She reached down to help Charlotte pick it up, but stomping boots and sneakers got in the way. Billy and Josh blocked the sudden stream of people, giving Tali and Charlotte enough time to rescue the blanket.

With the crowd jostling her, it took some effort for Tali to straighten up. When she did she saw hundreds of men, women and children moving into the street. They began chanting, "End the lawlessness." More people left their chairs to join them, grabbing signs that had been hidden under blankets. The signs read: "Children Deserve Education," "Only Teachers Can Teach," and "Kids Belong in Schools Not Out On The Streets!"

"What's going on?" Tali shouted in Josh's ear.

"It's some kind of protest."

"Has this happened before?" The pushing, shoving people made her nervous. She moved closer to him.

"No." He put his arm around her.

Tali lost sight of Mary, Chief Billiot, and the rest of the parade, though she did see Miss Simms hustling her dancers into the studio. She watched as people flowed in from the park and side streets yelling, chanting, and waving signs. She noticed the Carpe Diem townspeople were quiet, probably in shock. Then protestors moved aside for an approaching black limousine. A woman was lifted onto the car's roof.

"Is that the woman who stopped by the Inn yesterday?" Tali asked Quinn.

"*It is*," John Holden answered as he passed by them. "I'd better get over there." He disappeared into the mob.

The woman had shiny black hair and wore a tight red power suit and matching spiked heels. Amazingly, she didn't slip off the limo's roof. The woman said into a megaphone, "I am Raegan Colyer, chief of staff to Governor Michael Thomas."

"Good, maybe she'll break up the crowd. Tell them to go home," Josh said.

"I don't think so," Quinn replied.

"Good evening, Carpe Diem. I hope you don't mind that I brought a few friends."

Protestors cheered and shook their signs. "Tell 'em how it is, Ms. Colyer," a man shouted.

"Carpe Diem is a town of lawless anarchists who refuse to educate their children."

"You don't know what you're talking about!" Charlotte yelled.

"Oh, indeed I do. There are no teachers in this town."

The mob roared angrily. They began to chant, "No teachers, no education."

Raegan Colyer raised her arms. "Don't fear. The state of Illinois has arrived to rectify the situation. Beginning Monday, the state will provide buses to escort every Carpe Diem child to schools in nearby towns. This will continue until schools are built in Carpe Diem."

Quinn gasped. The mob shouted and cheered.

The woman bent down.

"What's she doing now?" Tali asked Josh, who was several inches taller and had a better view.

"Mary and Chief Billiot have made their way to the limo," he answered. "I don't see John, though. Oh geez, the limo driver is blocking Mary. I've never seen the chief so mad."

"Let her up! Let's hear what she has to say!" several people shouted.

"John's there now," Josh continued. "He and the chief are helping Mary up onto the limo's roof. Ms. Colyer is screaming at John. It looks like she knows him. He's trying to calm her down. The chief's stepped in, said something to Ms. Colyer. She's not screaming anymore."

"Mayor Mary Evans," a red-faced Raegan Colyer said, "for those of you who have lived under a rock this last week." She handed Mary the bullhorn.

The townspeople's cheers and applause were drowned out by the mob's boos.

"Ms. Colyer, members of the Association of Illinois School Teachers..." Mary began.

"They're from the teachers' union," Josh hissed in Tali's ear.

"We welcome you to Carpe Diem. We ask you to join us in celebrating our Fall Festival. Any concerns you might have about our community can be addressed at a later date."

"No, Mayor," shouted a woman holding a sign which read "Unschoolers Unwelcome." "You have to be held accountable!"

There were more angry screams. Several people started shoving each other.

"Where are the reporters now? Where's Leo?" Tali said to Josh.

He shook his head and pulled her close.

"Quinn, you have Leo's number, right?" she asked.

"I do. I'll text him."

"Please be calm," Mary said to the crowd, the shakiness in her voice amplified by the megaphone. "Carpe Diem isn't a threat to you or to anyone else."

"Like hell you say!" shouted a man with a child sitting on his shoulders.

"Let her speak," John shouted back.

"From what I can tell," Josh said, "John and the creep with the kid are shoving each other. Ms. Colyer's limo driver is there. Uh oh, I don't see John anymore. I hope he's okay. I don't see the chief either. I wonder where he is. Ms. Colyer's taken the microphone from Mary."

"The mayor is correct. Perhaps this isn't the proper venue. And perhaps there isn't a threat. Surely Mayor Evans doesn't advocate doing away with public schools, with public education. Why, that would destroy the whole fabric of our country."

"Destroy Carpe Diem first!"

"Traitors!"

Josh pulled Tali and shouted to Quinn, Will, and Billy, "Come on, I've got an idea." When they reached an opening in the crowd, he said, "We need to get Brendan and as many Carpe Diem teens as possible."

"Why?" Quinn asked.

"Just get on your phones and start texting. Quinn you take A through H. Will, I through P. I'll take the rest. Tell them to get to this spot as soon as possible."

"What's the plan?" Tali asked.

"I'll explain when everyone's here."

Within minutes, teens pushed through to them.

"It's getting crazier by the second," Brendan said. "I passed by a lunatic telling Stan Edwards that he was abusing Jimmy by unschooling him. The creep began taunting Jimmy, who cried. When Stan threw a punch at the guy, I nearly got hit."

"I overheard Charlotte Jansen explaining how natural unschooling is," a short girl said. "When I glanced over at her, I saw a woman spit in her face."

"That's nothing," a slender girl said. "Patrick Holden tried to get through the crowd on his motorcycle. He was shouting to people to just take it easy, but three men blocked his way. When he asked them to move, they actually pulled him off his bike." The girl trembled. "I don't know what happened. I was too scared to stick around."

"Poor Patrick," Tali said.

"He's tough. He survived the accident, didn't he?" Will said. "It's those three guys I'd be worried about."

"Where are the police?" Tali asked.

"Everywhere," the short girl replied. "But they're outnumbered. There isn't much they can do."

"There's something we can do," Josh said.

# 37

Trapped in traffic waiting for the Adams Street Bridge to lower, Leo called Mary several times but couldn't reach her. He then called Barnes at *The Examiner*. He dodged Barnes' questions about his testimony and talked the big man into joining him in Carpe Diem.

He suggested Barnes ask Sheila Lewis, a reporter friend at WCH-TV, to come along. By the time Leo was on I-90, the WCH-TV van was behind him.

Leo gave up trying to reach Mary and concentrated on getting to Carpe Diem as fast as possible without getting pulled over. As he passed through Elon, he received a text message from Quinn. His testimony must have bothered him more than he thought, because it never occurred to him to call Quinn when he couldn't reach Mary.

"Mob in CD. Hurry!" the text read. The word "mob" triggered in Leo's mind his brother, a younger, more improved version of himself engulfed in a mass of panicking people. He rubbed his jaw with a shaky hand and wiped the sweat forming on his forehead. His foot eased on the gas pedal. Why not turn around? Head home and stop at Kasey's Tavern for a cold one? Was it up to him to save Carpe Diem?

Then his phone sang out.

"Hey man, you're slowing down. What's up?" Barnes' deep voice came through Leo's Bluetooth headset.

*Jesus, I'm pathetic. Get a grip.* "Mayor Evans' daughter texted," he replied. "There's a mob in Carpe Diem. We've got to get there as soon as possible. Stay with me." He wiped a moist hand on his pants then punched the gas pedal. Speed trap be damned.

"No problem. You know how fast Kenny likes to drive."

He looked in his rearview mirror. Sure enough, the WCH-TV van was tailing him, a welcome sight, especially after receiving Quinn's text.

He pulled off Highway 20 onto the main road into Carpe Diem. A mile further, he passed school buses parked at precarious angles on both sides of the road. He estimated there were twenty buses surrounded by sedans, SUVs, cars, and trucks. The vehicles overflowed onto the farm. The pumpkin patch was a sea of chrome.

"Barnes, is the cameraman getting this?" he asked, looking in his rearview mirror.

"We're on it. Whoa, man." Barnes whistled. "Watch out for the sheep!"

Leo slammed on the brakes. A large herd of black and white sheep lumbered onto the road. Some idiot had backed his pick-up into the gate, busting it open. When the last animal passed, he stepped on the gas and swerved around cars parked in the road.

He floored it through the tunnel of trees and into the town square, then slammed on the brakes. Abandoned parade floats, antique cars, fire trucks, and a surging mass of people blocked the street. They were shouting, pushing, thrusting signs, throwing fists, and yelling in anger.

And then the memory of his brother's screams, suppressed so well for so long, assailed him. Leo's heart raced; the palms of his hands were so damp they slipped off the wheel.

For months those screams had echoed in his head. They kept him awake and when he finally drifted off to sleep, they amplified his nightmares. Only drunken stupors gave him a reprieve. But lately the dreams had no longer tormented him. He thought he was rid of them. But the sight of the mob in Carpe Diem unleashed them.

He pounded his fists on the steering wheel. *No, not now.*

Reminding himself that Barnes and the camera crew were following him, Leo willed himself to reach for the door and to pull on the latch.

KRISTIN A. OAKLEY

Somehow he managed to get out of the Mustang. The noise from the mob assaulted him. Steadying himself, he turned around to shout to the WCH-TV van. It wasn't there.

Hands shaking, stomach clenching, he got back inside the Mustang then closed the door. Safe and secure. In five minutes he'd be out of town. In thirty minutes he'd be at Carl's Tavern in Elon downing whiskeys.

He started the engine.

A black cat landed on the hood, its glowing yellow eyes accusing. Leo slowly put the car in reverse. The cat hunched its back and hissed. Leo stopped.

The cat hissed again then jumped off the hood, giving Leo a good view of a gap in the mob. Charlotte was on the ground in front of Joan and Dan's Diner, crouched over a body. John? Nearby, Mary, her face smeared with blood, shouted at a large, threatening man.

Anger overcame panic. Leo got out of his car and plunged into the crowd. He dodged people shoved into his path and ducked under signs waved in his face. He pushed through to Mary.

"Mary!"

She turned to him. Tomato seeds were stuck in her hair. Tomato juice, not blood. He shoved the large man out of the way.

"Hey man, what the f—"

"You don't want to mess with me."

The man scowled, then turned away. Leo hugged Mary, feeling her body quiver and realizing that his tremors had stopped. The screaming in his head had stopped, too. His heart still raced, but it urged him to take action, not retreat.

"It's gotten out of control," Mary said. "Some creep knocked John out cold."

Leo bent next to Charlotte as John came to.

"I'm fine, fine."

"Let's get him into the diner," Leo said. "He'll be safe in there."

Once they were back on Main Street, he asked, "How did this riot start?"

"Raegan. She's behind this." Mary pointed at a black limo parked diagonally in the street.

"She's in the limo?"

"Yes. She incited the crowd. I think she rounded up the protestors. Most are from the teachers' union. She's trying to destroy Carpe Diem."

A heavy lawn chair crashed through the plate glass window of Charlotte's Fair Goods Trading Center. People screamed as they scurried away from the raining glass. "Oh, my God, she's succeeding."

Leo spotted Barnes and the camera crew. "Not without an audience." Leo pointed down the street. "I've brought WCH-TV and they're filming. This is criminal. Everyone will know it."

"By then it'll be too late. The union will be so riled up the members won't stop until Carpe Diem has schools."

"That's right, bitch!" a short, chubby man shouted.

"Watch your language," Leo shouted back.

The round man shoved him. He shoved back. The man fell into two women with "Unschooling is Educational Abuse" signs.

"Stop it!" Mary shouted. "*Stop it! Listen.*"

"My Country Tis of Thee…" A wave of youthful singing cut through the mob's angry roar.

"What the—" Leo began.

Barnes came up to Leo. "Sorry we didn't get here sooner. Those damned sheep started chasing your car. We couldn't get past them. We ditched the van and came as quick as we could."

The singing grew louder.

"It's a bunch of kids," Barnes said. "They've locked arms and are marching this way."

Someone in the mob shouted, "Look out! It's a homeschool gang! They might have weapons!"

Leo spotted Josh, Quinn, Will, Billy, and Tali leading a group of teens through the crowd. They had help. Townspeople pushed back the mob and opened a path for the marchers. Other people joined the teens, hundreds of men, women and children. The singing grew louder and drowned out the angry rhetoric.

The short jerk and sign wielding women near Leo shouted, "stop them!" and tried to push past. Leo and Barnes blocked their path. "Don't even try," Leo hissed. The protestors backed down.

Other protestors stopped their yelling and shoving as the singers passed. The peaceful throng grew. A few protestors tried to shout over the singing and block the march, but they were drowned out and pushed aside. The townspeople had gained the advantage and the singing had the desired effect. The mob quieted, lowering their signs and their fists. They shifted uneasily. Many stared at their feet or the sidewalk.

The townspeople continued their march to the Town Hall. They gathered around the brick steps of the building and finished with a resounding, "… let freedom ring!"

The people of Carpe Diem cheered.

One of the women near Leo said, "Sue, Harvey, it's over. Let's go home." She took the "Educational Abuse" sign from the other woman and nudged the short man.

Others slowly gathered their signs, discarded lawn chairs and blankets, and trudged down Main Street to their vehicles.

Watching the mob disperse, Leo spied Raegan exiting the limo. He got to her just as she put the bullhorn to her lips.

He yanked it from her hand. "It's over."

"Give that back," she said, her face red with anger. She drew back her hand to slap him, then stopped. Something behind him caught her attention. She smoothed her hair and her skirt, and put on an inviting smile.

He turned around to see Barnes and the camera crew. Turning back, Leo spotted Chief Billiot coming from the other direction.

"Well, well. Sheila Lewis of WCH-TV News," Raegan said in a silky voice. "It's good to see you." She jerked her head around, "Hey, what do you think—"

"Raegan Colyer," Chief Billiot said, slapping handcuffs on her, "I charge you with inciting a riot. You have the right to remain silent—"

"This is ridiculous! What are you going to do, throw me in jail? You have no grounds. My attorney will have me out in an hour."

Chief Billiot remained calm. "No, Ms. Colyer. We'll merely hold you until the federal marshals come to pick you up. They've been notified and are on their way." He continued to Mirandize her.

"The federal government has no jurisdiction," she argued.

The police chief finished before he answered, "You're wrong. I talked to the bus drivers. Several of them drove down from Milwaukee. As I'm sure you're aware—"

"Crossing state lines to incite a riot is a federal offense," Patrick said, limping up to the group. There was a cut over his left eye and his hair was a long tangled mess. "Ms. Colyer, nice to see you again."

"You... you can't be..." she stammered. Her pale skin glistened with sweat.

"Alive? Yet here I am."

"Chief," Leo said. "You'll want to call Zachary Davies of the Cook County Sheriff's Office."

"Why?"

"He believes Chicago City Councilman Jim Harrison's car accident was sabotaged. The front tires' steel rims had melted away, just like on Patrick's motorcycle. And after his death, Ms. Colyer here took over Harrison's position on the board of FLASH."

"Damn," Patrick said.

"The Federation of Lawyers Advocating for School at Home?" the chief asked. "And if the homeschool laws in Illinois were to change—"

"Homeschoolers would need lawyers," Leo answered. "FLASH and our friend here would make a killing."

"I'm thinking our friend already has," the chief said.

Raegan gave the camera an oily smile. "You can't prove anything. You'll never make any charges stick. I have the right to—" The last of her words were lost as Chief Billiot shoved her into a nearby squad car.

"Chief, do you have a statement?" Sheila asked.

"No comment," he said as he got in the driver's seat and then drove away.

"Mayor, would you like to say anything?" Sheila held out the microphone.

Mary took the microphone and walked out into the street. She looked over at Patrick who smiled.

"I hate to admit it," Mary began, turning toward the camera, "but the townspeople of Carpe Diem may be partly to blame for this." She gestured all around her to the street littered with trash, broken glass and abandoned signs.

Leo walked up to her. "How can you say that?"

"We've hidden ourselves from the rest of Illinois. It's no wonder our alternative way of life seems threatening. People don't understand unschooling because they don't have enough information. People fear what they don't understand.

"Starting next week, I'd like to, in the words of my cousin Patrick Holden, cut a path of light through the darkness of misconception. I will begin a dialogue with educators across the state, spread the word about unschooling and show them how it works."

She looked at a Carpe Diem Fall Festival banner hanging in tatters from a nearby lamppost. "But for now, we'll clean up and go on with the festival as planned." She handed the microphone back to Sheila.

"Terrific. Thanks," the reporter said. "And thanks, Leo, for letting us tag along. This is a great story." She looked at Barnes. "We'd better get going. I'd like to get this on the ten o'clock news."

Barnes gave Leo a bear hug.

"Thanks for coming, man," Leo said, wondering when, or even if, he would ever see him again.

"I wouldn't have missed it for the world." The big reporter joined the camera crew as they jogged down Main Street, weaving around the debris and retreating protestors.

The townspeople and even a few protestors began cleaning up the debris.

Tali and Josh gathered up signs and stacked them on the sidewalk. Peyton Blaney offered Will and Quinn brooms to sweep up the glass from the Fair Goods Trading Center's storefront while Billy threw the larger pieces into a trash bin. Charlotte walked out of the diner with her arm around John. John saw Mary and gave her a thumbs-up.

Mary grabbed Leo and gave him a blazing kiss. "Thank you so much."

"You're more than welcome. But for what?"

"For finding out about Councilman Harrison's sabotaged car and bringing the press. It looks like we might finally be rid of Raegan Colyer."

"I wish I had gotten here sooner."

"You got to Carpe Diem just in time." She kissed him again then picked up a crumpled sign. "Once we've got this mess taken care of and I've made sure the festival is underway, how about coming back to the Inn with me?" She gave him a seductive smile. "I'll open a bottle of Joan and Dan's Merlot."

"You're not going to stay at the festival?"

She felt her matted hair and looked down at her tomato-stained shirt. "No, I'm a mess. Besides, I've had enough of crowds for awhile."

"I'm not a big fan of crowds myself." He picked a piece of tomato out of her hair. "And while you get cleaned up, there's a story I need to finish writing."

# 38

In The Signature Room at the 95th, the restaurant atop the John Hancock Center, Leo sat at the head of an elegant table. Gazing out the floor-to-ceiling windows, he could see a few yachts and cruise ships anchored alongside Navy Pier and a crowd under the giant Ferris wheel. White sailboats dotted the blue waters of Lake Michigan and lush trees, green grass, and flowering bushes lined the cream-colored beaches. Chicago in springtime, after the grimy slush dissolved and the bitter wind-chills thawed, was his favorite place to be.

"You were going to tell us why you're not in jail for lying to the grand jury," Patrick said, drawing Leo's attention back to the table. The man Leo once thought a hippie now resembled the courtroom lawyer he was, wearing a navy blue suit and red power tie. Only the brown ponytail and goatee betrayed more of Patrick's true nature.

"Patrick, I've told you already," Mary said, taking a sip of her merlot. Golden strands of hair grazed the soft skin of her cheek and the long curve of her neck. With Shaw locked safely behind bars for battery, Mary didn't need disguises. The mousey brown hair dye and tortoise shell glasses had disappeared months ago. She smiled at him and he instantly forgot Patrick's question.

"I don't know the whole story either," Tali said, her dark, inquisitive eyes dancing. Her plaited blond hair grazed the shoulder strap of her red-satin dress. On her right sat Josh. He looked more like a GQ model than a mechanic, his arm draped lazily over her chair.

"Neither do I," Quinn admitted, taking her last photograph of the city skyline and putting her camera on the table beside the china place setting. For tonight she had replaced the black lipstick with cherry red. But her spiky hair, cocktail dress and nail polish were still inky black. Leo had teased her about the shocking change in wardrobe. She had playfully punched him in the arm.

"I would like to hear it," Alexandra agreed. Leo could see the top of her cane leaning against the table. That and the faint scar above her left eyebrow, which she tried to hide with make-up, were the only remaining indications that she had been in a horrible car accident.

"Me, too," Will said, his suit jacket a little too snug. He had grown several inches taller since the fall. Mary couldn't buy new clothes fast enough.

"Come on, Leo, give the folks what they want," John said. He sat at the opposite end of the table, looking dapper in a tweed jacket, white shirt, and khaki tie, though the spring breezes had tossed his mane of white hair, making it as wild as ever.

"Okay, okay," Leo agreed. "After I testified, the grand jury adjourned for the day so the prosecutor could subpoena Raegan Colyer. Of course the federal marshal who tried to serve the subpoena didn't know she had left the city. Once they caught up with her in the Carpe Diem jail, there were other charges to deal with."

"Did they ever find out you lied about Ms. Colyer being your source?" Tali asked.

"Lied is a bit strong. I didn't actually know who my source was, though the person who called and told me about Smithson's embezzlement was a woman."

"You didn't recognize the voice?" Josh asked.

He remembered the raspy voice, interrupted by coughing. "No. She apologized for not speaking clearer, said she had a head cold. When she refused to give her name, I knew she was disguising her voice. It didn't matter to me, the evidence she gave panned out."

"But you told the grand jury Raegan was your source," Patrick interjected.

His grin became sly. "I testified that I *thought* she was the caller. When the prosecutor asked me point blank, I went right into my testimony about the three phone calls. The prosecutor was so excited about the possibility of nailing the governor's chief of staff that she didn't press me on that point."

"She'll ask you back to court, won't she?" Will asked. "To tell them your real source?"

"Oh, that's the beauty of it," Leo said. "Turns out, my source was Raegan. Her phone records proved it."

"Wait," Tali said, "Ms. Colyer was your source all along?"

"Yes."

"You are one lucky bastard," Patrick said. Everyone laughed.

"And," Leo added once the laughter subsided, "Raegan's going to be locked away for a long time. They discovered she poured nitric acid onto Senator Shaw's scarf right before he touched it, to frame him."

"There's some comfort in knowing he didn't cause the accident," Alexandra said. "I don't know if Tali told you, but they've expelled Christopher from the state Senate. His license to practice law has been revoked because of the battery charge and his involvement with Raegan Colyer. He'll be in jail for several more months and then he's leaving the state. We doubt he'll be back." She squeezed her daughter's hand.

Tali gave her mother a sad smile then turned back to Leo. "What about your job at *The Examiner?*"

"I met with my editor, the managing editor, and the publisher, all of whom had various run-ins with Raegan over the years. They aren't sad to see her behind bars. They realized if I hadn't given the grand jury a name, I would be sitting in jail while Raegan would have gotten away with the murder of Jim Harrison.

"Also, Carl Smithson's embezzlement charges would have been dropped, Senator Shaw would have been found guilty of attempted murder, and who knows what would have happened to Carpe Diem. They decided to let me finish writing the Carpe Diem piece."

"Good call on their part," Patrick said. "That story has made you, once again, a Pulitzer Prize finalist."

Leo grinned and ran his hand through his thick brown hair. "*The Examiner's* main concern was whether confidential sources would be able to trust me again. And they're right, several sources have refused to talk to me though others have approached me after they've understood the circumstances. Anyway, once I handed in my story, *The Examiner* put me on probation for an indefinite period." He smiled at Mary and touched her cheek. "I don't give a damn. It was all worth it."

John rose from the table and lifted his wine glass. "I'd like to propose a toast," he said. "To Leo, soon-to-be Pulitzer Prize winning journalist and the champion of unschoolers everywhere."

"Here, here!"

The celebration continued late into the night, until the Carpe Diem residents decided they had better head home. After a round of goodbye hugs, John, Patrick, Alexandra and the kids left Mary with Leo outside the John Hancock Center while they retrieved the Bradbury Inn van from a nearby parking garage.

"I'm missing you already," Mary said to him after giving him a goodbye kiss. The wind dancing down Michigan Avenue played with her hair.

"I'll see you in a month." He tucked the wayward strands behind her ear and kissed her again. "Then I'll have you all to myself in New York. We may even skip the Pulitzer Prize luncheon."

"We will do no such thing, mister."

She played with his tie. "A month is a long time."

"You and I will be busy until then."

Mary sighed. "You're right. I've got lots to do before the Carpe Diem teachers' convention next weekend. We're expecting teachers from around the world. I'm nervous about it, though John and Patrick say it's the right thing to do. Patrick claims it'll help ward off any future Raegan Colyers from invading our town."

"I think he's right."

"And you've got your hands full, mister novelist," Mary said, as the van pulled up to the curb. "When are you going to let me read your manuscript?"

He gave her a dimpled grin. "If I let you read it, what will you do for me?"

"I'm sure I'll think of something." She grabbed the back of his neck and kissed him.

"Break it up," Patrick chided, stepping out of the van and walking over to them. Mary gave Leo one last hug.

Patrick held out his hand. "We haven't seen eye-to-eye on a lot of things, but I do want you to know I've appreciated all you've done for Mary and our town."

"Take care, Patrick." Leo shook the activist's hand.

"You too," Patrick said, and then helped Mary into the van. He turned back to Leo and winked. "I'll be seeing you around."

Leo waved as the van pulled into the throng of cars, cabs, and city buses.

*I Shot the Sheriff* rang from Leo's suit coat pocket. He took out his cell phone and noted the number.

"Ted. I'm sorry you and Barnes missed the party." He loosened his tie and began walking down Michigan Avenue.

"Me, too. We couldn't get an earlier flight back from the coast."

"No, no, I understand. Hey, it's pretty late. Is something wrong?"

"No," the editor paused. "Something has come up."

"What is it?"

"A hell of a story and it's all yours."

# ACKNOWLEDGEMENTS

Many thanks to my parents, Elizabeth and Clyde Oakley, for introducing me to Dr. Seuss, E. B. White, and William Shakespeare; to my daughters, Caitlin and Jessica Podemski, for pointing out in draft one that teenagers don't talk that way; and to my sister, Lisa Schroeter, for not being able to put down draft two. Jamie, Benjamin, and Jay Schroeter, my niece, nephew, and brother-in-law, I'm counting on you to make Leo famous in cyberspace.

I would never have finished this book if my critique group, originally called "The Chicks of the Trade," hadn't kicked me in the butt. Thanks to Mary Lamphere, Pat Noel, Carol Kuczek, Kelly Epperson, Katie Vanderjack, Kathleen Tresemer, Catherine Conroy, and Linda Kleczkowski for passing along their writing expertise and their never-ending support. An additional thank you to Mary Lamphere, whose creative insight and critical analysis was invaluable. She helped make Leo come to life.

Because I've never been a reporter, I turned to the Chicago Writers Association and asked journalists Pamela Ferdinand and Lynn Blumenthal and former journalist Randy Richardson to help me with Leo's career. Because I've never been a man, I asked Rich Brandt, Matt Corey, and Randy Richardson for their input on Leo's masculinity. I am the mother of two unschooled daughters, but thought it best to ask Illinois unschooling activists Rebecca Jaxon and Dorothy Werner to double-check my homeschooling facts. Unschoolers Laura Endres, Bonni Gullak, Sonia Nelson, and Jacqui Reddy added valuable information. Thank you!

Thanks also to Bob Futrell, estimator at Alpine Body Shop in

KRISTIN A. OAKLEY

Rockford, IL, who explained that a Harley going eighty miles an hour has been known to pick up the vehicle it hits; to the knowledgeable staff at Kegel Harley-Davidson in Rockford who helped me pick out Patrick's motorcycle, a 1997 Harley-Davidson Heritage Softail Classic; to Drs. Bill and Matt Banholzer who pointed out the properties of nitric acid and its effects on motorcycle tires; and to law professor Susan Brenner of the University of Dayton School of Law who answered my questions about federal grand juries.

Christine DeSmet, Gale Walden, Kathy Steffen, and Laurie Scheer of the UW-Madison Division of Continuing Studies taught me how to form my idea into a manuscript. I can't begin to tell you how much you've inspired me.

Karyn Saemann, my editor at Inkspots, Inc., made my manuscript sing. Kristin Mitchell, my publisher at Little Creek Press, put *Carpe Diem, Illinois* into my hands.

Thank you to all the members of In Print for showing me how to seize the day.

Finally, many, many thanks to the late John Holt, founder of the unschooling philosophy, for trusting in children.

# ABOUT THE AUTHOR

Carpe Diem's unschooling lifestyle is based upon Kristin Oakley's own homeschooling experiences. Kristin unschooled her two daughters, founded two homeschooling support groups, wrote for Home Education Magazine, and offered workshops at the InHome Homeschooling Conference in St. Charles, IL. Kristin is a founding member and former president of the professional writers' organization, In Print, a board member of the Chicago Writers Association, and teaches an online writing course through the UW-Madison Division of Continuing Studies. She lives with her family in Madison, Wisconsin, just down the road from Carpe Diem, Illinois. You can find her online at www.kristinoakley.net.

# COMING SOON
## IN THE LEO TOWNSEND SERIES

## *God on Mayhem Street*
### By Kristin A. Oakley

*Chicago Examiner* reporter Leo Townsend has landed the interview of a lifetime with openly gay, front-running US presidential candidate Griffin Carlisle. But when Leo is forced to abandon the interview to rush to the side of his estranged father, who has suffered a near-fatal heart attack, his personal and professional worlds collide. When Griffin offers to visit the Townsend farm for an interview, secrets are exposed that jeopardize not just Leo's family, but an entire nation.